Alex's hair fell in great soft brunette waves around her shoulders, the tendrils framing her face shining in the light that came from the firepit, and it was every bit as exciting as he'd imagined.

"What are you doing?" Max said, shock and desire turning his voice into almost a growl.

"I thought I would let my hair down."

"It's beautiful," he said before he could stop himself.

"Thank you."

"All of you is beautiful."

"Do you really think so?"

"Yes."

She took a deep breath and leaned forward an inch, dizzying him with her scent and confusing him beyond belief, because what was she doing? "You're the most attractive man I've ever met," she said, the words coming out of her mouth in a rush. "And the most dangerous."

His heart gave a great lurch. "In what way?"

"You make me want to break my own rules."

# Lucy King

## THE BILLIONAIRE WITHOUT RULES

# HARLEQUIN®
# PRESENTS®

**Recycling programs
for this product may
not exist in your area.**

ISBN-13: 978-1-335-56921-9

The Billionaire without Rules

Copyright © 2021 by Lucy King

All rights reserved. No part of this book may be used or reproduced in
any manner whatsoever without written permission except in the case of
brief quotations embodied in critical articles and reviews.

This is a work of fiction. Names, characters, places and incidents
are either the product of the author's imagination or are used fictitiously.
Any resemblance to actual persons, living or dead, businesses,
companies, events or locales is entirely coincidental.

This edition published by arrangement with Harlequin Books S.A.

For questions and comments about the quality of this book,
please contact us at CustomerService@Harlequin.com.

Harlequin Enterprises ULC
22 Adelaide St. West, 40th Floor
Toronto, Ontario M5H 4E3, Canada
www.Harlequin.com

**Printed in U.S.A.**

**Lucy King** spent her adolescence lost in the glamorous and exciting world of Harlequin when she really ought to have been paying attention to her teachers. But as she couldn't live in a dreamworld forever, she eventually acquired a degree in languages and an eclectic collection of jobs. After a decade in southwest Spain, Lucy now lives with her young family in Wiltshire, England. When not writing or trying to think up new and innovative things to do with mince, she spends her time reading, failing to finish cryptic crosswords and dreaming of the golden beaches of Andalucia.

## Books by Lucy King

### Harlequin Presents

#### *Passion in Paradise*

*A Scandal Made in London*

#### *Lost Sons of Argentina*

*The Secrets She Must Tell*
*Invitation from the Venetian Billionaire*

### Other books by Lucy King

*The Reunion Lie*
*One Night with Her Ex*
*The Best Man for the Job*
*The Party Starts at Midnight*

Visit the Author Profile page
at Harlequin.com for more titles.

For the parents at my kids' school, whom I shamelessly mined for info on many topics that pop up in this trilogy, from adoption to postpartum psychosis to how to get stranded in Venice to Caribbean floating bars to hacking into Times Square billboards. You know who you are!

# CHAPTER ONE

'Great, Alex, you're back. You'll never *guess* who's waiting for you in your office.'

Having shrugged off her jacket, Alexandra Osborne hung it and her bag on the coat stand and levelled her assistant and sometime associate, Becky, a look. She was in no mood for games. Or, right now, for Becky's perennially bubbly enthusiasm. She'd just ended yet another call informing her that a promising lead had gone absolutely nowhere and her gloom and anxiety were at an all-time high.

The absence of progress with regard to the case she'd been working on for the past eight months was both teeth-grindingly maddening and desperately worrying.

Last December, after discovering an adoption certificate while going through his late father's papers, billionaire hotelier Finn Calvert had hired her to look into the circumstances surrounding his birth.

Despite there being exceptionally little to go on, Alex had nevertheless eventually managed to trace the trail to a derelict orphanage on the Argentina-Bolivia border, where paperwork had been found in a battered filing cabinet that suggested her client was one of a set of triplets. Finn had immediately instructed her to locate the others, and she'd poured considerable time and resources into it, to depressingly little avail.

One of Finn's long-lost brothers, Rico Rossi, had turned up six weeks ago, in possession of a letter that gave details of the agency his parents had used to adopt him thirty-one years before and, with the injection of new information, Alex had had high hopes. But the agency no longer existed and so far no one had been able to locate any archived records.

After a promising start she'd hit brick wall after brick wall. Even the interview that Finn and Rico had recently recorded, in which they'd entreated their third missing brother to come forward, had produced no genuine leads. It had been eight long months of precious little development and she desperately needed a breakthrough, because she could *not* allow this assignment to fail.

For one thing, she had a one hundred per cent success rate that her pride would not have ruined. For another, Finn Calvert was a hugely powerful and influential client who, upon successful completion of the mission, would be paying her not only the remaining half of her fee but a staggeringly generous bonus. His recommendation would open doors and his money would pay off debts that were astronomical since London premises and the kit required to do the job didn't come cheap.

Both, she'd realised when she'd accepted the case, would accelerate her expansion plans by around four years and all those people who should have supported and encouraged her when young, but who'd instead believed she'd never amount to anything and hadn't hesitated to tell her so, would be laughing on the other side of their face far sooner than she'd anticipated. Her success would be cemented and she'd have proved once and for all that she'd conquered not only the environmental obstacles she'd encountered growing up but also the fear that with one false move she could end up like her deadbeat family.

There was no way she'd *ever* pass up the chance of that, so she'd thrown everything at it, even going so far as to turn down other lucrative work in order to devote all her time and resources to this one job, which would secure her future and realise her dreams.

She'd assumed it would be as straightforward as other similar cases had been, that she'd easily track down the adoption paperwork and from there find the answers Finn craved. She'd never expected to be in this position all these months later. Having to admit the possibility of defeat and being forced to move on to different assignments in order to stave off the threat of looming bankruptcy made her want to throw up.

'Who is it?' she asked, mustering up a smile while reminding herself that it wasn't Becky's fault progress was so slow and she had no right to take her worry or her bad mood out on her assistant.

'Only our missing triplet.'

Alex stopped in her tracks, the smile on her face freezing, the floor beneath her feet tilting for a second. All her churning thoughts skidded to a halt and her head spun. Seriously? The man she'd invested so much time and so many resources in looking for was here? Actually here? After so much disappointment and despair, it was hard to believe.

'You're joking.'

'I am *not*,' said Becky, practically bouncing on her seat. 'His name is Max Kentala and he arrived about five minutes ago.'

'Oh, my God.'

'I *know*. I was literally just about to text you.'

'I was beginning to give up hope of ever finding him,' said Alex, a rush of relief colliding with the shock still zinging around her system.

'Well, technically he found you,' her assistant pointed out in an unhelpful way that Alex decided to ignore.

'He must have seen the interview,' she said instead, her pulse racing as she tidied her shirt and smoothed her skirt.

'Ah, so that I *don't* know,' Becky admitted ruefully. 'I tried to find out how he came to be here but he was incredibly tight-lipped. Impossible to read. And, to be honest, it was kind of hard to concentrate. He's every bit as gorgeous as his brothers, maybe even more so, although I don't see how that's possible, given they're identical give or take a haircut and the odd scar or two. We're talking not just hot, but *scorchio*,' she added, her expression turning dreamy as she gazed into the distance. 'I think it's the eyes. That blue… They kind of make you forget your own name… I wonder if he's single…'

'Becky.'

Her assistant snapped back and pulled herself together. 'Yes, sorry,' she said with a grin as she fanned her face. 'Phew. Anyway, I showed him into your office and made him a coffee. I'll move around the appointments you have.'

'Thanks.'

'Brace yourself.'

Used to Becky's dramatic tendencies—not entirely helpful in a trainee private investigator, she had to acknowledge—Alex ignored the warning and headed for her office, the adrenaline powering along her veins kicking her heart rate up to a gallop.

Max Kentala's hotness was irrelevant, as was his marital status. That he was actually here was very definitely not. On the contrary, depending on what information he brought with him, it could be exactly the breakthrough she was so desperate for. It could be game-changing. If there was the remotest possibility her current predicament could be reversed, she'd grab it with both hands and never let go, so she needed all her wits about her.

Taking a deep breath to calm the shock, relief and anticipation crashing around inside her, Alex pulled her shoulders back, fixed a smile to her face and opened the door to her office.

'Good morning,' she said, her gaze instantly landing on the tall figure standing at her window with his back to her.

A broad back, she couldn't help noticing as her stomach clenched in a most peculiar way. Excellent shoulders. A trim waist, lean hips and long, long legs. Then he turned and his eyes met hers and it was as if time had stopped all over again. The air rushed from her lungs and goose bumps broke out all over her skin. And was it her imagination or had someone turned the heating on?

Well, Becky certainly hadn't been exaggerating, she thought dazedly as she struggled to get a grip on the extraordinarily intense impact of his gaze. *Scorchio* was an understatement. Max Kentala was quite possibly the best-looking man she'd ever come across in her thirty-three years. Not that she particularly went for the dishevelled surfer look. In fact, when she *did* date these days—which was rarely since firstly she tended to work unaccommodating hours and secondly, with a cheating ex-husband in her background, she had a whole host of issues to do with self-esteem and trust—her dates were generally clean-cut and tidy.

This man's unkempt dark hair was far too long for her liking and he was badly in need of a shave. His faded jeans had seen better days, although they did cling rather lovingly to his powerful thighs, and the untucked white shirt he wore so well had clearly never been introduced to an iron.

No. He wasn't her type. So why her stomach was flipping and her mouth had dried was a mystery. Maybe it was the eyes. They really were arrestingly compelling. Blue and deep and enigmatic, they looked as if they held a wealth of secrets—catnip to someone whose job it was to uncover hidden truths—and she wanted to dive right in.

And to do more than that, if she was being honest. She wanted to run her fingers through his hair while she pressed up against what looked like a very solid chest. She wanted to plaster her mouth to his and urge him to address the sudden throbbing ache between her thighs.

It was bizarre.

Alarming.

And deeply, horrifyingly inappropriate.

This man was part of her biggest, most important assignment. He might well hold key information about it. It wouldn't do to forget that. However attractive she found him—and there seemed little point in denying she did—she could not afford to get distracted. So what if he wore no wedding ring? That meant nothing. And as for the throbbing, what was that all about? It hadn't been that long since she'd had sex, had it? A year? Eighteen months at most? And why was she even thinking about sex?

Snapping free from the grip of the fierce, very unwelcome desire burning through her and putting an end to all thoughts of sex, Alex gave herself a mental shake and pulled herself together.

'Alex Osborne,' she said crisply, stepping forwards into the room and holding out her hand for him to shake.

He gave her a brief smile and took it. 'Max Kentala,' he replied, a faint American accent tingeing his deep voice which, to her irritation, sent shivers rippling up and down her spine despite her resolve to withstand his appeal.

'I'm very pleased to meet you, Mr Kentala.'

'Call me Max.'

'Alex,' she said, withdrawing her hand from his and resisting the urge to shake it free of the electricity the contact had sent zapping along her fingers and up her arm. 'Do take a seat.'

'Thank you.'

See, she told herself as she walked round to her side of the desk and smoothly lowered herself into her chair. Cool and professional. That was what she was. Not all hot and quivery and ridiculous. Still, it was good to be able to stop having to rely on her strangely wobbly knees and sit down.

'I take it you saw the interview,' she said, sounding remarkably composed considering she still felt as if she'd been thumped in the solar plexus with a flaming torch.

He gave a brief nod. 'I did.'

'When?'

'Yesterday.'

And now he was here. He hadn't wasted time. Finn was going to be thrilled. 'Can I also assume you'd like me to set up a meeting with your brothers?'

'I set up my own,' he drawled. 'I've just come from seeing them.'

Oh? That wasn't right. In the interview, Rico had told anyone with any information to contact *her*. He and his brother protected their privacy and she'd known the interview would generate more false leads than real ones, as had turned out to be the case. So what did Max think he was doing, bypassing her carefully laid plans like that?

'You were meant to go through me,' she said with a frown, not liking the idea of a potential loose cannon entering the arena one little bit. 'Those were the instructions.'

'But I don't follow instructions,' he said with an easy smile that, annoyingly, melted her stomach. 'I make my own arrangements.'

Not on this, he didn't, she thought darkly, pulling herself together and ignoring the dazzling effect of his smile. Uncovering the truth surrounding the triplets' birth and adoption was *her* assignment. Right from the start, Finn had given her total autonomy. She'd set the rules and established procedure. She was in charge. However glad she was that Max had shown up like this, he had no business meddling. She was not having her entire future potentially snatched away from her simply because he'd decided he was going to do things his way. Her blood chilled at the very thought of it.

Despite the laid-back look and the casual smile, the set of his jaw and the glint of steel in his eye suggested he wasn't to be underestimated, but she wasn't to be underestimated either. She'd given up a steady career in the police force to set up her own private investigating business. She'd taken a huge risk and she'd worked insanely hard. She'd come far but she had a lot further to go. Her dreams were of vital importance. They drove her every day to do more and be better. At one point, as a confused and miserable teenager, they'd been all she had. They were not going to be dashed by anyone or anything. Almost as bad, if everything went to pot and she lost her business, she could well find herself having to re-join the police, where she'd run the risk of bumping into her ex, who'd been a fellow officer and was still in the force, she'd last heard, and no one wanted that.

She needed Finn's good opinion and she needed his money, which meant *she* had to be the one to find the answers. So from here on in the man lounging so casually in the chair on the other side of her desk, looking as if he owned the place when he absolutely didn't, would be toeing *her* line.

'Why are you here, Max? What do you want?'

Sitting back and eyeing the coolly smiling woman in front of him with deceptive self-control, Max could think of a thing or two.

For a start he wanted her to carry on saying his name in that low husky voice, preferably breathing it right into his ear while he unbuttoned her silky-looking shirt and peeled it off her. Then she could shimmy out of the fitted skirt she had on, hop onto the desk and beckon him close. In an ideal world, she'd tug off the band tying her hair back and shake out the shiny dark brown mass while giving him a sultry encouraging smile. It was the lamest of clichés, he knew, but hey, this was his fantasy, albeit an unexpected one when he generally didn't go for the smart, tidy professional type.

But he had to admit she was stunning. Beneath the fringe she had wide light blue eyes surrounded by thick dark lashes, high defined cheekbones and a full, very kissable mouth he was finding it hard to keep his gaze off.

The minute he'd turned from the window and

laid eyes on her the attraction had hit. He'd felt it in the instant tightening of his muscles, the savage kick of his pulse and the rush of blood south. The intensity of his response, striking with the force of a tsunami, had made him inwardly reel. He couldn't recall the last time he'd been so affected by a woman he'd only just met. Ever?

Not that any of that mattered. The startling impact of her clear blue gaze on him, which he'd felt like a blow to the gut and the effects of which still lingered, was irrelevant. As were her trim curves. He wasn't here for a quick, steamy office encounter, even if in an alternative universe Alex Osborne *had* decided to throw caution to the wind and do as he'd imagined.

He was here because of recent events.

Fifteen hours ago, all Max had known of family was a difficult, demanding mother who lived in New York with husband number four and a father who, after the bitterest of divorces, had abandoned him to move to Los Angeles, where he'd remained determinedly on his own for a decade until he'd suffered a fatal heart attack seven years ago.

To Max, up to the age of fourteen, family had meant endless disapproval and cold stony silences. It had meant constantly walking on eggshells in an environment devoid of true affection and respect, and bending over backwards to please yet failing every single time. It had meant a devastating awareness of not being good enough and living with the relentless guilt at never meeting expectations, all of which worsened after his mom had been granted sole custody of him in the wake of the divorce.

Since then it had involved coming to terms with having had a father who'd essentially abandoned him for good and managing a tricky, complex relationship with a woman who was needy, self-absorbed, hypersensitive and controlling. But he'd done it because she was his mother. Or so he'd always believed.

Then he'd seen the interview given by two men who were the spitting image of him apart from a few superficial differences, and what he'd understood of family had blown wide apart.

Max had been in his study at his home in the Caribbean when the video had been forwarded to him by his assistant with an instruction to click on it immediately. As a cyber security expert with global businesses and governments among his clients he never clicked on anything immediately, regardless of whence the recommendation came. When, at Audrey's insistence, he eventually had, yesterday afternoon, the shock had knocked the air from his lungs and drained the blood from his brain.

Pulse pounding, he'd watched the twenty-minute footage of Finn Calvert and Rico Rossi a further three times, pausing each time on the final frame in which Rico looked straight down the lens and urged their missing triplet to get in touch. He'd stared into the eyes that were identical to his own, the dizziness and chaos intensifying to the point he'd thought he was going to pass out, before gradually calming down enough to allow logic and process to take over.

In urgent need of answers to the myriad questions ricocheting around his head, he'd put in a quick, rare call to his mother, who'd confirmed that he had indeed been adopted from an orphanage in Argentina thirty-odd years ago and had then proceeded to try and make it all about her. Stunned and shaken to the core, Max had hung up before saying something he might regret, and had then hacked into the systems that would disclose as much information as there was about these men who could quite possibly be brothers he'd never known anything about.

Having established, among other things, that Finn and Rico shared his date of birth and were both currently in London, he'd booked himself onto the next flight. On landing this morning, he'd sent them each a message with details of where he'd be and when, should they be interested in meeting up.

Two hours later, the three of them were sitting in the bar of Finn's flagship central London hotel, swapping coffee for vintage champagne in celebration of having found each other after so long apart and firing questions back and forth, as if trying to cram half a lifetime into half a morning.

'Here's to long-lost brothers,' Finn said with a smile that could have been one of Max's own as he lifted his glass and tilted it towards his brothers.

'*Saluti*,' said Rico, following suit.

'Cheers.' Max tapped his glass against the other two and then knocked back half the contents, the fizz of the bubbles sliding down his throat adding fuel to the maelstrom of thoughts and emotions churning around inside him.

With the revelation that he was adopted, so many questions that had dogged him all his life had suddenly been answered. Such as how on earth he could ever be related to either of his parents, people who bore no resemblance to him either physically or in temperament. Such as why he'd always felt an outsider. Why nothing he'd ever done was good enough. Why his father hadn't fought harder for him in the divorce. The strange yet deep-rooted sense that he wasn't where he was meant to be and he wasn't with the people he was meant to be with.

*These* were the people he was meant to be with, he knew with a certainty that he felt in his bones. His brothers. Who shared his dislike of milk and his skill with numbers, and who, like him, had had encounters of varying degrees with the law. Who he instantly got and who instantly got him. With whom he felt more of a connection in half an hour than he ever had with either of his so-called parents.

'Any idea how we ended up in an Argentinian orphanage or why we were separated?' Finn asked him and he snapped back.

'None,' he said with a quick frown.

'Nor me,' said Rico.

'Alex has hit a brick wall.'

Max raised his eyebrows. 'Alex?'

'Alex Osborne,' Finn clarified. 'The private investigator I hired. Progress has been virtually non-existent lately, which has been frustrating as hell, but then there isn't a whole lot to go on.'

'How about I look into it?'

'Could you?' asked Rico.

'Sure,' said Max.

Having just come to the end of one contract and the next starting in a month, he had time. He also had resources. But, more than that, he needed to get to the bottom of this. He'd spent the last decade believing he knew exactly who he was and where he was going. The news of his adoption had turned his world on its head. It might have answered many of the questions and cleared up much of the confusion he'd always had, but it had also thrown up even more. Who was he? Where had he come from? How had he ended up where he was? And that was just the start of it. The need for an explanation, for information, burned inside him like the hottest of fires. 'I have an extensive data network and know where to look, so that's a start.'

'It would be good to get to the truth,' Rico said. 'Whatever it may be. Anything you need, let me know.'

'Here are Alex's details,' said Finn, handing him a card.

'Leave it with me,' Max replied.

And now here he was, his pulse beating a fraction faster than usual and his senses oddly heightened as Alex continued to look at him while waiting expectantly and somewhat challengingly for him to tell her what he was doing here.

'I want everything you have on the case,' he said, ignoring the awareness and the buzz of desire firing his nerve-endings, and focusing on what was important.

Her eyebrows arched, her chin lifted and the temperature in the room seemed to drop thirty degrees. 'Why?'

Because he'd worked hard to get over the traumas of his childhood and as proof had spent the last decade living in at least some degree of peace. Because yesterday that peace had been shattered and he badly needed it back. Because he valued his brothers' kinship, wanted their approval and their acceptance—old habits died hard, clearly—and would do anything to get it. And, frankly, because she hadn't exactly got very far.

'Because I'll be taking things from here.'

# CHAPTER TWO ·

*WHAT?* NO. NO WAY.

Alex stared at the man oozing arrogance from the other side of her desk, the outrage shooting through her doing a very good job of obliterating the inconvenient attraction still fizzing along her veins.

She'd been absolutely right to consider him a loose cannon with the potential to wreak havoc. He clearly posed a greater danger to her plans than she'd originally assumed. But if he thought he could swan in here and take over the investigation, he could think again. She was *not* meekly handing him what little she had just because he demanded it. This was *her* assignment, and her reputation and her *future* were at stake.

'I'm afraid that's not possible,' she said coolly.

He arched an eyebrow and languidly hooked

the ankle of one leg over the knee of his other.
'Why not?'

'The information is confidential and Finn's
my client,' she said, determinedly not glancing
down and following the movement, 'not you.'

'If I needed my brother's authority to act on
his behalf—which I don't—I'd have it. He was
the one who gave me your card.'

Right. OK. So why had Finn done that? she
wondered, her confidence suddenly plummet-
ing for a moment. Was he unhappy with progress? Had he instructed Max to effectively fire
her? She couldn't let that happen. She was *not*
going to fail and have her dreams crumble
to dust.

'You are not taking over this case,' she said,
stiffening her spine and lifting her chin. Why
would he even want to? She was the expert here.

'How long have you been working on it?' he
asked with a deceptive yet pointed mildness
that instantly put her hackles up.

'A while,' she said, wincing a little on the
inside.

'Eight months, I heard.'

'It's complicated.'

'I don't doubt it.'

'Information is scarce.'

'Then you're looking in the wrong place.'

Really. She'd put in hundreds of hours of

research and mined every database available. She'd built a network of operatives in Argentina and hired subcontractors of whom she asked a lot without enquiring too closely how they were going to get it. She'd looked everywhere there was to look. 'And what would you know of it?'

'Information is my business.'

'What do you do?'

'Cyber security.'

'And?'

'I have access to resources I imagine you can only dream about.'

The faint patronising tone to his words grated on her nerves even as his easy smile was setting off tiny fireworks in the pit of her stomach, and yet she couldn't help thinking, what kind of resources? Legal ones? Illegal ones? *Better* ones?

'But I have people on the ground and they're working hard.'

'They wouldn't be too difficult to find,' he countered with a casual shrug that didn't fool her for a moment because she could hear the implication and the threat behind his words. He didn't need her cooperation. There was nothing stopping him going ahead and embarking on an investigation of his own. He was just here to get a head start.

But if he *did* strike out on his own, *and* got the answers the brothers wanted, then where would she be? Bankrupt. Redundant. The failure that everyone had always expected her to be. And she wasn't having that. Max might not be the type to give up—that steely glint of his had sharpened, she saw—but then neither was she. Whether or not he had the authority to fire her or intended to do so, she was not backing down on this.

Quite apart from her professional pride and the monumental fee she was due to collect, she liked Finn and Rico. She wanted to track down every existing snippet of information about the birth and adoption of these triplets, piece together the story and give them the answers they craved. She'd started the job. She had every intention of finishing it, however hard. It was *her* responsibility, and that was all there was to it.

'I've pursued every avenue there is, Max,' she said, keeping the cool she'd developed over a decade in the police.

'I very much doubt that.'

Behind a casual smile of her own she gritted her teeth. She wasn't incompetent, despite what he clearly thought. 'I've looked into personnel records and bank accounts,' she said with what she considered to be impressive calm under very trying circumstances. 'I've examined company records and sent off freedom of information requests. Every lead has come to nothing. The orphanage was run by nuns and closed around twenty years ago. Everyone who worked there has either died or disappeared. There was a massive earthquake shortly after it shut and all the archives that were held in the town hall basement were destroyed. It was only by some fluke that your birth certificates, which were found at the actual orphanage, survived.

'The adoption agency, which was owned by a holding company, was originally registered in Switzerland,' she continued. 'It also closed down years ago. I've found no records relating to either entity. The only possible link I've established between the agency and the orphanage is three large payments that arrived in the orphanage's bank account around the time of your adoption, originally made in Swiss francs before being converted to pesos. Freedom of information requests have come back with nothing. Swiss banking secrecy at the time hasn't helped. The only end that isn't yet a completely dead one is a possible future DNA match. I sent Finn's off for analysis four months ago.'

'With no result to date.'

'No.'

'It's a long shot.'

At the dismissive tone of his voice, she bristled. 'I am aware of that.'

He regarded her for one long moment, then arched one dark eyebrow. 'So is that it?'

'I've done everything I can.'

'Except for one thing.'

Her brows snapped together. 'What?'

'Actually going there.'

She stared at him. 'To Argentina?'

'No. The moon. Yes, Argentina.'

OK, so, no, she hadn't done that, she had to admit while choosing to ignore Max's derision. She'd considered it, of course, in the beginning. At great length. But she'd come to the conclusion that it could well have been an expensive wild goose chase, which, if she'd found nothing, would have eaten substantially into the budget and, worse, damaged Finn's confidence in her. So she'd stayed in London and opted for a network of local operatives instead to do the legwork on the ground, and told herself that she could always go herself as a last resort.

And that was the point she was at now, she realised with a start. She'd reached the end of the road with what she could do from London. She was all out of options, bar one.

'That was my next plan,' she said smoothly, as if it always had been, while frantically trying to remember how much she had left to spend on her credit card. 'I'll be looking at flights this afternoon.'

'No need.'

The glimmer of triumph that lit the depths of his eyes sent a double jolt of alarm and wariness shooting through her that had nothing to do with the precarious state of her finances. 'Why not?'

'I'm leaving for La Posada first thing in the morning.'

What? *What?* She guessed he'd learned about the abandoned town in which the ruins of the orphanage were located from his brothers but God, he'd worked fast. 'First thing in the morning?' she echoed, reeling.

'Rico's put his plane at my disposal. I'm making use of it. So I'd like everything you have on the case, Alex. Names. Dates. Places. Everything. And I'd like it now.'

In the face of Max's implacability and the realisation that he'd done it again, Alex's brain swirled with frustrated panic and angry confusion. How dared he go behind her back like this? These decisions weren't his to make. Why wouldn't he play by the rules? Did he think they didn't apply to him? Was he really that arrogant?

Whatever his motivation, whatever his methods, whether or not he even *knew* about the rules, he'd backed her into a corner, she realised, a cold sweat breaking out all over her

skin. Her least favourite place to be. She had
no room for manoeuvre. She was trapped.

But she wasn't going down without a fight.
In fact, she thought grimly as a plan to get out
of the tight spot he'd put her in began to form
in her head, she wasn't going down at all. However high-handed, disagreeable and infuriating
Max might be, she was not letting him go off
on his own and potentially snatching a victory
that was rightfully hers from the jaws of defeat. He was unpredictable and a threat to everything she'd worked so hard for. He needed
to be reined in and controlled. How would she
be able to do that if he went to Argentina all on
his own? And how was she supposed to know
what he found, if by some miracle he did indeed find anything, if she stayed in London?

There was only one thing for it. She was
going to have to go with him. It needn't be so
bad. He might even turn out to be useful. She
hadn't yet established what he knew about the
past. He might hold crucial information. And
what were these resources of his that she could
only dream about? She'd be a fool not to enquire about those.

'All right,' she said, setting her jaw and snapping her shoulders back in preparation for battle. 'On one condition.'

'Which is?'
'I go with you.'

In response to Alex's demand, every fibre of Max's being stiffened with resistance. No. Absolutely not. What she was suggesting amounted to teaming up and working together. He did neither. He operated alone. He always had. He'd grown up an only child and had learned at a very early age that he could rely on no one but himself. Now, the highly confidential nature of his work meant he trusted few. Collaboration was something he'd never sought and certainly never wanted.

That Alex's performance wasn't as flawed as he'd previously assumed didn't matter. He didn't want her involvement. Or anyone else's, for that matter. The quest for the truth was going to be intensely personal. He needed to get a grip on the resentment and anger that the call with his mother had sparked and now simmered inside him. He had to find out whether he'd ever been wanted by someone, whether he'd ever mattered. Netting all the emotions that had escaped Pandora's Box and shoving the lid back on them could get messy and no one else needed to be along for that particular ride.

'Absolutely not,' he said curtly.

Her jaw set and her shoulders snapped back.

'Absolutely yes,' she countered with steel in her voice.

'I work alone.'

'Not any more.'

'I'll match what Finn's paying you.'

'It's not just about the money.'

'I find that hard to believe. The bonus he's offered you is exorbitant.'

He could practically hear the grind of her teeth. 'My fee structure is none of your business. If you want me to share with you the information I have,' she said bluntly, 'I go with you. Otherwise you get nothing. That's my offer, Max. Take it or leave it.'

The resolve flashing in the depths of her eyes and the jut of her chin told him she was adamant. That she wasn't going to back down. Which was absolutely fine. He didn't appreciate ultimatums. He'd had enough of those growing up and just the thought of them made his chest tighten and his stomach turn. So he'd leave it. He had no doubt he could get what Alex had already found. He'd never come up against a problem he hadn't been able to solve, family conundrums aside. He didn't need her. He didn't want her—or anyone—in his space and never had. His world was his and his alone, and he'd be far more flexible and focused if he pursued the mystery surrounding his birth on his own.

And yet...

He had to admit he found Alex's fiery determination intriguing. Why was this assignment so important to her? he couldn't help wondering. Why not just take the money and move on? What was she fighting for?

And that wasn't all that was intriguing, he thought, his pulse hammering hard as he let his gaze roam over her beautiful animated face. Her prickliness was having an incredibly intense and wholly unexpected effect on him. It was electrifying his nerve-endings and firing energy along his veins. Lust was drumming through him with a power he'd never have imagined when she was the polar opposite of what he usually found attractive.

She was so defensive, so rigidly uptight. It ought to have been a turn-off, yet he badly wanted to ruffle those sleek feathers of hers, to butt up against her defences. What would it take to break them down? How far would he have to push?

She wasn't immune to him, despite her attempts to hide it. He'd caught the flash of heat in her eyes the moment they'd met. He'd noted the flush on her cheeks before she'd pulled herself together and coolly held out her hand for him to take. She was as attracted to him as he was to her. How satisfying would it be to unravel her until she was in his arms, begging him to undo her completely? How explosive would they be together?

The urge to find the answers to all the questions rocketing around his head thrummed through him. The need to hear her panting his name while writhing beneath him was like a drug thumping in his blood. So what if, instead of rejecting her proposal, he accepted it? What if he did actually allow her to accompany him to Argentina in return for everything she knew? There was little point in replicating the work she'd already done. It would only waste time. Undoubtedly, two heads would be more efficient than one.

And while they investigated he could work on unbending her. They'd have to find *something* to occupy themselves in the downtime, and seducing her would provide a welcome distraction from the more unsettling aspects of learning he was adopted.

Alex need pose no threat to his goals. He had no interest in sharing with her anything other than hours of outstanding pleasure. He wasn't cut out for anything more. He'd witnessed first-hand how thankless and manipulative relationships could be and the unhappiness they wrought. He neither believed in nor wanted commitment. He needed that kind of toxicity in his life like a hole in the head, which was why the women he dated never lasted long. The shorter the encounter, the less chance there was of disappointment and dashed expectations, of having to accommodate the feelings that someone else might develop, of becoming trapped and gradually losing the control and power to end things when he chose. Alex, despite the novel intensity of the chemistry that arced between them, would be no exception. All he had to do was persuade her to agree to a fling. It wouldn't take long. He gave it thirty-six hours tops.

'All right,' he said with a slow smile as heady anticipation at the thought of embarking on a short, sharp, scorchingly hot affair with her began to surge through him. 'London City Airport. Jet Centre. Seven a.m. Don't be late.'

Alex, with her better-to-be-twenty-minutes-early-than-twenty-seconds-late approach to timekeeping, wasn't the one who was late.

After Max had left her office she'd thrown herself into rearranging her diary, issuing instructions to Becky—who'd agreed to hold the fort—and then going home to pack. After a couple of hours of research followed by an annoyingly restless night, she'd risen at dawn and arrived at the airport with her customary two hours to spare. She'd taken immediate advantage of the private jet lounge to fortify herself with coffee while going over the notes she'd made last night and the list of questions she wanted to ask him.

Of the man himself there'd been no sign, and there still wasn't. She supposed that one of the advantages of this kind of travel was not being beholden to a schedule but she'd been told the time of their slot for take-off and in her opinion he was cutting it extremely fine.

However, that was OK with her. The more time she had to brace herself against the frustratingly edgy effect he had on her, the better. To her despair, he'd been on her mind pretty much constantly from the moment he'd walked out of her office. His scent—spicy, masculine, delicious—had lingered on the air. The intensity with which he'd looked at her was singed into her memory and she could still feel a strange low-level sort of excitement buzzing in her stomach.

Last night's dreams hadn't helped. Every time she dropped off, there he was in her office, smouldering away at her, only when he eventually rose, it wasn't to leave. It was to pull her up off her chair and spread her across her desk, and then proceed to take her to heaven and back, thoroughly and at great length. She'd lost count of the number of times she'd jerked awake, hot and breathless and aching, with the sheets twisted around her.

Why Max should evoke this strong a response in her when his brothers—so similar in looks—left her completely unmoved she had no idea. He might be mind-blowingly attractive but he still wasn't her type and she still didn't trust him one inch.

That last smile he'd given her—slow, seductive and devastating—was particularly worrying. It spoke of secrets, of being privy to information that she wasn't, and if there was one thing she detested it was secrets. Her ex-husband had had many—mainly of the female kind—and when she'd found them out they'd crucified and humiliated her.

What did Max have to be secretive about? she wondered, draining her fourth coffee of the morning and setting the delicate porcelain cup in its matching saucer. She wished she knew. She had the disturbing feeling that it somehow involved her.

Not that what lay behind the smile really mattered, of course. She wasn't interested in any of his secrets, even less in ones in which she might feature. She was here to work, nothing more. And she could easily manage the strangely wild effect he might still have on her.

As a thirty-three-year-old divorcee with a career like hers, she was no naïve innocent. She'd seen things, met all manner of people and been through her fair share of struggles. She'd become adept at hiding her true feelings beneath an ultra-unflappable surface and she saw no reason why that shouldn't be the case now.

It wasn't as if Max was similarly affected by her. It had been very clear that he wasn't interested in anything other than the information in her possession, which was a huge relief. The assignment was far too important to risk screwing up by either or both of them getting distracted.

As soon as he showed up she'd make a start by finding out what he knew. Assuming he was still intending to actually catch this flight, of course. Personally, she didn't know how he could operate like this. What was the point in stipulating a time to meet if you were going to completely disregard it? His website had revealed that he consulted for clients across the globe. Apparently he was some kind of computer genius, in constant and high demand. Truly, the mind boggled.

On the other hand, she had first-hand experience of how deceiving appearances could be. Look at the nonchalant way she'd sauntered into the private jet lounge as if she travelled this way all the time when she very much did not. Take her work, which proved it on a daily basis. Or her ex-husband, who'd been impossibly charming, handsome and initially doting, yet had also been a lying, cheating rat. And then there were her parents and siblings, whose willingness to break the law was staggering, who lied, cheated and stole as naturally as breathing while managing to maintain a perpetual air of injured innocence.

Just because Max chose to live life on the edge timewise, it didn't automatically mean he was reckless and rash. And just because he'd turned up in her office dishevelled and wearing crumpled clothes, it didn't mean he couldn't don a suit if necessary.

He'd certainly look good in one, she thought absently, staring out of the window and remembering the breadth of his shoulders and the leanness of his frame. A navy one, perhaps, to match the colour of his irises. With a crisp pale blue shirt open at the collar to reveal a wedge of chest. Although, frankly, he'd probably look better in nothing at all…

No.

This wasn't on. She had to get a grip. She really did. How Max conducted his affairs was none of her business. His attitude towards timekeeping and clothing was entirely up to him.

The reason her reaction to him yesterday had been so strong was because the shock and the relief at the breakthrough he presented, followed by the fear and panic that he intended to take the case over and cut her out of it, had momentarily rocked her foundations. Now, however, those foundations were solid, unassailable. Now she was prepared, She had to be.

Breathing deeply to ease the tension in her muscles and calm the annoying anticipation nevertheless rippling through her, Alex reached into her bag for her laptop. She flipped it open and determinedly concentrated on her emails, but barely two minutes passed before she felt the air around her somehow shifting. A prickly awareness washed over her skin and a pulse kicked in the pit of her stomach. Stiffening her spine and reminding herself of just how impregnable she was, she abandoned her emails and glanced up.

Max stood at the entrance to the cabin, being accosted by one of the two cabin crew on board, who seemed overly concerned with a desire to assist him. Alex mentally rolled her eyes, because how much help could an athletically built six foot plus man of thirty-one really need? But to her relief—because, quite honestly, she could do without having to sit through thirteen hours of simpering and flirting—he responded to the inviting smile with a quick, impersonal one of his own and a minute shake of his head.

'Good morning,' he said, heading towards her and tossing his bag on one of the two soft leather sofas the colour of buttercream.

'Good morning,' she replied, reminding herself sternly that it was of no concern to her how he responded to an invitation. 'So much for not being late.'

At her arch tone, his dark eyebrows lifted. 'Am I?'

Well, no. Technically, he wasn't, but for some reason it felt as though a swarm of bees had made their home in her stomach and as a result everything had the potential to make her tetchy. 'You're cutting it extremely fine.'

'Let me guess, you've been here for hours.'

'There's no need to sound quite so dismissive,' she said, bristling at the hint of mockery she could hear in his voice. Admittedly, she might have been a tad overzealous with the two hours, but then she'd only ever flown economy. She'd never had the luxury of private jet travel, with its gorgeous gleaming walnut surfaces, cream carpet and real china. 'Punctuality isn't a bad thing.'

'Punctuality is the thief of time.'

Hmm. 'I think you'll find it's procrastination

that's the thief of time. But, either way, mine is equally valuable as anyone else's.'

'I don't disagree. But, seeing as how I'm not late, the point is moot.'

Max folded his large frame into the seat opposite hers and buckled up. His knee bumped against hers and the jolt it sent rocketing through her could have powered a city for a week.

What was wrong with her? she wondered dazedly, her heart pounding like a jack hammer. One brief contact and she'd felt it like lightning. She was normally so steady and calm. Where was her composure? What was going on? Why him? Why now? More importantly, when was the air-con going to kick in? It was so hot in here.

Thankfully, Max was looking at his phone so couldn't have noticed her absurd overreaction to his touch. A minute later the engines started up and they were taxiing away from the terminal. As the plane accelerated down the runway, Alex gave herself a severe talking to. Her response to the gorgeous man once again sitting opposite her was not only ridiculous, it was wholly unacceptable. She had to pull herself together. How was she going to make any headway on the case if she couldn't work alongside him without turning into a quivering wreck?

That wasn't who she was. And how dangerous would it be if he knew how strongly he affected her? That she'd been dreaming about him? He might well consider her unprofessional as well as incompetent and neither was the case.

By the time they were in the air, the slow steady breaths she'd been taking to calm her raging pulse and the pep talk had had the desired effect and she'd got herself under enough control to at least make a start on the questions she'd compiled.

'How was lunch?' she asked, determined to focus on the job. When she'd spoken to Finn yesterday afternoon to subtly check that he wasn't intending to fire her, he'd mentioned the three brothers planned to spend the afternoon together. Max must have told him that they were teaming up and heading to Argentina together because Finn had also, bizarrely and unexpectedly, requested she take care of him. She knew that both he and Rico had had issues concerning their adoption but, quite honestly, in Max, she'd never met a man who needed taking care of less.

He glanced up and, despite all her efforts to control her response to him, her breath nevertheless caught at the bright intensity of his gaze. 'Good,' he said. 'Lengthy. It stretched into dinner and then drinks. I ended up crashing in one of Finn's hotel rooms.'

'You must have had a lot to catch up on.'

'We did,' he said with the quick flash of a genuine blinding smile.

'Do you get on well?' she asked, determined not to be dazzled.

'Exceptionally.'

He was obviously over the moon at having found his siblings, Alex thought, unable to prevent a dart of envy lancing through her. She had three siblings, with whom she had absolutely nothing in common other than a mutual lack of understanding.

How great would it be to have or find just one person who instinctively got you? Who unconditionally accepted you for who you were, warts and all. Not even her ex had truly understood her, or genuinely loved her for herself, possibly not even at all. But then, repenting at leisure was what came of marrying in haste. If she hadn't been so desperate for security and conventionality she could have saved herself years of heartache.

'Did you know you were adopted?' she asked, yanking her thoughts back on track since her relationships with her siblings and her ex weren't remotely relevant to the conversation.

'Not until the day before yesterday.'

'How did you feel when you found out?'

'Relieved.'

'Oh?'

'It's complicated.'

'In my experience, family generally is.'

His gaze sharpened and turned quizzical. 'In what way is yours complicated?'

Hers? Hmm. In what way *wasn't* it complicated? She was so different to the rest of hers that, ironically, for years she'd thought *she* had to be adopted.

She'd grown up on a rundown council estate, her parents and siblings largely relying on state support and the odd cash-in-hand job to keep them afloat. She'd been clever and wanted more, but aspiration had been thin on the ground both at school and home.

When she'd expressed an interest in university she'd been asked why she thought she was so special and told to get back in her box. In the face of such lack of encouragement she hadn't been brave enough to pursue that avenue, but had sought another way out instead. She hadn't fancied the army, with its olive drab and international danger zones, so she'd joined the police. Her family, who harboured a deep distrust of the authorities with whom they'd had more than one or two run-ins, had seen the move as a betrayal and never forgiven her.

She'd long since realised that their acceptance, their love, was conditional on conformity and it had been a price that ultimately she hadn't been willing to pay. But it still hurt, and she still wished things could have been different.

However, *her* family issues bore no relation to this case.

'I wasn't referring to mine,' she said, while thinking, well, not entirely. 'I simply meant that I've seen a lot of it through my work. Tell me about yours. It could be helpful.'

'It won't be,' he said with a frown, his jaw clenching in a faint but intriguing way.

'Let me be the judge of that,' she countered. 'Despite what you might think, Max, I am good at my job. There's a reason Finn hired me over one of the bigger, more established agencies. Not only was I highly recommended by an acquaintance of his, for whom I did some work, I leave no stone unturned. I'm tenacious like that. But I can only be the best if I have all the facts.'

He regarded her for a moment then gave a short nod. 'Fair enough. My father had a fatal heart attack seven years ago.'

'I'm sorry to hear that,' she said, feeling a

faint twang in her chest, which was baffling when she hardly knew him.

'My mother lives in New York. They divorced when I was fourteen.'

'Have you spoken to her about your adoption?'

'Briefly.'

'What did she say?'

'She claims not to recall much of the detail.'

From across the table, Alex stared at him in shock. His mother didn't recall much of the detail relating to the adoption of her son? Was she ill? Had he not asked the right questions? 'How is that possible?'

'She can be difficult.'

Or could it be that his family was as dysfunctional as hers? 'I'd like to talk to her.'

'There'd be little point.'

'It's an avenue I can't leave unexplored,' she said, noting the tension suddenly gripping him and the barriers shooting up.

'It's too early to call now.'

'The minute we land, then.'

'Have you had breakfast?'

'No,' she replied, intrigued by the abrupt change in topic but letting it go until she figured out a way of bypassing the barriers.

'Well, I don't know about you, but I'm ravenous.'

# CHAPTER THREE

UNBUCKLING HIS SEATBELT, Max got up and strode to the buffet bar, upon which sat a platter of cold meats and cheeses, bowls of fruit and a basket of pastries and rolls. He didn't want to talk about his mother to anyone at the best of times. He certainly didn't want to discuss her with Alex right now, he thought darkly as he took a plate and handed it to her.

Generally, he tried to think about Carolyn Stafford née Warwick née Browning née Kentala née Green as little as possible. He'd described her as difficult but that was an understatement. She was impossible and always had been. Everything was about her, nothing was ever good enough and her ability to find fault knew no bounds.

He could still vividly recall the time he'd broken his leg at the age of eight. She'd had to cancel a lunch date to take him to hospital and on the way there had let him know in no uncertain terms exactly how inconvenient he was being. The memory of the chilly silences she'd subjected him to as a child, when he'd failed to live up to one expectation or another, had had the ability to tighten his chest and accelerate his pulse for years.

Even now, she twisted words and situations for her own benefit and tried to manipulate and control him. The difference these days was that the armour he'd built over the years to protect himself from her—and from his father, for that matter—was inches thick and strong as steel. Everything now simply bounced off it.

So no, he thought, excising all thoughts of his mother from his head and piling breakfast onto a plate of his own, what he *wanted* to do was grab Alex by the hand, lead her into the bedroom he'd spotted at the back of the cabin and keep her there until they landed.

After departing her office yesterday morning, he'd put her from his mind and headed back to Finn and Rico, the need to reconnect with them before the flight out his number one goal. Lunch had extended into the afternoon and then to dinner and drinks late into the night, the conversation and his fascination with his brothers absorbing every drop of his attention.

Yet the minute he'd stepped onto the plane

he'd felt Alex's gaze on him like a laser, and every single thing discussed and learned and every accompanying emotion that had swept through him had vaporised. It was as if he'd been plugged into the national grid. The tiny hairs at the back of his neck had shot up and electricity had charged his nerve-endings, the effects of which still lingered.

This morning she was wearing a smart grey trouser suit, her hair up in a neat bun, her glossy fringe not a strand out of place, but, once again, none of that was as off-putting as he might have assumed. On the contrary, it only intensified his intention to unwind her and find out exactly what lay beneath the icy cool surface.

Was it a concern that he was so tuned to her frequency? No. The tiny gasp she'd let out when his knee had bumped hers was merely encouraging. The hint of defensiveness and the faint stiffening of her shoulders he'd noticed when they'd been talking about complicated families was nothing more than mildly interesting, because he didn't buy for one moment that she hadn't been referring to hers.

Nor was the fact he found her obvious disapproval of him so stimulating anything to worry about. Sure, it was unusual and unexpected—especially given how much censure he'd grown up with—but it wasn't as if he was after anything other than a purely physical relationship with her. She'd already turned what he'd always considered he found attractive on its head and her opinion of him was irrelevant.

And, quite honestly, there was no need to overthink it.

'So, by my calculations,' said Alex, cutting through his thoughts and snapping him back to breakfast, 'if you factor in the change in time zones, we should be landing at La Posada some time this afternoon.'

'We're making a stopover in the Caribbean first,' Max said, breaking open a roll and drizzling olive oil onto it.

A pause. Then, 'Oh?'

'Isla Mariposa. It's an island off the north coast of Venezuela. I live there. We should land mid-morning local time. We'll leave for Argentina tomorrow.'

There was another, slightly longer pause. 'I see.'

At the chill in her voice, Max glanced up and saw that her eyes were shooting daggers at him and her colour was high, which was as fascinating as it was a surprise. 'Is that a problem?' he asked with a mildness that totally belied the arousing effect her glare was having on him.

'Yes, it's a problem.'

'We'll need to refuel and the crew will need

a break,' he said, shifting on the seat to ease the sudden tightness of his jeans. 'I also need to pick up some clothes. It's cold where we're heading.'

La Posada stood three thousand four hundred metres above sea level and had a cold semi-arid climate. At this time of year, August, the temperature, which averaged seventeen degrees centigrade by day, plummeted to minus four at night.

'I know that,' said Alex somewhat witheringly. 'I checked. *That's* not the problem. Nor is refuelling and giving the crew a break, obviously.'

'Then what is?'

'You are,' she fired at him. 'You unilaterally making decisions that involve me without discussing them *with* me is the problem.'

In response to her unanticipated wrath, Max sat back, faintly stunned. 'If I'd known it was so important I'd have sent you the flight plan.'

'It's not just the flight plan,' she said heatedly. 'It's the way you set up a meeting with Rico and Finn when you were specifically requested to go through me. And then the commandeering of Rico's plane to fly to Argentina completely on your own.'

'Would you rather have flown commercial?'

'That's not the point. I'm the expert here. This is my field, Max. And it's *my* case.'

'No, it's not,' he replied, unable to resist the temptation to see how far she could be pushed.

'Yes, it is.'

'I prefer to think of it as *our* case.'

Alex threw up her hands in exasperation and he could practically see the steam pouring out of her ears, which would have put a grin on his face if he hadn't thought it would result in her throwing a croissant at him.

'But you're right,' he said a touch more soberly when it looked as if she was going to get up and storm off in vexation. 'I apologise. This is the first time I've worked with someone.'

Alex eyed him suspiciously for a moment but remained seated. 'Seriously?'

'I have a great respect for confidentiality.'

'You trust no one?'

'Not with work.' Or with anything else, but she didn't need to know that.

'Well, you're going to have to start,' she said, stabbing a chunk of kiwi with her fork. 'You'll soon get used to working with me.'

No, he wouldn't. This was a one-off and temporary. Joking aside, he didn't do 'our' anything and never would. A long-term relationship was way out of his reach, even if he had wanted one. Any hope he might have once had for love had been eroded so long ago he couldn't remember what it felt like, and thought of emotional intimacy, the kind he supposed might be required for such a thing, made him shudder. However, constant confrontation would hardly entice her into his bed.

'I'll endeavour to do better,' he said with what he hoped was the right amount of conciliation. 'And, with that in mind, my villa has a guest suite that I thought you might like to use, but feel free to book into a hotel if you'd prefer.'

The scowl on her face deepened for a moment, but then it cleared and she seemed to deflate, as if he'd whipped the wind of indignation from her sails. 'No, your guest suite would be great,' she said grudgingly. 'I wouldn't want to incur any unnecessary costs.'

'You're welcome.'

'Thank you.'

'This investigation means a lot to you, doesn't it?' he said, deeming it safe to continue with breakfast and adding a slice of ham to the roll.

'Every investigation means a lot to me,' she said archly. 'And they all come with rules.'

Did they? 'I'll have to take your word for it.'

'So I'd appreciate it if you would respect them as much as you say you respect confidentiality.'

Respect them? She had no idea. 'No can do, I'm afraid.'

'Why on earth not?'

'Rules are made to be broken.'

'Mine aren't.'

'You seem very definite.'

'I *am* very definite.'

Max watched her neatly slice a pain au chocolate in half and thought that if that kind of a statement wasn't irresistible to someone who'd never come across a rule he hadn't instinctively wanted to trample all over, he didn't know what was.

His days of rebelling against authority and challenging the system were over long ago. A brush with the Feds at the age of twenty for hacking into the digital billboards of Times Square had made him reassess his need to foster anarchy and create chaos, but that didn't mean the urge had disappeared altogether. 'That sounds like a challenge.'

She looked up and glared at him warningly. 'Believe me, it absolutely isn't.'

'What's the attraction?' He took a bite of his roll and noted with interest that her gaze dipped to his mouth for the briefest of moments before jerking back to his.

'Well, for one thing,' she said with a quick, revealing clearing of her throat, 'society wouldn't function without them. They maintain civilisation and prevent lawlessness. Everyone knows what's what, and there's security in that.' She paused then added, 'But on a personal level I will admit to liking order and structure.'

'Why?'

'I grew up without much of either. I came to see the benefits.'

'The complicated family?' he said, catching a fleeting glimpse of disappointment and regret in her expression.

'Maybe,' she admitted with a minute tilt of her head. 'My upbringing was chaotic.'

'In what way?'

'It just was.'

Her chin was up and her eyes flashed for a second and he thought that if she didn't want to talk about it that was fine with him. Her family problems were no concern of his. He had enough of his own to deal with. 'Chaos can be good,' he said instead, reflecting on how it had got him through his teenage years before his arrest had given him the opportunity to reassess.

She sat back and stared at him, astonishment wiping out the momentary bleakness. 'Are you serious?'

'The most disruptive periods of history have produced the finest art and the best inventions. Think the Medici.'

'So have the quietest. Think the telephone. What do you have against rules anyway?'

What *didn't* he have against them? They stifled creativity. They put in place boundaries that were frequently arbitrary and often unnecessary. Mostly, though, they represented authority that he'd once seen no reason to respect.

Max had started hacking at the age of twelve as a way of escaping from the rowing at home, his mother's constant criticism and his father's lack of interest in him. Not only had he got a massive kick out of breaking the law; more importantly, he'd found a community to become part of, one that considered failure a valuable learning tool, celebrated the smallest of successes and accepted him unconditionally. It had given him the sense of belonging that he'd craved and that had been addictive.

His early talents had swiftly developed into impressive skills and by the age of seventeen he'd gained a reputation as being the best in the business. He'd had respect—of the underground type, sure, but respect nevertheless—and he'd welcomed it.

While some of his acquaintances had stolen data to sell to the highest bidder and others held companies to ransom by installing malware, the more nefarious paths he could have chosen to take had never appealed. His interest had lain wholly in breaking systems and creating chaos. He'd relished and needed the control and the power it had given him when home was a place where he had none.

Now he had control and power that he'd acquired through legitimate routes and chaos no longer appealed, but there was still part of him that missed those days and always would.

'I'm a rebel at heart,' he said, giving her a slow grin which, intriguingly, made the pulse at the base of her neck flutter.

'Well, just as long as you don't make it your mission to lure me to the dark side,' she said pointedly, 'we should get along fine.'

It was all very well for Max to dismiss her need for rules, thought Alex, smiling her thanks to the flight attendant, who was clearing away breakfast with an obligingly professional rather than flirtatious manner, to treat them as some kind of joke. He couldn't possibly understand the hunger for stability and peace that she'd developed growing up.

Home had been a noisy, disruptive place. There'd been six of them initially, living in a cramped three-bedroom flat on the eighteenth floor of a tower block decorated with graffiti, lit by dim, flickering light bulbs and littered with cigarette ends and fast-food packaging.

She'd shared a bunk room with her sister and then the baby, her niece, as well, when she'd arrived. Her older brothers, who'd shared another of the rooms, had come and gone at all hours, where and to do what she'd never dared to enquire. Her parents had considered discipline and regular meals too much of a challenge to bother with properly, and school had been optional. Somehow, though strangely, there'd always been enough money.

Since it had been impossible to study at home with the racket that went on, Alex had spent much of her time at the local library and it was there that she'd happened upon Aristotle and his thoughts on the rule of law.

What she'd read had been liberating. When she'd realised that there was nothing to celebrate about the reckless, irresponsible way her family lived, she'd stopped trying to mould herself into something they could accept—which was proving impossible anyway when she'd rejected the idea with every fibre of her being—and turned her sights on escape.

Rules had given her a path out of the chaos. She'd diligently followed the school curriculum despite little encouragement, taken every exam available and set her sights on a career in the police, which, with its hierarchy and methodical approach to things, had appealed to her need for structure.

Sticking to them was hardly an adventurous or daring course of action, but it was a safe one and one which she knew she could rely on. She'd experienced the fallout from zero adherence: the worry about where her father was and when he'd be back; jumping every time there was a knock on the door and knowing with a feeling of dread that the law stood on the other side; a diet so deficient it gave you anaemia that made you faint.

The knowledge that she shared her family's DNA was a constant worry. What might happen if she let go of her grip on her control? How quickly would genes win out and consign her to a future of petty crime and little hope? She couldn't let that happen. She didn't want to live the way her parents and siblings did. She wanted a steady, law-abiding, chaos-free existence, one in which she knew where she was going and how she was going to get there.

Max, on the other hand, for some reason evidently saw rules as something to bend and to break. A challenge. So what did that mean going forwards? Would he try and break hers? If he did, how many and which ones? How far would he go? And how would she respond?

Well, she'd fight back with everything she

had, of course, because his love of breaking rules was not more important than her need to abide by them. That had been set in stone years ago and further cemented by embarking on a career as a woman in a man's world, which meant that she'd had to work twice as hard for her reputation.

Besides, she would not have him messing with her plans, her *life*, just because he felt like it. That tiny little thrill she could feel rippling through her at the thought of being the object of his focus could take a hike. It was wholly unacceptable and not to be indulged. She didn't want to be the object of his focus. Of *anyone's* focus, for that matter. She was very happy on her own, and had been since her divorce. She didn't need the stress and potential failure of another relationship, even if she ever could find it in her to trust again. The occasional date whenever she started to feel a bit lonely, where *she* called the shots, was more than enough.

Not that Max fell into the date category or ever would. Even if he had shown any sign of being attracted to her, he was too unpredictable, too much of a threat to her peace of mind. He was chaos with a capital C and therefore completely off-limits, despite the insane attraction she felt for him.

But he was also nothing she couldn't handle,

she told herself sternly as she turned her mind
to work. She'd come across far more temper-
amental personalities. He might have broken
through her unflappable exterior with his de-
cree about the stopover, but there'd been ex-
tenuating circumstances. She'd been provoked
one time too many. It wouldn't happen again.

And, in any case, they'd be busy with the
investigation. There wouldn't be time or space
for Max to challenge her rules. There'd be no
upheaval, no chaos. It would be fine.

While Alex set up a workspace at the table,
Max grabbed his laptop from his bag, kicked
off his shoes and stretched out on the sofa, still
thinking of interesting and inventive ways to
'lure her to the dark side'.

It might not be as simple as he'd first imagined, he acknowledged, firing up the machine
and revisiting their conversation. He hadn't
counted on rules. But he didn't envisage too
much of a problem. However mighty her will
and however noble her intentions, the attraction they shared was a thousand times stronger. If it drummed through her the way it did
through him—hot, insistent, all-consuming—it
wouldn't take long for her resistance to buckle
under the pressure. Maybe not quite within
the thirty-six hours he'd so confidently pre-

dicted yesterday lunchtime, but well within forty-eight.

'Making yourself comfortable?'

At Alex's dry question he glanced over and saw that her gaze was fixed on his bare feet. No doubt she disapproved, which naturally made him want to do something even more unprofessional—say, strip off his shirt—just to see her reaction.

'Why don't you join me?' he said with a grin, briefly wondering what the chances were of her letting her hair down in both senses of the phrase and taking up a position on the sofa that sat at right angles to his.

'Thanks,' she muttered, returning her attention to her laptop, 'but I'm fine over here.'

As he'd thought. Minuscule. But that was all right. Now he was beginning to see how she operated, he could adapt his strategy to seduce her into his bed accordingly. 'What are you doing?'

'Emails.'

'Haven't you forgotten something?'

She frowned. 'What?'

'Your side of our deal. If I allowed you to accompany me this morning,' he said, his choice of words deliberately provocative, 'you'd give me all the information you have on the investigation so far.'

Her eyes narrowed for a moment and he felt

a little kick of triumph. She was too easy to
wind up. Less clear was why he found it so
tempting to try.

'Sure,' she said with a disappointing return to
her customary cool. 'I'll send everything over
right now.'

The emails dropped into his inbox, one after
the other, and as Max clicked on the attachments, opening up reports, birth certificates, a
letter from Rico's adoptive parents to their son
and even the analysis of Finn's DNA, his pre-
occupation with undoing Alex and pulverising
her rules evaporated.

Reading the names of his birth parents, Juan
Rodriguez and Maria Gonzalez, made his
throat tight and his pulse race. Were they still
alive? Who were they, what were they like, and
did he resemble them in any way? What were
the chances of finding them? And which of the
three certificates was his? Would he ever get
to know who he truly was? Would he ever find
out why he'd been given up?

Rico's letter, a translation into English from
the original Italian, was deeply personal and
filled with loving thoughts as well as the name
of the adoption agency. Somewhere deep inside
Max's chest the words and the sentiments det-
onated a cocktail of resentment and pain that
he hadn't experienced in years, followed hot on

the heels by searing envy, which he wasn't particularly proud of since Rico's parents had died in a car accident when he was ten. But at least his brother had had a decade of affection and love, which was more than Max had ever had.

The analysis of Finn's DNA was less affecting but equally gripping. Their heritage was seventy-five per cent Latin American, twenty per cent Iberian, with a smattering of Central and Eastern European representing the remaining five per cent. Revelations included the low likelihood of dimples and the high possibility of a lactose intolerance. He scoured the data for similarities and found many.

Alex might consider this to be her field and her case, Max thought, methodically going through the reports supplied by her subcontractors, the details spinning around his head. But it was his history, his *family*. She could have no idea what it was like growing up sensing that somehow you were part of the wrong one, that you were unwanted but didn't know why. Nor could she know what it was like to obsessively wonder now how different things might have been if you'd grown up loved, wanted and happy in the right one. He'd spent thirty years not knowing his real parents. Thirty years apart from his brothers, with whom he'd shared a womb. So many memories unformed and opportunities lost...

'You mentioned having resources that I could only dream about,' Alex said, jolting him out of his thoughts, which was welcome when they'd become so tumultuous and overwhelming.

'You've been pretty thorough,' he said, clearing his throat of the tight knot that had lodged there. 'However, I can call in a few favours to see if we can't get round the Swiss banking secrecy issues and access Argentina's national archives.'

'Some favours they must be.'

'They are.' He'd once resolved the hack of a major Swiss bank and fixed a number of issues in systems controlled by the Argentinian government. 'But, other than that, I'm not sure what more I could legitimately add.'

'An interesting choice of words,' she said shrewdly. 'What about illegitimately?'

'It's a quick and efficient way of getting things done.'

Her mesmerising blue eyes widened for a second. 'Would you be willing to break the law for this?'

'I could,' he said, instinctively working through how he might go about it. 'And once upon a time I would have done so without hesitation. But not now. Now I have no intention of screwing up my career for a quick thrill.' These days he exerted his control and power in other ways, and accessing the systems to locate his brothers had been risky enough.

She looked at him steadily and he could practically see the pieces slotting into place in her brain. 'Were you a hacker?'

He nodded. 'A long time ago.'

'Is that how you got into cyber security?'

'It seemed like a good career move.'

Following his arrest, in an unlikely turn of events, Max had been offered a deal by the FBI: if he worked for them, he'd avoid jail. Initially he'd rejected the proposal. He hadn't even needed to think about it. Every millimetre of his being had recoiled at the thought of being employed by the authorities he despised. A sentence, however lengthy, would be infinitely preferable to selling out his principles.

But they'd given him forty-eight hours to reconsider, two days in a cell with nothing else to think about, and eventually he'd changed his mind. He was now on the authorities' radar. Escaping them in the future would be tough and actually he quite liked his freedom. The risks were beginning to outweigh the rewards, so maybe it was time for the poacher to turn gamekeeper.

From then on he'd been inundated with

job offers, which ranged from finding weaknesses in firewalls and fixing them to providing advice on how to stay one step ahead of the hackers and disrupters in an exceptionally fast-moving field. None of his prospective employers had a problem with his brush with the law. His incomparable skills easily overrode what had gone before.

Despite being presented with some exceptionally generous packages once he'd paid his debt to society via the FBI, he'd opted to go it alone, to take his pick of the work. He'd never regretted the decision to be in sole control of his future, and not just because he had millions in the bank.

'How long have you been doing it?'

'Ten years.'

'I read you have clients all over the world.'

'I do.'

'Then I'm surprised you have time to work on the investigation.'

'I'm between contracts.'

'Handy.'

'I'd have made time regardless.'

Her gaze turned quizzical. 'It means that much to you?'

'Yes.'

'Why?'

There was no way he was going into detail

about his upbringing, his efforts to overcome it and the emotional disruption the discovery of his adoption had wrought. He could barely work it out for himself. 'I'm good at solving puzzles,' he said with a casual shrug. 'I developed that particular skill while I was at MIT.' Or at least he had until his arrest, at which point he'd been stripped of his scholarship and kicked out.

'Computers are your thing.'

'They are,' he agreed, glancing at his laptop and feeling a familiar sense of calm settle over him. They were a damn sight simpler than people, that was for sure. They were devoid of emotion and didn't demand the impossible. They were predictable, easy to read if you knew what you were looking for and generally did what they were told. 'Like rules are yours.'

'Tell me more about the hacking.'

'What do you want to know?'

'Everything,' she said, getting up and moving to the sofa next to his, taking up a position that was too far away for his liking. 'Call it professional interest. There's a big gap in my knowledge of this particular area. How did you get into it?'

'I was given a computer for my tenth birthday,' he said, remembering with a sharp stab of pain how excited he'd been until his mother had told him in no uncertain terms that she expected it to improve his grades, otherwise it would be removed. 'I spent hours messing about on it, learning the language and writing programs, before discovering forums and chats. I got talking. Made friends. Things went from there.'

She leaned forward, avid curiosity written all over her face. 'How?'

'What do you mean?' he said, slightly taken aback by her interest in him and faintly distracted by the trace of her scent that drifted his way.

'Well, lots of people mess about on computers and chat online,' she said. 'Not many go down the hacking route.'

'Not many are good enough.'

She tilted her head. 'You say that with pride.'

'Do I?'

'You shouldn't.'

'Probably not.'

'What sort of things did you get up to?'

'The first thing I did was change a grade for a math test when I was twelve. I got an F. I should have got an A. I just hadn't studied. The F was a mistake.' More than that, though, he'd been terrified his mother would act on her threat and take his computer back.

She stared at him, appalled. 'How on earth could you not have studied for an exam?'

Because, since it was a subject he'd found easy, with the arrogance of youth, he'd assumed he'd wing it. 'Surely that isn't the point.'

'You're right,' she agreed. 'It isn't. What else?'

'I regularly set off the fire alarms and sprinkler systems at high school. I travelled round the city for free and was behind a handful of denial of service attacks. At one point I ran an operation cancelling parking tickets.'

'That's really bad,' she said, tutting with disapproval he'd come to expect. 'If the US authorities treat that kind of thing the same way the UK ones do, you risked years in jail.'

And that had been part of the appeal. The power, the control, the extremely high stakes and the respect he'd garnered that had made him feel so alive. It had given him a sense of identity, of purpose and he'd revelled in it. 'The commission I earned paid my rent while I was at college. I never caused anyone harm. I never even wanted to. Maximum disruption was my only goal.'

'And making money.'

'That was just a coincidence.'

'What did your parents think of what you were doing?'

'They never knew,' he said, hearing the trace

of bitterness he was unable to keep from his voice and hating that old wounds he'd assumed were long gone appeared to have been ripped open. 'They were too wrapped up in themselves.'

'Ah,' she said, with a nod and smile he couldn't quite identify but which, for some reason, shot a dart of unease through him. 'Did you ever get caught?'

'Eventually. While I was at MIT, I hacked into the billboards in Times Square. I took down all the adverts and announcements and replaced them with my avatar.'

'Why?'

'Because I could. Because I was young and hubristic. Twenty-four hours later I had the FBI knocking on my door.'

'How did they find you?'

'A dark net contact of mine got sloppy and then did a deal to save his own ass.'

'Did you go to jail?'

He shook his head. 'I traded my principles for my freedom.'

'You got off lightly.'

'I was lucky.'

Very lucky, in retrospect. Forty-eight hours in the cells had been ample time to contemplate the journey that had landed him there. It hadn't taken him long to figure out that everything he'd done had been a reaction to the environment at home. His father's neglect, his mother's emotional vampirism. Operating in the shadows had given him the respect, approval and appreciation that he hadn't even known he'd been missing. His many successes had earned him recognition. His few failures had fuelled his determination to be better.

But he hadn't liked thinking about how weak and vulnerable he'd been as a kid. Nor had he enjoyed dwelling on why he'd carried on with his double life even when he'd escaped to MIT. He didn't want to admit to the fear that without it he didn't know who he was.

He'd never get the opportunity to work that out if he didn't give himself a chance, he'd eventually come to realise. And he had to stop being so angry. It didn't mean he'd forgiven his parents for the effects of their behaviour on him, but he could either allow the bitterness to take over or let it go. He'd chosen the latter, determinedly putting it all behind him, and gone on the straight and narrow, building his business and maintaining minimal contact with his parents. And everything had been going fine until he'd seen the video of his brothers and the fragile reality he'd created for himself had imploded.

'You'd get on well with my family,' said Alex

with a dry smile that bizarrely seemed to shine through the cracks in his armour and light up the dark spaces within.

'In what way?' he asked, absently rubbing his chest.

'They have an unhealthy disrespect for the law too. Not quite on your level, admittedly. One of my brothers has a habit of shoplifting. My sister claims benefits but also works on the side. My father describes himself as a wheeler-dealer, but he treads a fine line.'

'Yet you went into the police.' Yesterday, he'd looked her up. The idea of a former law enforcement officer hooking up with a former criminal—albeit a non-convicted one—had held a certain ironic appeal.

'It was *my* escape.'

'How did that go down?' he asked, conveniently ignoring the comparison while thinking that she was way too perceptive.

'They've never forgiven me.'

'That I can understand. My mother's never got beyond my arrest.' Not even his subsequent success, which she tended to either diminish or ignore, could make up for that.

'I'm very much the ugly duckling of my family.'

'There is nothing ugly about you.'

'Nor you.'

A strange kind of silence fell then. Her cheeks flushed and her gaze dipped to his mouth. He became unusually aware of his heartbeat, steady but quickening. Her eyes lifted back to his, darkening to a mid-blue, and she stared at him intently, as if trying to look into his soul, which shook something deep inside him. The tension simmered between them. The air heated. He was hyperaware of her. The hitch of her breath. The flutter of her pulse at the base of her neck. He wanted to kiss her so badly it was all he could think about.

And then she blinked.

'Right,' she said briskly, snapping the connection and making him start. 'I'm going for a nap. Unlike some, I had a very early start. See you later.'

And as she leapt to her feet and fled the scene, Max had the oddly unsettling feeling that it was going to be a very long flight.

# CHAPTER FOUR

NEVER HAD SHE been so glad of fresh air and space, Alex thought six hours later as she sat at the back of Max's speedboat, which was whisking them from Simón Bolívar International Airport, just north of Caracas, to Isla Mariposa, where he lived. She lifted her face to the glorious mid-morning sun while the warm Caribbean Sea breeze whipped around her, willing it to blow away the excruciating tension gripping every cell of her body.

So much for a nice refreshing nap. She felt as refreshed as a damp, dirty dishcloth, on edge and gritty-eyed, but then that was what came of not being able to catch up on a broken truncated night. She wished she could have blamed her tossing and turning on turbulence, but the flight had been smooth and uneventful. The only turbulence she'd experienced had been within.

She'd met many criminals in her time, but

never a hacker and none as devastatingly attractive as the man standing at the wheel, handling the boat so competently. Beneath the blazing sun she could make out fine golden streaks in his dark hair. His eyes were even bluer in the bright mid-morning light. Once again he'd kicked off his shoes and once again she was transfixed.

Alex had never had a thing about feet before. If she'd had to provide an opinion on them she'd have said function over form was generally the case and the more hidden away they were the better. It would appear she had a thing about his, however, because they were things of beauty. She could stare at them for hours. She had, in fact, at length, on the plane, when he'd been talking about his early career and she'd been rapt. But at least it made a change from trying not to stare at his mouth, which was proving an irritatingly hard challenge.

What was the matter with her? she wondered, taking a sip of water from her bottle and surreptitiously running her gaze over him. Why were Max Kentala and his many physical attractions occupying so much of her brain? He really wasn't her type. It wasn't about his looks any longer. In that respect, it had become blindingly obvious that he was exactly her type, hair in need of a cut and jaw in need of a shave or not.

But with regard to everything else they were chalk and cheese. Their poles apart attitudes towards time-keeping notwithstanding, he'd been a law-breaker. She'd been a law-enforcer. He clearly embraced turmoil while she craved the security of stability and predictability. He considered engaging in criminal activity *a quick thrill*. They couldn't have more opposing values or be more different.

What she couldn't understand, however, was why she found this dichotomy so fascinating. The pride she'd noted when he'd been talking about the illegal ways he'd deployed his considerable IT skills, which had lightened his expression and made him look younger, more carefree and, unbelievably, even more gorgeous, wasn't something to be applauded. Hacking into the Times Square billboards wasn't cool or fun or imaginative. It was reckless, irresponsible and downright illegal.

The walk on the wild side he'd once taken was everything she abhorred, everything she avoided like the plague. That he'd so obviously enjoyed it should have dramatically diminished his appeal. But it didn't. Instead it seemed to have *augmented* it, which was baffling and more than a little concerning, as was the still unacceptable thrill that was begging to be indulged with increasing persistence.

Could it be that their many differences were somehow mitigated by their few similarities? They were both problem solvers who'd forged successful careers from nothing. They'd both had disapproving parents and had once upon a time sought an escape from their families. Both were equally invested in uncovering the truth, although she didn't quite believe that for him it was just a problem to solve.

So could their unexpected commonalities somehow explain her one-eighty swing from reproach to sympathy? *Something* had to account for that oddly heart-stopping moment they'd shared just before she'd legged it to the bedroom.

She hadn't meant to confess that she found him attractive. She was sure there was nothing to read in his comment along the same lines. Yet he'd suddenly looked so sincere it had caught her off-guard. Her gaze had collided with his and the intense heat she'd seen darkening the blue to navy had dazzled her. Her mouth had dried. Her pulse had pounded. She'd wanted to get up and move to his side. To lean down, pin him to the sofa and cover his mouth with hers. She'd very nearly done it too, to her horror, hence the sudden excuse of a nap.

She had to put the whole plane journey from her mind, she told herself firmly for what felt like the hundredth time in the past hour. She might not be able to make head or tail of her attitude towards Max but one thing was certain: his ability to derail her focus was wholly wrong. The unexpectedly sexy way he put on his sunglasses, pulling them from the V of his shirt and sliding them onto his nose, bore no relevance to anything. That the fine hair on his beautifully muscled forearms was a shade lighter than that on his head was not something she needed to concern herself with. And who cared that he'd been strangely monosyllabic and tight-jawed ever since they'd landed?

All she wanted was to crack this case and secure her future.

As they rounded a small headland Max slowed the boat and Alex turned her gaze to the shore. At the sight of the house that hove into view, her jaw dropped. Beyond the water that sparkled jade and turquoise and was so clear she could see right down to the bottom, above the curving swathe of palm-fringed white sand, the villa stood nestled among the trees that rose up behind. Four low-level triangular wooden roofs stretched out above huge glass windows and doors. In front, overlooking the sea, was a series of connected terraces. On one she thought she could make out a pool. At each end, a flight of wooden steps descended between the boulders to the beach.

Even from this distance she could see that it was a building sympathetic to its surroundings and stunningly beautiful. It was the kind of place she'd only ever seen in magazines, in which, incredibly, *she* was getting to stay. And yes, it was for work, just as the private jet had been, but that didn't stop her mentally sticking two fingers up at the teachers who'd told her repeatedly and scornfully that with her family she didn't stand a chance of ever making anything of herself. Nor did it stop her wishing her parents could see her now, not that there was any point to that at all.

Max brought the boat to a near stop and lined it up to the dock. He tossed a loop of rope over a mooring bollard with easy competence and a flex of muscles that, to her despair, made her stomach instinctively tighten, but she had the feeling that for the greater good she was just going to have to accept the way she responded to him and ignore it.

Displaying an enviable sense of balance, he unloaded their luggage and then alighted. He bent down and extended his arm. 'Give me your hand.'

For a moment Alex stared at his outstretched

hand as if it were a live grenade. She couldn't
risk taking it. If she did, she might not be able
to let go. But she didn't have his sense of balance. One wobble and she could well end up
in the sea, and quite frankly she felt jumpy
enough around him without adding looking
foolish into the mix.

'Thanks.'

After hauling Alex up off his boat and then
dropping her hand as if it were on fire, Max
grabbed their bags and strode up the steps to
the house without bothering to see if she was
following. He was tense. Tired. On edge.

As he'd suspected, it had been a very long
flight. Once he'd rid his head first of images
of Alex lying on the bed in the cabin of the
plane alone and then of what would happen
if he joined her, he'd found himself revisiting
their conversation. Every detail, no matter how
minute, appeared to be etched into his memory,
and his unease had grown with every nautical
mile, twisting his gut and bringing him out in
a cold sweat.

Which was odd.

Generally he had no problem talking about
his career or what he'd done to get there. He
didn't have anything to hide. Most of it was
in the public domain for anyone interested

enough to go looking for it. It wasn't as if he'd given away a piece of himself or anything. He'd long ago come to terms with his mother's ongoing ignominy of having a son with a criminal background.

So why had their conversation unsettled him so much? Alex clearly disapproved of the things he'd got up to in his youth, but so what? Her opinion of him genuinely didn't matter. They were absolute opposites in virtually every respect, and he wasn't interested in her in any way except the physical.

Perhaps it was her curiosity in him which, despite her assertion to the contrary, had seemed more personal than professional. He couldn't recall the last time anyone had genuinely wanted to know what made him tick. Neither of his parents ever had. And these days most people just wanted to hear about his exploits. But Alex had wanted to know what lay behind them. She'd looked at him as if trying to see into his soul and it had rocked him to the core.

Or perhaps it had been that 'ah' of hers, the one she'd uttered when he'd told her that his parents couldn't have cared less about what he'd got up to. It suggested she'd caught the trace of bitterness that had laced his words and it smacked of sympathy and understanding, which he really didn't need. That they had parental disapproval and lack of forgiveness in common meant nothing. What did it matter that she was as much of a disappointment to her family as he was to his?

He was beginning to regret accepting Alex's ultimatum and allowing her to come with him. He should have stuck to his guns and listened to his head instead of his body. He had more than enough going on without her adding complications. He hated the confusion and uncertainty currently battering his fractured defences. He'd thought he'd overcome that sort of thing a decade ago. To realise that he might not have dealt with the past as successfully as he'd assumed was like a blow to the chest. At the very least he should have booked her into a hotel for tonight.

But there was nothing he could do about any of that now. However tempting it might be, he could hardly leave her here while he continued to Argentina alone. They'd made a deal and, for all his many faults, for all his crimes and misdemeanours, he'd never once gone back on his word. And booking her into a hotel now, when he'd already offered her his guest suite, would indicate a change of plan he didn't want her questioning.

At least where he was putting her up was separated from the main house, he thought grimly, striding past the infinity pool and heading for the pair of open doors that led to the suite. It wouldn't be too hard to ignore her for as long as it took for him to get a grip on the tornado of turmoil that was whipping around inside him. His plans for seduction could handle a minor delay while he regrouped.

'Here you go,' he said, stalking through the doors and dumping her bag beside the huge bed that stood before him like a great flashing beacon. 'Make yourself comfortable.'

'Thank you. This is an incredible house.'

'I like it.'

What he *didn't* like, however, was the fast unravelling of his control. Him, Alex, the bed… On top of everything else, the hot, steamy images now cascading into his head were fraying his nerves. The sounds she'd make. The smoothness of her skin beneath his hands and the soft silkiness of her hair trailing over him as she slid down his body.

He shouldn't be in here. He should have simply handed her her bag and pointed her in the right direction. He had to get out before he lost it completely. He whipped round to leave her to it, but she was closer than he was expecting. He slammed to a halt and jerked back, as if struck.

'Are you all right, Max?' she said with a quick frown.

No. He wasn't all right at all. 'I'm fine.'

'You don't look fine.' She put her hand on his arm and her touch shot through him with the force of a thousand volts. 'Your jaw looks like it's about to snap. You've been tense ever since we landed. Has something happened?'

What *hadn't* happened? Forget the fact that the last forty-eight hours had been more tumultuous than the last ten years. *She'd* happened. He couldn't work out why that should be a problem, but it was. As was the compassion and concern written all over her beautiful face. He didn't need that any more than he needed her sympathy or understanding. What he *did* need was space. Air to breathe that wasn't filled with her scent. Time to get himself back under control.

And yet he could no more move than he could fly to Mars. She was close. Very close. He could see a rim of silver around the light blue of her irises and he could hear the soft raggedness of her breathing. The concern was fading from her expression and the space between them started cracking with electricity, the air heavy with a strange sort of throbbing tension. Her pupils were dilating and her gaze dipped to his mouth and still her hand lingered on his arm, burning him like a brand.

The desire that thudded through him was firing his blood and destroying his reason, but he welcomed it, because this he understood. This he could command. She leaned into him, only the fraction of an inch, so minutely she probably wasn't aware she'd done it, but in terms of encouragement it was the greenest of lights and one he couldn't ignore.

Acting on pure instinct, Max shook her hand off him and took a quick step forwards. He put his hands on either side of her head and, dazed with lust, lowered his mouth to hers. Her scent and heat stoked his desire for her to unbearable levels and his ability to think was long gone, but he nevertheless felt her jolt and then stiffen and was about to let her go when she suddenly whipped her arms around his neck, pressed herself close and started kissing him back.

With a groan of relief, he pulled her tighter against him and deepened the kiss, the flames shooting through him heating the blood in his veins to bubbling. The wildness of her response, the heat and taste of her mouth robbed him of his wits. He was nothing but sensation, could feel nothing but her, could think only of the bed not a dozen metres away and the painful ache of his granite-hard erection, against which she was grinding her pelvis and driving him mad.

He deftly unbuttoned her jacket and slid a hand to her breast, rubbed his thumb over her tight nipple, and she moaned. He moved his mouth along her jaw, the sound of her pants harsh in his ear, sending lightning bolts of ecstasy through him. She burrowed her fingers into his hair, as if desperate to keep him from going anywhere, which was never going to happen—

And then a door slammed somewhere inside the house.

In his arms, Alex instantly froze and jerked back, staring at him for what felt like the longest of moments, her cheeks flushed and her eyes glazed with desire. But all too soon the desire vanished and in its place he could see dawning dismay. She shoved at his shoulders and he let her go in a flash, even though every cell of his body protested.

'What's wrong?' he muttered dazedly, his voice rough and his breathing harsh.

'What's wrong?' she echoed in stunned disbelief. 'This is.'

'It seemed very much all right to me.'

'It was a mistake,' she panted, smoothing her clothes and doing up the button of her jacket with trembling hands while taking an unsteady step back. 'I'm here to work.'

It very much hadn't been a mistake. It had been everything he'd anticipated. More. 'Work can wait.'

'No. It can't,' she said, swallowing hard.

'We're not leaving until tomorrow. There's no rush.'

'I'd planned to call your mother as soon as we landed. Now would be that time.'

At that, Max recoiled as if she'd slapped him. What the hell? If that door hadn't slammed they'd be on the bed getting naked just as fast as was humanly possible. She'd clung to him like a limpet. Kissed him as if her life had depended on it. And now she was talking about his mother? Well, that was one way to obliterate the heat and the desire.

Had that been her intention? If it was, she'd succeeded, because now instead of fire, ice was flowing through his veins, and instead of lust and desperate clawing need, all he felt was excoriating frustration and immense annoyance.

'Sure,' he said, reaching into the back pocket of his trousers and pulling out his phone, while his stomach churned with rejection and disappointment. He scrolled through his contacts and stabbed at the buttons. 'I've sent you her num-

ber,' he added as a beep sounded in the depths
of her handbag.

'Thank you.'

'Call her whenever you like.'

'Don't you want to be in on it?'

'I already know what she's going to say.' And
he didn't need to hear it—or anything else she
might choose to add—again. What he needed
was to get rid of everything that was whirling
around inside him as a result of that aborted
kiss, the agonising tension and the crushing
disillusionment. 'Help yourself to lunch when
you're done,' he said curtly. 'I'm going for
a swim.'

Alex watched Max stride off, six foot plus of
wound-up male, and sank onto the bed before
her legs gave way.

What on earth had just happened? she wondered dazedly, her entire body trembling with
shock and heat and confusion. One minute
she'd been filled with concern for his well-being since he'd looked so tormented, the next
she'd been in a clinch so blistering she was surprised they hadn't gone up in flames.

Touching his arm had been her first mistake,
even though she'd desperately wanted to know
what had been troubling him. Her fascination
with the clench of his muscles beneath her fin-

gers and the feel of his skin, which had meant she hadn't wanted to let him go, had been her second. Then she'd become aware that he'd gone very still and was looking at her with an intensity that robbed her of reason and knocked the breath from her lungs, and the mistakes had started coming thick and fast.

She shouldn't have allowed the enormous bed and the two of them entwined on it to dominate her thoughts. She should have spun on her heel and fled to the sanctuary of the terrace. But she hadn't. She'd been rooted to the spot, utterly transfixed by the inferno raging in his indigo gaze. Unguarded, fiery, havoc-wreaking heat, directed straight at her.

She didn't have time to wonder at the startling realisation that the attraction she'd assumed to be wholly one-sided could, in fact, be mutual. Or to even consider what was happening. A second later she'd been in his arms, her heart thundering so hard she'd feared she might be about to break a rib.

And, oh, the feel of him… The strength and power of his embrace and the intoxicating skill of his kiss. Her head was still swimming from its effect, her blood still burned. His mouth had delivered on every single promise it made. Heat had rushed through her veins, desire swirling around inside like a tropical storm. When he'd moved his hand to cup her breast the shivers that had run through her had nearly taken out her knees. If it hadn't been for that door, she'd have ended up in bed with him and she wouldn't even have cared. She'd have *relished* it, and that was so wrong she could scarcely believe it.

Where had that response come from? It had been so wild, so abandoned. Mortifyingly, she'd practically devoured him. So much for the professionalism she'd always prided herself on. She hadn't so much blurred the lines as erased them altogether.

What on earth had she been *thinking*? she asked herself, going icy cold with stupefied horror at what she'd done. Had she completely lost her tiny little mind? And where the hell had her rules been in all of this? Max had simply taken what he wanted and she'd let him. She'd had ample opportunity to push him away but she hadn't until it had been shamefully late. And before that she hadn't even thought about it. He might have taken her by surprise when he'd first kissed her but she hadn't for a moment considered not kissing him back.

God, she had to be careful. He was so much more dangerous than she'd imagined. He was such a threat to her rules, not because he saw them as a challenge necessarily, but because he made her want to break them herself. He made her forget why she had them in the first place.

But that couldn't happen. She couldn't afford to have her head turned or give in to the blazing attraction they clearly shared. Her future plans were at stake, and how good would it look if Finn ever got wind of what had just happened? He'd have every right to fire her after that lapse of professionalism. If it happened again or, heaven forbid, went any further—which it absolutely wouldn't—and got out, her reputation would never recover.

A chill ran through her at the thought of how easily she could lose everything she'd worked so hard for. How precariously she teetered at the top of a very slippery slope. She couldn't allow another blip when it came to reason. Or make any more mistakes. She would not be governed by forces which threatened her very existence and over which she had no control. She would not turn into her family. She had an entirely different future to forge.

Three hours after Max had disappeared to go for his swim, Alex sat on a sofa beneath the shades that covered the terrace, nursing a glass of mint tea while largely ignoring the laptop open in front of her. How on earth could she concentrate on emails when she had so many other things occupying her mind?

Like that kiss…

No, not the kiss, she amended firmly. Hadn't she decided she wasn't going to think about it ever again? Wasn't she supposed to be completely ignoring the irritating little voice inside her head that demanded more of the delicious heat of it? She had and she was, and besides, it wasn't as if she didn't have anything else to think about. Such as the extraordinary conversation she'd just had with Max's mother.

As he'd told her, Carolyn Stafford had nothing to add to the investigation. With regard to Max's adoption, her then husband, the first of four and Max's father, had dealt with all the practicalities. He was the one who'd found the agency, arranged the payment and booked the flights to Argentina. She couldn't even recall filling in any forms. When it came to actually picking Max up, she had the haziest of recollections involving a woman whose name she couldn't remember, which struck Alex as very peculiar when it had to have been a momentous occasion.

The minute she'd established that Mrs Stafford could be of no further help, Alex should have hung up. The rest of the conversation had borne no relevance to anything. She didn't need to know about the issues in the marriage, the troubles they'd had conceiving and the belief that adopting a baby would somehow fix everything. The impact the divorce had had on Mrs Stafford was neither here nor there, although the way she hadn't spared a thought for how Max might have taken it was telling. She evidently held her son to blame for failing to repair the marriage, which didn't seem at all fair, and obviously considered him lacking in pretty much every other area. The digs and barbs had been well wrapped up and so subtle as to be easily missed, but Alex had noted them nonetheless.

But, to her shame, she hadn't hung up. Instead she'd listened to his mother's litany of complaints with growing indignation. She hadn't recognised anything about the man being described and at one point a sudden, inexplicable urge to put things right had surged up inside her, the force of it practically winding her.

But she'd known it would achieve precisely nothing.

Firstly, given that she'd only met Max yesterday, she was hardly qualified to provide an in-depth commentary on his character, even if she did have an extremely thorough knowledge of his mouth. Secondly, early on in her career with the police, Alex had done a course on psychopathic personalities and it sounded as if Max's mother was a narcissist. She'd come across as self-absorbed, condescending and unfairly critical. Everything had been about her. Any attempt to stand up for Max would have fallen on deaf ears, and that wasn't part of the job anyway.

She couldn't exactly start questioning him on it, she reminded herself, taking a sip of tea and staring out to sea, regardless of how much she might want to deep down. Not only was it none of her business, she was here to work, nothing more. She didn't need to know and, in any case, he wasn't around to ask.

And that was something else that was beginning to bother her, even though it surely shouldn't. Max had been gone for three hours. Wasn't that quite a long time for a swim? What if something had happened? Could he have been caught in a rip tide? What if he'd got a cramp and drowned? He might be a grown man who lived by the sea and presumably swam a lot, but maybe she ought to contact the coastguard. Just in case.

Trying to keep a lid on her growing alarm, Alex picked up her phone and opened up the browser to look for the number, when her gaze snagged on something moving in the water. A figure broke through the shimmering surface of the azure water, and she froze.

First to emerge was a sleek dark head, followed by a set of broad shoulders that she hadn't had nearly enough time to explore before. A swimmer's shoulders, she thought dazedly as she put the phone down, since there was clearly no need to contact the coastguard. Max, looking like some sort of Greek god, rising from the deep, master of all he surveyed, had not perished in the waves.

As he waded through the shallows, giving his head a quick shake that sprayed water off him like droplets of sparkling sunlight, more of his body was revealed. She was too far away to make out the details, but his bronzed shape was magnificent and by the time his long powerful legs emerged, undiluted lust was drumming through her, drugging her senses and heightening her awareness of everything. Her mouth was dry. Her breasts felt heavy and tight, and she was filled with the insane urge to get up and meet him and pull him down onto the sand with her and finish what they'd started back there in the guest house.

Having reached the shore, Max bent and picked up a towel off a lounger. He rubbed it over his head, slung it around his neck and started striding up the beach towards the steps, which gave her approximately thirty seconds to compose herself. It wasn't nearly enough, she realised, taking a series of slow deep breaths to calm her racing pulse and rid her body of the dizzying heat that she'd thought she'd obliterated hours ago.

But she managed it somehow, until he came to a stop right in front of her, blocking her view of the sea with an even better one, and she realised that her efforts had been in vain.

He didn't have an ounce of fat on him. He was all lean hard muscle. The depth of his tan suggested he spent a lot of time shirtless in the sun. Judging by the definition of his six-pack, he wasn't completely desk-bound. And she didn't need to wonder what might lie at the base of the vertical line of golden-brown hair that bisected his abdomen and disappeared enticingly beneath the waistband of his shorts because she'd felt it. She'd pressed her hips against it and wanted it hard and deep inside her, and that was exactly what would have happened if only that door hadn't slammed.

But she wasn't going to think about earlier. She certainly wasn't going to bring it up. If Max did, she'd brush it off as if it had meant nothing. Which it hadn't. And she was *relieved* that door had slammed, not disappointed.

But whatever.

Denial was the way forward here, even though she generally considered it an unwise and unhelpful strategy. In her line of work, knowledge was power. If her clients could accept what was going on, they could handle it. Right now, however, confronting what had happened when she was on such unsteady ground around him seemed like the worst idea in the world, and if that made her a hypocrite then so be it.

'How was the swim?' she said, nevertheless struggling to keep her tone light and her gaze off his chest.

'Good.'

'You were gone a long time.'

A gleam lit the depths of his indigo eyes. 'Were you worried about me, Alex?'

Maybe. 'No.'

He gripped the ends of the towel, which drew her attention to his hands and reminded her of how warm and sure they'd been, first on her face and then on her body.

'There's a floating bar the next bay along. I stopped for a drink.'

'A floating bar?' she echoed, determinedly keeping the memory of his kisses at bay. Was there no end to the incredibleness of this place?

'I'll take you for dinner there this evening.'

'I didn't bring a swimsuit.'

His gaze roamed over her, so slowly and thoroughly that she felt as if her clothes were simply falling away like scorched rags, and he murmured, 'That's a shame.'

No, it wasn't. The assignment didn't include swimsuits, dinner in a floating bar or the shedding of clothing. 'This isn't a holiday for me, Max,' she said, setting her jaw and pulling herself together. 'I was expecting to be heading straight to La Posada.' Which was situated six hundred kilometres inland. 'I didn't pack for a Caribbean island stopover.'

'All right. Forget the swimsuit,' he said, which immediately made her think of skinny-dipping with him in the gorgeous water beneath the moonlight. 'We'll go by boat.'

'No.'

'I apologise,' he said with a tilt of his head and a faint smile that lit an unwelcome spark of heat in the pit of her stomach. 'How would you feel about going by boat?'

The same. It wasn't going to happen, however he phrased it. She wasn't here for fun, and dinner out felt strangely dangerous. 'I'd rather you called in the favours you mentioned.'

'I already have.'

What? 'When?' she asked with a frown. How could he have wrong-footed her yet again?

'Earlier. On the plane.'

'What happened to working together?'

'What do you mean?'

'We had a deal, Max. You asked me to hand over everything, which I did. The least you could do is include me in your decision-making.'

'You were taking a nap.'

His reasonableness riled her even more than his unpredictability. 'Still,' she said frostily, not quite ready to accept that he'd done the right thing, given what had happened when the two of them had found themselves in close proximity to a bed. 'You should have told me.'

'I just have.'

*Agh.* 'You're impossible.'

His grin widened. 'Did you eat lunch?'

'No.' She hadn't felt comfortable raiding his fridge.

'Neither did I, and it seems neither of us is at our best on an empty stomach. So shall we meet back here in, say, half an hour?'

To her despair, Alex was all out of excuses. Any further protest and he might start questioning what was behind it. There was no way she wanted him guessing how much their kiss had unsettled her. Or how confusing she found the switch in demeanour when the last time she'd seen him he'd been all troubled and tense. And she badly needed him and his near naked body out of her sight. His mention of stomachs was making her want to check out his and she feared she wouldn't be able to stop there.

'Sounds great.'

# CHAPTER FIVE

STALKING INTO HIS en-suite bathroom, Max stripped off and grabbed a towel. He secured it round his waist, rolled his shoulders to ease the ache that had set in as a result of his lengthy swim and, with a quick rub of his jaw, turned to the sink.

As he'd hoped, vigorous exercise, a cold beer and easy conversation had assuaged his earlier excruciating tension. It had taken a while, however. He'd been ploughing through the warm tropical water for twenty minutes at full speed before he'd been able to stop thinking about what would have happened had he and Alex not been interrupted.

His imagination had been on fire, and it had occurred to him as he'd cracked open a beer at La Copa Alegre that that was unusual because, despite his mother constantly telling him that his was very vivid whenever he'd tried to correct her memory about certain things as a kid, he'd never thought he had much of one. His ability to see outside the box and apply lateral thinking to problem-solving was second to none, but it was always done in the context of data. Facts. Systems, processes and algorithms. Lurid was not a word that had ever applied to his thoughts. It was now.

On emerging from the sea he'd intended to head straight for the house. But he'd felt Alex's eyes on him like a laser and had instead deviated towards her as if drawn by some invisible force. She'd taken off her jacket, he'd noticed once he'd been standing in front of her. The pale pink T-shirt she'd had on had been tight. The alluring curve of her breasts had not escaped his notice, and as a bolt of heat had rocketed through him at the memory of how she'd felt in his hand, tightening his muscles and giving him an erection as hard as granite, he'd been grateful for the loose fit of his shorts.

She might have chosen to opt for denial with regard to the chemistry they shared, he thought now, lathering up his jaw, reaching for a razor and setting about methodically cutting swathes through the foam, but he wasn't. That kiss had blown his mind. He wanted more. A lot more. And so did she. She'd barely been able to keep her eyes off his bare chest just now. The hunger in her gaze had been illuminating. It gave him ideas. Would it be playing dirty to capitalise on her interest in his body? Might it not simply lead her to realise that little bit faster that making out with him hadn't been a mistake?

He couldn't deny that the idea of pushing more of her buttons appealed. He liked the way her eyes narrowed and flashed when she was riled. It gave him a kick, as did the thought of demolishing her barriers and persuading her to break her own rules. The end would more than justify the means. Based on the wild heat of the kiss, he had little doubt the end would be spectacular.

There was no need to dwell on the other ways in which Alex bothered him, he told himself as he rinsed his face. He wasn't interested in any similarities in their upbringings. Or their myriad differences in outlook. He'd never meet her family. It didn't matter that she'd looked very comfortable sitting on his sofa on his terrace drinking his tea. Or somehow *right*. No one had been or ever would be right.

Love didn't exist, in his experience—certainly not the unconditional kind that people banged on about—and he was through long ago with trying to conform to someone else's expectations in the futile hope of reward. But even if he had believed in it, even if he had deserved it, he would have steered well clear.

Love, he'd decided while cooling his heels in that prison cell all those years ago, was likely to be unpredictable and tumultuous. It would follow no formula and the outcome would not be dependent on the input. If love were a flow-chart, it wouldn't be nice and neat, with square boxes and straight arrows. It would be a mess of thought bubbles filled with dramatic declarations and angst amidst a tangle of wiggly lines, a constant state of confusion and turmoil, and who needed that kind of hassle?

Sure, he'd had a few wild and wacky girl-friends as a youth, but he'd subsequently come to the conclusion that it was far safer to focus on his own world and his place in it. To be in total control of his actions and opinions and emotions, and responsible for those alone. Relationships meant having to take someone else's feelings into account, and he'd never been shown how to do that. He wouldn't know how to do such a thing even if he'd wanted to.

No, when it came to women, he was supremely content with keeping things short and simple, one or two nights, a week at most, avoiding emotional involvement and un-meetable expectations, and how he felt about Alex was no different. The strength of his desire for her might be unique, but she wasn't. All he wanted, he thought as he stepped into the shower and switched on the water, was her in his bed. Anything else was totally irrelevant. So tonight he'd focus on that.

La Copa Alegre was as fabulous as Alex had imagined. The two-floor wooden platform was anchored to the seabed three hundred metres offshore and floated on the surface of a literal sea of cerulean. In the centre stood the grass-roofed bar. At one end, giant sails of fawn fabric shaded the deck, upon which sat half a dozen double sunbeds. At the other was the grill that had cooked the sublime seafood platter which had arrived at their table twenty minutes ago. Strings of softly glowing lights looped around the structure and sultry Latin American beats thumped out of the speakers situated on the top floor that was a sun deck by day and dance floor by night.

So in no way was it the venue making Alex regret not being firmer in putting her foot down about dinner. That was all down to Max, who for some reason had decided to switch on the charm.

It was hard enough to resist him when he was being irritatingly unpredictable and immensely frustrating. It was almost impossible when he kept up a flow of easy conversation while flashing her devilish smiles. And then there was the revelation that he was fluent in Spanish. She didn't speak a word, so she could only take an educated guess at what he actually said when he issued greetings and ordered drinks and food, but the sexy accent and the deep timbre of his voice when he rolled his 'r's were spine-tingling.

So much for her intention to stick to mineral water and keep a clear head, she thought exasperatedly, taking a sip of her drink and despairing of how badly wrong this whole occasion was going. She'd given in to his suggestion of a margarita with embarrassing speed. But then she'd needed something strong to dampen the insane heat and desire that had been rushing along her veins and repeatedly knocking her sideways ever since he'd reappeared on the terrace on the dot of the appointed hour.

That he'd been on time had been a surprise. The fact that he'd shaved was another. On the one hand it was rather exciting to be able to gaze at the strong line of his jaw, but on the other she missed the stubble that had, only this morning, grazed the ultra-sensitive skin of her neck and whipped up such a whirlpool of sensation inside her.

And then there were all the tiny touches that had happened along the way. The warm palm at the base of her spine as he'd led her to the boat, burning through the fabric of her top and scorching her back. The firm grip of his fingers around hers when he'd helped her first board and then alight on arrival at the bar. Why hadn't he let her go as abruptly as he had this morning? Why had his hand lingered on hers? More annoyingly, why couldn't she stop thinking about the kiss?

Under any other circumstances, with the attention Max was paying her, this evening might feel like a date. Yet it wasn't. It couldn't be. Nor was any of it remotely relaxing. The margarita was doing nothing to assuage the desire flooding every inch of her being. Her pulse thudded heavily in time to the music vibrating through her. She'd changed into a sleeveless top and a pair of loose trousers, but her clothes felt too tight. Every time she moved, the fabric brushed over her body and her hypersensitive skin tingled.

She was overdressed, that was the trouble. The rest of the select, beautiful clientele were far more scantily clad, and that included Max. He was wearing a pair of sand-coloured shorts and a white shirt that he hadn't bothered to button up, and that was yet another source of discomfort. His bare chest, just across the table, was insanely distracting. She couldn't look away. She wanted to lean over and touch. To put her mouth to his skin and see if she could taste traces of salt from his swim. At one point he'd lifted his bottle of beer to his mouth and a drop of condensation had landed on his right pec. It had sat there, not going anywhere, snagging her attention, and she'd wanted to lick it off. She'd wanted to trace her tongue over the ridges of his muscles and run her fingers over the smattering of hair that covered them.

The clamouring urge to do all this—and more—was not only crazy, it was intolerable. She would never give in to it. It would not be professional to embark on anything with someone who was part of an assignment. If she did and it got out, her reputation would be destroyed. But even if there had been no assignment and they'd met under entirely different circumstances, Max would still be off-limits. Firstly, he'd never allow her to call the shots and, secondly, he posed a huge threat to her control and could easily give her a push down the genetic slippery slope she feared so much.

No, she had to focus on work and stay strong. Her resolve must not weaken, however great the provocation. She had to call a halt to the nonsense going on inside her.

She set her glass down with rather more force than was necessary and determinedly pulled herself together. 'So I spoke to your mother,' she said, taking a prawn from the platter and peeling it. 'You were right. She doesn't have anything to add to this case.'

'I thought not.'

Max appeared to have nothing further to add to that, but she needed to pursue this line of questioning if she stood any chance of keeping her thoughts out of the gutter. 'Aren't you interested in what she did have to say?'

'I can't think of anything I'm less interested in right now.'

His languid gaze drifted over her, electrifying her nerve-endings, and the prawn she'd just put in her mouth nearly went down the wrong way, but she was not to be deterred.

'You said she was difficult,' she said, clearing her throat and ignoring the sizzling heat powering through her veins. 'I can see what you mean.'

'Have I told you how lovely you look this evening?'

At his compliment her temperature rocketed, despite her best efforts to stay cool. 'We only met yesterday,' she said, determined not to let it or the unsettlingly alluring gleam in his eyes detract her. 'I look like this all the time.'

'And still very professional.'

Now that was a compliment she could get behind. If he recognised that their relationship was to remain purely professional it would make her life a whole lot easier for the next week or two. 'Thank you.'

'Do you ever let your hair down?'

She frowned. What did that have to do with anything? 'Literally or metaphorically?'

'Either. Both.'

'Metaphorically, I run. The generally wet, perpetually grey pavements of London aren't a patch on your lovely Caribbean waters, but I like them.' And literally, her hair was tied back in a ponytail this evening, which was really rather relaxed for her. But they were getting off topic. 'So. Back to what I was saying, I—'

'Alex.'

'Yes?'

'Stop.'

'Stop what?'

'I'm not going to talk to you about my mother,' he said, the cool evenness of his tone totally belying the shutters she could see slamming down over the gleam. 'Not this evening. Not ever.'

Why not? What was the story there? She badly wanted to know, because there definitely was one, and these days she couldn't come across a mystery without needing to solve it. But his jaw was set and his shoulders were tight, and what could she do? Wrestle the information out of him?

'All right,' she said, suppressing the instant vision of exactly how that wrestling might play out and parking the topic of his mother until later.

'Good.'

'Have any of those favours you called in produced anything useful?'

'Not yet.'

'It's insanely frustrating.'

'And far too nice an evening to be talking about the investigation,' he said, his eyes glittering in the candlelight and the faint smile now curving his lips doing strange things to her stomach. 'There'll be plenty of time for that when we arrive in La Posada tomorrow. Why don't you take a break tonight?'

Take a break? He had *no* idea. 'I haven't taken a break in years,' she said, flatly ignoring his effect on her.

'All the more reason to do so now.'

What did he know about it? 'How much time do you take off?'

'Three or four months a year.'

Seriously? 'What do you do?'

'I surf. Hang out with friends. Travel.'

Alex stifled the pang of envy and then consoled herself with the realisation that he'd been his own boss twice as long as she had. 'Has your business never given you a moment's concern?'

He leaned forwards and regarded her thoughtfully for a second. 'Honestly?' he said, turning his attention to the seafood platter. 'No. Ever since I was arrested I've had so much work come my way that I've been able to pick and choose.'

'An unusual outcome to an arrest, I imagine, but lucky you.'

'It's not luck. I'm exceptionally good at what I do.'

And what else might that be? she couldn't help wondering as her gaze snagged on his hands, which were deftly dealing with a lobster claw. How skilled would they be on her? Not that they'd ever *be* on her again, obviously. The kiss had been a never-to-be-repeated aberration, and he was still talking.

'Your website says that you were in the police for ten years before you started up your own agency five years ago.'

'That's right,' she said, ruthlessly removing the scorching images of his hands on her body from her head and biting into the slice of lime that garnished her margarita in the hope that the sharp acid hit might jolt some sense into her.

'What made you swap?'

This was better. A conversation about work she could handle. 'Years ago, when I suspected my then husband was cheating on me, I hired a private investigator to find out what was going on and report back to me. Which he did. But not with a whole lot of sympathy or tact. I saw a gap in the market for a more sensitive approach and decided to fill it. We started off investigating cases of suspected infidelity, then expanded to work on missing persons and fraud. There's very little we don't now cover.'

'Impressive.'

She put down the slice of lime and sat back. 'I have big plans, which I will allow nothing and no one to ruin,' she said pointedly.

'I'm surprised that you'd take the risk.'

Oh? 'Why?'

'You said you liked order and structure. A career in the police reflects that. Setting up your own business doesn't.'

Hmm. So that was true. She'd never really thought about it like that. She'd only ever focused on her need for security. But maybe she was more of a risk-taker than she'd thought. Professionally, at any rate. Only time would tell whether hers would pay off, but if it didn't it wouldn't be because she hadn't tried her hardest.

'Yes, well, there was also the complication that my ex worked for the police too,' she said, hauling her focus back to the conversation. 'We met on the training course and were posted to the same area. The divorce made things difficult. I was under no obligation to leave but it was hard. Especially when he started dating another colleague.'

'He should have been the one to go,' Max said bluntly.

'I agree,' Alex replied. 'But once I got my head around it and started making plans it was exciting. I wanted to move on anyway. From everything.'

'What went wrong?'

So that was none of his business. That strayed from the professional into the personal, and it was a step she wasn't sure she wanted to take. She didn't like to talk about the mistakes she'd made or even think about how naïve and foolish and desperate she'd once been.

And yet, if she shared more of herself with Max, maybe he'd feel obliged to do the same with her. Her curiosity about his relationship with his mother was killing her. She wanted to know everything about it, for the case, naturally, but she suspected it would not be forthcoming without serious leverage. Perhaps not even then, but she had to give it a try, and since she'd got over the disaster of her marriage long ago, it wouldn't exactly be traumatic.

'I got married far too young and far too quickly,' she said, twirling her glass between her fingers and resisting the urge to down the remainder of her drink. 'I'd already left the chaos of my family behind. A solid relationship seemed to me to be the next step and I guess I thought that in one I'd find the emotional connection I'd been missing at home. I was embarrassingly desperate to go down the conventional route. I thought I'd found a partner for life and we were engaged within three months.'

'So it was a whirlwind romance.'

'Hardly,' she said dryly. 'He broke our vows within months of the ink drying on the certificate. Yet it took me five more years of trying to fix things before realising that I had to end it for good.'

'That's a long time.'

'Far too long, in hindsight. God knows where my self-respect was. But I hated the thought of failing. I gave him endless chances and believed too many of his promises. I tried to change, more fool me. I even turned down a promotion because it meant more time away from home and he wasn't happy about that.'

'You left no stone unturned.'

'Exactly. But none of it worked.' She shook her head and gazed at the shadowy horizon for a moment before giving herself a quick shake. Regrets were futile. All she could do was ensure that if she ever did get over her trust issues enough to embark on another relationship, she wouldn't make the same mistake again. 'Looking back, I don't know what I was thinking. I guess I was going through some kind of identity crisis. Police officers are supposed to have sound judgement. Mine was a disaster.'

'The man was an idiot.'

'Well, he was young too,' she said, a little confused by the ribbon of warmth that was winding through her at Max's terse pronouncement. 'And my career was moving faster than his, which I think he found intimidating. He used to make these sly little comments to undermine my confidence and belittle me.'

'Like I said, an idiot.'

'The only good thing to come out of the whole sorry mess was that I made a promise to myself that never again would I try and be what someone else expected me to be. I've learned to be exceptionally resilient on that front. Very little shocks me these days. Except people's propensity for self-centredness. That still floors me every time. I don't know why.'

'What did your parents want you to be?'

'Definitely not a police officer,' she said, unable to prevent a quick stab of hurt and regret from piercing her heart. 'I grew up in a very working class area of east London, except "working" class is a bit of a misnomer. It was a sink estate with lots of crime and many social problems. My school had a forty per cent truancy rate. No one cared. I once told my teacher that I wanted to go to university and she first just stared at me and then burst out laughing. At that point I realised that if I wanted to achieve anything I'd have to do it on my own. Joining the police was a way out.'

'Do your parents still live there?'

'Yes.'

'Your job must have made visiting tricky.'

'It made it impossible. But then I wasn't welcome anyway. I'm still not.'

'Do you want to be?' he asked, something about the intensity of his expression suggesting that he was really interested in her answer.

'I'm not sure,' she said with a sigh. 'Sometimes I think I do, which is nuts, right?'

'Not at all. As we've already established, families are complicated. Yours is probably jealous.'

She stared at him for a moment as that sank in. 'Do you think so?'

He shrugged. 'It's a possibility, I guess, although I'm no expert. But, ultimately, whatever lies at the heart of it, it's not your problem. You can't change anything. You'd be better off letting it go.'

Easy for him to say. 'And how do I go about that?'

'I wish I knew.'

A shadow flitted across his expression and she wondered suddenly if perhaps it wasn't easy for him to say. Could it be that he wasn't as laid-back as he liked to portray, and was, in fact, far more complex a character than she'd thought? It was a more appealing idea than it should have been. 'Let me know when you figure it out.'

'Likewise. But, for what it's worth,' he said, 'I think that what you've achieved under the circumstances is remarkable.'

Did he? She scoured his face for signs of insincerity but found none. Well, well, well. A little boost to her self-esteem from a man who was her opposite in almost every way. Who'd have thought? 'Thank you.'

'You're welcome. Would you like some dessert?'

Yes, was the answer on the tip of her tongue. For dessert she wanted him. A little salt, a little sweetness, a whole lot of spice. However, since that wasn't going to happen and she was full of shellfish and margarita, she ought to de-cline. But, for some bizarre reason, she couldn't get the 'no' out. Despite how very on-edge she was feeling, she didn't want the evening to end. And, besides, he owed her now, and this time she wouldn't be letting the debt go unpaid. 'Dessert would be lovely.'

# CHAPTER SIX

MAX DUG HIS spoon into a bowl of coconut sorbet and thought that he could easily understand Alex's determination not to conform to someone else's expectations. How many times as a kid had he tried to do the exact same thing, with equally disappointing results? How long had he spent pointlessly trying to figure out what it was his mom wanted from him and then attempting to provide it, to no avail? It had never ended well. The inevitable failure ate away at a person's confidence and crushed their spirit until either they were ground to dust or got out. Like him, Alex had chosen the latter. He wondered if, also like him, she inwardly recoiled at the word 'compromise'.

Her ex-husband was the biggest fool on the planet. She was beautiful, intelligent and capable. To be cherished, not cheated on, if a long-term relationship was your thing. Any idiot could see that. How pathetically insecure must he have been, to handle her successes with such disparagement. How difficult that must have been to live with. Max had experienced both, having been on the receiving end of endlessly crippling insincerity and belittling while growing up, and his admiration for her grew.

Not that Alex's marriage was any of his concern, beyond the fact that it had ended and she was now single. How much he admired her was irrelevant. The stab of sympathy he'd felt when she'd been talking about disappointing her family had been wholly unnecessary.

What was important here was that his plan to get her into bed worked and, infuriatingly, with the way things were going, it didn't look as if it was going to. All evening he'd been as charming as he knew how—which had had great results in the past—and he'd deliberately left his shirt undone, but she'd seemed remarkably unmoved by his efforts. She'd generally responded to his flirting with an arch of an eyebrow and a glare of disapproval and hadn't ogled his chest once.

He, on the other hand, was anything but unmoved by her. She'd changed out of the trouser suit of earlier into a pair of loose-fitting trousers and a sleeveless top and looked effortlessly chic, which was a result he was sure she hadn't intended. The breeze had loosened her ponytail so that tendrils of hair fluttered around her face. He wanted to peel the clothes from her body and pull the band from her hair with a need that bordered on desperate.

While eating, she kept making all these appreciative noises, even groaning at times, and he'd instinctively contemplated all the ways *he* might be able to make her groan, should the opportunity arise. Desire was drumming through him and he was so hard it hurt and all he could think about was what it would take to erode her resolve. What more could he do? The not knowing, the possibility of failure, was driving him nuts.

'What you've achieved is remarkable too,' she said, cutting through his frustration and making him glance up at her.

'What do you mean?'

'It doesn't sound like you had the easiest of childhoods either.'

He didn't want to talk about that. He wanted to talk about the chemistry they shared that she seemed determined to ignore, or, better still, act on it. And what did she know of his childhood anyway? How long had her conversation with his mother lasted?

'As I told you before,' he said so smoothly she'd never guess how churned-up inside he was feeling, 'that subject is off-limits.'

'Was it that bad?'

It had been traumatic and difficult and he had no wish to take a trip down that particular memory lane. 'It bears no relevance to anything.'

The look she levelled at him was pointed. 'Neither did mine.'

Now what was that supposed to mean? That because she'd talked to him he was under some sort of obligation to reciprocate? To hell with that. He'd hardly forced her to spill out the details of her marriage. He hadn't even been that interested. He owed her nothing.

And yet…

Maybe it wasn't such a bad idea. What if opening up to her succeeded where the flirting and his bare chest hadn't? What if she was the sort of woman to be lured into bed with sincerity and connection rather than flattery and visuals?

He wanted her more than he'd wanted anyone and failure hadn't been an option since the moment he'd left the police station a reformed character. So perhaps he should take a leaf out of her book and leave no stone unturned in his quest to seduce her.

Any connection created would hardly be deep and it sure as hell wouldn't be binding. It wasn't as if his experiences were any great secret. It was just that he'd never felt the need to share before. He'd never had a conversation where this aspect of his past came up. But it had now, and if he continued to deflect she might suspect there was more to it than there really was, and for some reason that didn't appeal. Besides, with her background, she'd hardly be likely to judge.

'All right, fine,' he said, nevertheless bracing himself as he set his spoon into his empty bowl and met her gaze. 'The environment I grew up in was a toxic one.'

She sat back and regarded him steadily, and he was strangely relieved to see in her expression no sign of victory that she'd succeeded where no one else ever had. 'You said your parents argued.'

'It was more than just that,' he said darkly. 'It was frequently a full-on war. My mother is obnoxious.'

'Your mother is a narcissist.'

At her blunt observation, Max frowned. 'What makes you say that?'

'Well, I'm no expert, obviously, but I once did a course on psychopathic personalities and, from what I recall, she fits the profile.'

'Which is?'

'A constant demand for praise and attention,

ignoring the needs of others and a belief of being special, for a start.'

That sounded very familiar. 'How about an inability to tolerate criticism, never-ending attention-seeking and an obsessive need to control the lives of others?'

She nodded and took a sip of her drink. 'All that too.'

'Then you could be right.' He'd always known his mother was utterly self-absorbed, but he had to admit now that was probably the least of it.

'The conversation I had with her earlier today was extraordinary.'

'What did she say?'

Alex tilted her head and regarded him for one long heart-stopping moment. 'I thought you didn't want to know.'

Well, no, he hadn't then. But he did now. Because, to be quite honest, he was sick to the back teeth of being in the dark. The dark was where a man could get hurled off course, where doubts set in and chaos reigned, and three days of it was more than enough. 'Humour me.'

'It's not pretty.'

'I can take it,' he said, thinking that that was hardly news. Nothing about his family background was pretty. How bad could it be?

'You won't shoot the messenger?'

He had entirely different plans for the messenger if this strategy of his played out. 'No.'

'OK, then,' she said, taking a deep breath, her gaze unwavering. 'She told me that the marriage was in trouble and that she'd decided a baby—you—would fix things. Your father initially refused but she told him that if he loved her he'd do this for her, and fast.'

Even though he'd been expecting the worst, the information still struck him like a blow to the gut. Yet another ultimatum, he thought, acid and bitterness swilling around inside him. How he hated them. So he really *hadn't* been wanted by his parents. He didn't know why it was such a shock when the evidence had always been there, but it was nonetheless.

'She said she doesn't remember anything about picking you up,' Alex continued, oblivious to the turmoil he was experiencing, 'and I don't know if that's genuinely the case or if, once it had been done, it had served its purpose and didn't require any more thought. Given her narcissism, I suspect the latter. She laid a lot of the blame for things at your feet, wholly unfairly. That kind of behaviour can be very destructive. I'm so sorry.'

He loathed the pity in her eyes and wished he could shrug casually, but he couldn't. 'It's not your fault,' he said, thinking that the old adage 'be careful what you wish for' had never been more appropriate.

'My father should have stood up to her. He should have been stronger. He should have said no.'

'Narcissists can be very persuasive and manipulative.'

She was right about that. To the outside world, his mother was beautiful and charming. It was only with her family that she showed her true monstrous self. Appearances were everything, which was presumably why their disaster of a marriage had limped on for so long. But still.

'He was weak. He was worse than I was in his efforts to please an unappeasable woman.'

'A toxic environment indeed.'

'And yet he left me there.' For which Max had never forgiven him. But perhaps the adoption explained that. Perhaps he'd never considered Max his true son.

'Didn't they share custody of you?'

'My mother was keen to keep control over me and my father couldn't have cared less.'

'How devastating.'

'It wasn't great.'

'Did you see much of him before he died?' she asked, her voice cracking a little and her eyes shimmering.

'Twice.' That was it. Neither visit had been a success. He'd harboured a lot of anger and his father had clearly just wanted to put everything behind him. 'He moved to Los Angeles after the divorce,' he said flatly, ruthlessly clamping the lid down on all the old memories and feelings that were bubbling up.

'The other side of the country.'

'It wasn't a coincidence.'

'And you choosing the Caribbean as your home, which is what, two thousand miles from New York?'

She was too clever by half. 'That's not a co-incidence either.'

'I didn't think so. What about your step-fathers?'

'They were never around for long.'

'Used and then discarded?'

'Either that or they swiftly saw through the deceptively beautiful facade and got the hell out.'

She shook her head. 'I can't imagine what it must have been like.'

He was glad she couldn't. He wouldn't wish it on anyone. 'It wasn't much fun,' he said with staggering understatement. 'My dad couldn't have cared less about me while my mom was obsessed. She had to control everything. My friends, my clothes, even the music I listened to. Weakness and failure weren't allowed. They reflected badly on her. Expectations were impossibly high and I rarely met them, and the criticism was relentless. Nothing I did was ever good enough and she had no problem with letting me know that. If I put a foot out of line, she'd go very still and very quiet and then simply walk out of the room. In the end I figured it was less hassle to keep my opinions and feelings to myself. She wouldn't let me stay out of her way, so I just bided my time and bit my tongue until I got accepted at MIT.'

'How on earth did you get through it?'

'I had the hacking and its community.'

'Like I had studying,' she said with a slow nod of what looked like understanding. 'I spent most of my time at the library. That was where I realised my family chose to live the way they did and that I could choose not to.'

'Hence the rules?'

'Via the classics.'

'Everyone needs some form of escape.'

'And everyone has expectations to face,' she countered, 'although in my case, they were low rather than high. I still don't meet them and I've come to terms with that, so I have no idea why I still feel guilty about it.'

Her too? 'I was angry for a very long time.'

'I think I still am.'

'You should try a couple of days in jail. There's nothing like it for reflecting on what's going wrong and why. Break a law or two. It's a lot cheaper than therapy.'

'I'll bear that in mind,' she said with a faint smile. 'But you do realise your parents' behaviour is none of your fault, don't you?'

'In theory, yes. In practice, it's complicated.'

'As I know only too well. So is all that why you're so keen to track your biological parents?'

'I need to know who I am and where I come from,' he said, once again struck by her perception as much as the effect of her smile on his lungs. 'How I ended up with parents who didn't give a crap about me. With a mother who can't even remember travelling halfway across the world to pick me up and a father who barely spared me a thought. I've spent the last decade believing I'd dealt with it and living in relative peace. But one twenty-minute interview three days ago blew that peace to smithereens and I need it back. I hate not knowing what's going on. With so much information about my history missing, I suddenly feel like half a person. I need that information. I need answers.' Deep down, he also desperately hoped he'd find out that, whatever the circumstances that had led to his adoption, he'd once been wanted, but there was no way in hell he was going to share that with her. Exposing that level of vulnerability to another human being was never going to happen. Instead, he said, 'You have no idea what it's like to have your life so suddenly torn apart.'

'Well, I do have some idea,' she said with a tilt of her head. 'When I first found out my husband was cheating on me, my world collapsed. Not just my marriage, but everything I'd been working towards. Structure. Normality. A life of conventionality. It took me a while, too, to get back on track, and God knows it wasn't easy, but I did, and nothing will push me off it again.'

'Which is why the success of this assignment is so important to you, why you wouldn't just take my money and move on.' She was fighting for her future like he was fighting for his identity.

She nodded. 'When I was young I was repeatedly told I'd never amount to anything. I've worked hard to overcome that. You were right about the importance of the fee Finn's paying me. It does matter. But his good opinion is invaluable. Much of my work comes via word-of-mouth and his recommendation would open all kinds of doors. I have big expansion plans and I won't have them derailed.'

Yeah, well, he had big plans too and didn't

want them derailed either. He was done with
talking about the past. It was all water under
the bridge anyway. He was infinitely more interested in the present and the imminent future.
The conversation had taken an unexpectedly
heavy turn but that didn't mean it couldn't now
be steered in a different direction. It was still
early and he wanted her as much as ever. It was
time to wrap things up here and move on.

'Are you done?' he asked, wiping his head of
the conversation and everything it had stirred
up and contemplating his next step instead.

'Yes. Thank you.'

'Then we should head back.'

The boat journey back to Max's house was conducted in silence, the warm dark night acting
like a sort of blanket that prevented further conversation, which was more than all right with
Alex, who was feeling all churned up inside by
what she'd learned about his upbringing, such
as it had been.

She couldn't get the look of torment that had
appeared on his face when she'd revealed what
his mother had said to her on the phone out of
her head. Or the shock and the hurt that had
flashed in the depths of his eyes, even if he had
got it all under control with remarkable speed.

Should she have told him? was the question

that kept rolling around her thoughts. If she'd known the effect it was going to have on him, she might have thought twice. But, on the other hand, if they asked, didn't everyone deserve to know the truth, however messy, whether it was to do with a faithless spouse, an embezzling employee or a narcissistic mother? Hadn't she always believed that ignorance wasn't necessarily bliss?

One of the things she recalled from her course on psychopathic personalities was that the effects of narcissistic behaviour on those around the narcissist could include feelings of not being good enough, a deep-rooted need for approval and the suppression of emotion. Before this evening, if she'd put much thought to it, she'd have remembered Max's pride in his former life as a hacker and his general air of supreme confidence and assumed that he'd overcome any suffering he might have experienced or even escaped totally unscathed.

But she'd have been wrong.

How could he not have been affected? she reflected, her heart wrenching at the thought of it, while the Caribbean breeze whipped at the scarf she'd tied around her head to protect her hair. He'd essentially been bought by a pair of people who didn't deserve to be parents, and then shamelessly used by one while being wholly neglected by the other. It was hard to know which one of them had been worse. An insecure, manipulative mother or a father who'd bailed on him and left him to the cruel whims of a woman who only thought of herself?

What a horrible, wretched environment he'd been brought up in. He'd had no siblings, no one who was going through the same thing to talk to. What must it have been like to grow up knowing that his father didn't want him? That while his mother had been physically present, every interaction she'd had with him had had an ulterior motive? Where had the love been? The affection? Not that she knew much about it, having had little of either herself.

No wonder he'd sought out an online community among which to find what he'd been missing at home. She couldn't imagine it would have been the place for a discussion of the kind of angst his upbringing must have generated, but the comradeship he had clearly found there had to have been the only way to survive, just as studying and a plan to escape had for her. If there'd been anything remotely amusing about any of it she'd have thought it was funny how they'd both drawn the short straw on the family front, but really there wasn't.

Once they were on dry land and heading up the steps to the house, Alex wondered how he felt about it all now and what effects still lingered in a way that had nothing to do with the filling of a gap in her professional knowledge. She was intrigued by the many complicated layers to him and the insanely tough journey he'd had. She couldn't imagine what he was going through now, having had his world turned so upside down by the discovery of his adoption. Her identity crisis wasn't a patch on the one he had to be undergoing.

'Nightcap?' he offered as he headed for the outdoor bar, his deep voice making her shiver despite the balminess of the evening.

'No, thank you,' she said, managing to muster up a smile to mask the thoughts rocketing around her head. 'I think I'll head to bed.' Where she would no doubt revisit their conversation at the bar and wonder if there was some way she could help him deal with everything. Where she would ponder his insight into her family's possible jealousy and her blamelessness for it instead of the way he made her feel. Where her resolve to stay strong and resist him wouldn't be challenged by the burning desire to know more about him and the dark, sensual intimacy of the terrace that was softly lit by hundreds of tiny discreet solar-powered lights.

'The night is young.'

'But today's been a big day,' she pointed out,

slightly dazed by how eventful it had been, 'and tomorrow's an even bigger one.'

He turned to face her and leaned against the worktop of the bar. 'Just one drink.'

'Jet lag is catching up with me.' It was a lie. She'd never felt so energised. But she didn't trust herself. The intensity of his gaze was a threat to her reason. Where was the flirting? Where was the charm? That she could bat away. This sudden serious intent of his, on top of the intimate conversation they'd had earlier, felt so much more dangerous.

'Coward.'

She went very still. His eyes were dark, his expression unsmiling and her pulse skipped a beat. 'What makes you say that?'

'Your determination to ignore what's between us.'

Her heart thumped and her mouth went dry. So they were doing this, then. 'There's nothing between us.'

The fire burning in his gaze nearly wiped out her knees. 'Our kiss this morning would suggest otherwise.'

'Like I said, that was a mistake.' And the less said about it the better.

'I disagree,' he said, his voice low and rough. 'It nearly blew the top of my head off. If that door hadn't slammed when it did, you know we'd have ended up in bed together. And you know we'd probably still be there.'

She envied how easily he could accept what he wanted from her. He was so sure, so confident. In this, she was quite the opposite and, despite the envy, she couldn't help wishing that he'd opted for denial like she had.

She swallowed hard and fought for control. 'I know nothing of the sort.'

'I'm very attracted to you, Alex,' he said, running his gaze over her so slowly and thoroughly that a wave of heat rushed over her, tightening her nipples in a way she desperately hoped he wouldn't notice. 'As you are to me. You can carry on burying your head in the sand if you want, but that won't make it go away.'

Wouldn't it? He was probably right. The pressure crushing her was immense. How much longer could she stand it? Perhaps if she confronted the attraction, the intoxicating mystery of it would disappear and along with it the heat and the desire. Denial wasn't working and facing up to things was something she encouraged in her clients, so maybe she ought to put her money where her mouth was.

'All right,' she said, mentally crossing her fingers and wishing her heart would stop hammering quite so hard. 'It's true. I want you.

A lot. And I'm not in the slightest bit happy about it.'

'I know you aren't,' he said, the tension in his shoulders easing a fraction and the ghost of a smile curving his mouth. 'But do you have any idea how rare the chemistry between us is?'

'Not really,' she admitted, thinking that if she was in for a penny she might as well be in for a pound. 'I imagine I'm considerably less experienced than you.'

'We'd be explosive together.'

Like phosphorus and air. There she was, happily sitting surrounded by water, all nicely inert and safe, and then along he came, luring her to the surface and encouraging her to break through it, at which point things would go bang.

'It's not going to happen,' she said, having to believe that for the sake of her future.

'Why not?'

'There's a huge conflict of interest.'

'As we've established, I'm not your client.'

'That's not the point,' she said, struggling for a moment to remember quite what the point was when her head was filling with images of the two of them being explosive together. 'Finding the truth about your adoption is too important to me to screw up by fooling around and getting distracted.'

'Who says we can't do both?'

'I do.'

'You want me.'

'That doesn't matter.'

He regarded her for one achingly long moment. 'You know I could prove you wrong, don't you?'

In a heartbeat. Desire was flooding through her, weakening her knees and her resistance. All he'd have to do was touch her and she'd go up in flames. 'I'd hope you have more integrity than to try,' she said, inching back out of his mind-scrambling orbit and wondering if she was expecting too much from a criminally minded former hacker.

'On any other occasion, I'd say I absolutely do,' he said with an assessing tilt of his head. 'Right here, right now, however, I'd put it at fifty-fifty.'

Her heart gave a lurch and for one appalling moment she couldn't work out which fifty she wanted. But then she pulled herself together. 'I have rules about this sort of thing.'

'Of course you do.'

'Don't mock me.'

'I'm not. But would it really be so bad if they got broken?'

'Yes,' she said firmly, squashing the little voice in her head yelling, *Would it? Really?* The risks vastly outweighed any potential reward.

She couldn't allow herself to think about possible explosions.

'Why?'

'I've worked insanely hard to get where I've got and my reputation is everything to me. I would stand to lose a lot if it got out that I fraternise with people involved in a case.'

'Who would ever know?'

'I would.'

'But think of the fireworks.'

'There'd be fireworks?' What was she saying? Of course there'd be fireworks. Mini Catherine wheels were spinning in her stomach and they weren't even touching.

He ran his gaze over her yet again, as if he *knew* the effect it would have on her, and those Catherine wheels nearly took off. 'I know what I'm doing.'

That didn't help one little bit, because now all she could think about was how spectacularly good in bed he would be. 'I wish I did.'

'You do,' he said. 'You're successful and well-respected. Finn sang your praises. He described you as tenacious and determined. He wouldn't have hired you if you hadn't come highly recommended. Your reputation would be in no danger from sleeping with me.'

Maybe it would. Maybe it wouldn't. But, actually, that wasn't the real issue.

'You're wasting your time, Max,' she said with a shake of her head, although who she was trying to warn she wasn't sure. 'We are totally different. Sleeping with you would bring chaos to my life. You're unpredictable, a loose cannon. And I don't want that, however briefly. I need to stay in control of everything. My rules aren't just about order and structure. They keep me focused. On the right track. Every morning I wake up with the feeling that if I'm not careful I could well end up like the rest of my family. That all it will take is one slip, one "it'll be fine just this once", and genes will take over and I'll lose everything I've worked so hard for. You can't have any idea what that's like.'

'I know exactly what that's like,' he said, his eyes dark and glittering. 'I've done everything in my power not to turn out like either of my parents. Doesn't matter that we share no genes. Nurture trumps nature in my case.'

'I won't risk it.'

'Some risks are worth taking.'

'Not this one.'

He took a step towards her, and her breath caught while her heart hammered. 'I don't want anything long-term, Alex,' he said, his gaze so mesmerising she couldn't look away. 'I'm not cut out for that. I simply want you, for as long as we're working together.'

'And then what?'

'We go our separate ways with no regrets.'

But she would have regrets. She knew she would. She wouldn't be able to help throwing herself into it one hundred per cent, the way she did with everything, and while it would undoubtedly be fabulous while it lasted, the fallout would be huge. He was too overwhelming, too potent—too everything. The impact of a fling with him would be immense and she didn't want to have to mop up the mess afterwards. She wasn't willing to make that mistake again and that was all there was to it.

'This might be some kind of game to you, Max,' she said, the thought of history repeating itself injecting steel into her voice, 'but it isn't to me.'

'It's no game.'

'Then have some respect for my rules. Have some respect for me. And back off. Please.'

# CHAPTER SEVEN

WATCHING ALEX SPIN on her heel and head off in
the direction of the guest wing, Max grabbed a
beer and cracked it open, disappointment and
frustration coursing through him like boiling
oil. Her resolve was stronger than he could have
possibly imagined. Under any other circumstances he'd applaud it. Under these circumstances, tonight, he hated and resented it.

Not that that was her fault, of course. She had
every right to turn him down and she'd given
a perfectly reasonable, understandable explanation for why she was so reluctant to yield
to the attraction that arced between them. He
knew what it was like to fear turning into your
family. He'd spent half his life concerned that
both his father's general weakness of character and his mother's manipulation could be he-
reditary and had done everything in his power
to avoid both.

But right now all he could think was that

he'd given it his best shot with Alex and he'd failed. The physical attraction, although mutual and scorching, wasn't enough. Opening up and allowing her a glimpse into parts of him that hadn't seen the light of day for years wasn't enough. *He* wasn't enough.

Rejection spun through him at the idea of that, leaving the sting of a thousand darts in its wake and stirring up memories of his childhood that he'd buried deep long ago. Such as seeking out his father's attention for help with a school project, only to be dismissed with a glance of irritation and a mutter of 'later'. Such as once making a birthday cake for his mother, who'd showered him with thanks before telling him that she was watching her weight and tossing it in the trash. But he shoved aside the memories and ignored the tiny stabs of pain, loathing the weakness they represented.

The impact on him of Alex's rejection was ridiculous, he told himself grimly as he lifted the bottle to his mouth and necked half its contents. It wasn't as if she were the only woman on the planet he'd ever wanted, and it wasn't as if he'd never want anyone else. There were plenty of other women in this world who would be only too pleased to spend a night or two in his bed.

Why had he tried so hard with her? What made her worth an effort he'd never had to make before? Had he really been so keen for a distraction from the disruption caused by the discovery that he was adopted? Didn't that somehow make him a bit of a coward rather than her?

Well, whatever his motivations, whatever they made him, the result was the same. Despite the sizzling chemistry that she'd even acknowledged, she didn't want him. So he'd back off. He had no interest in pursuing someone who didn't want to be pursued and she'd made it very clear that she was that someone.

Starting now he'd withdraw the smiles and the charm she disdained and channel the pure professionalism that she valued so highly. He'd prioritise the investigation, the way she had. He'd get the answers he so badly needed and haul his life back on track. It was faintly pathetic that it mattered so much. He was a grown man of thirty-one, for God's sake. Professionally, he was at the top of his game. He was envied by the best of the best. Personally, however, the events of the last few days had revealed that he languished somewhere at the bottom, unable to claw his way up, and it was frustrating as hell. He needed to get to the truth, whatever it might be, so he could move on.

None of this was a game to him, despite Alex's accusation. It mattered. A lot. And that was all there was to it.

Max and Alex had arrived in La Posada late the following evening, having landed at the airport in La Quiaca in the afternoon and picked up a top-of-the-range four-by-four to cover the hundred-and-fifty-kilometre distance by road.

The Quechuan town, home to six thousand inhabitants and situated on the eastern edge of the Andes, stood on the top of a dramatic ridge. It had been rebuilt after a devastating earthquake twenty years before, some thirty kilometres from the original site. The air was dry and dusty. The surrounding landscape was rocky, the vegetation was sparse and the sun was harsh. The contrast to the sparkle and lushness of the Caribbean could not have been sharper.

But it wasn't the lack of humidity, the aridity or even the altitude that accounted for her irritability, Alex had to admit as she breakfasted alone on coffee and bread in the restaurant of the only hotel in town. It was her apparent and alarming contrariness.

Despite knowing she'd done absolutely the right thing by laying her cards on the table, bidding Max goodnight and marching off into the house, she'd still spent a large part of the night fretting about how things between them would turn out come morning.

What would she do if he completely ignored her plea and launched a concerted effort to change her mind? she'd agonised as she'd stared at the ceiling and listened to the chirrup of the crickets that inhabited the thickets beyond the terraces. Realistically, how long would she be able to resist his considerable charms? She'd like to think for ever, but she was only human, the attraction was impossibly strong and it had been so long since she'd had any attention.

And why had he set his sights on her in the first place? She was nothing special. Surely he had to know far more appealing women than her, gorgeous, interesting ones who were totally on his wavelength and shared his approach to rules. No doubt she was merely convenient, popping into his life at a moment when he was in between contracts and looking for a challenge to fill the time. It could hardly be anything else. Despite the intimacy of the conversation they'd had at La Copa Alegre, he was so out of her league he might as well be on another planet.

In fact, her concerns had become so troubling that at one point she'd actually considered telling him to go to Argentina on his own and simply report back, which was so baffling and downright wrong that she'd had to give herself a mental slap to get a grip while reminding herself at length that never again was she going to allow how she felt about a man get in the way of work. Nor was she going to keep on wondering how explosive was explosive.

However, she needn't have worried. Max had clearly taken on board what she'd said. The smiles had gone and had been replaced with polite distance. He hadn't touched her once since they'd met on the deck to catch his boat to the airport. He'd barely even looked at her. On the plane he'd been professionalism personified. He'd opened his laptop the minute they'd taken off, and had only stepped away to make some calls.

Alex, on the other hand, had hardly been able to concentrate on anything. She'd been restless, as if sitting on knives, and the plane had felt oddly claustrophobic. Even Becky, with whom she'd checked in somewhere over north Brazil, had queried her distraction, for which she hadn't had much of an answer.

Bizarrely, with every nautical mile, she'd found herself growing increasingly irritated by Max's aloofness. Surely it was over-the-top. Surely they could have settled on somewhere in between flirty and frosty. To her confusion and consternation, that irritation still lingered.

None of it made sense, she thought frustratedly, taking a sip of freshly squeezed orange juice to wash down the last few flakes of delicious buttery *medialuna*. She should be glad he'd backed off. She shouldn't be feeling piqued that he'd done what she'd asked. And as for the disappointment that had lanced through her yesterday evening when the hotel he'd booked had had another room available, which he'd accepted without a moment's hesitation, what on earth had that been about? She didn't want to be put in a situation where they had to share a room. Or at least she shouldn't. And she ought to have been delighted not disappointed when, after checking in, he'd ordered room service before heading off, not to be seen again for the rest of the evening.

She couldn't work out what was wrong with her. Max was showing respect for her rules, for *her*, so where was the satisfaction? Where was the relief? Why was she missing the smiles, the conversation and even the dangerous edge of the night before last? Why did she keep willing him to actually meet her gaze for longer than a fleeting second or two? When exactly had she become so obsessed with his hands that she could practically feel them on her body?

She'd had nearly twenty-four hours to ruminate these baffling questions but, to her exasperation, she was no closer to an answer. But at least his imminent arrival at her table would give her a welcome break from that particular madness.

God, he was gorgeous, she thought, watching as he made his way across the room, weaving through the tables, all lithe grace and powerful intent. This morning he'd foregone the shave and her fingers itched to find out whether the light stubble adorning his jaw was as electrifying as she remembered. His hair was damp and, as a vision of him in the shower, standing beneath the jets while hot, steaming water poured over him and ran in rivulets down the contours of his body, flew unbidden into her head, she felt a throb between her legs.

'Good morning,' he said with a quick impersonal smile that she'd inexplicably grown to loathe.

Was it? It seemed very hot for this time of day. And she clearly hadn't got used to the altitude because she was suddenly finding it hard to breathe. 'Good morning.'

'Did you sleep well?'

To her surprise she had, but maybe it shouldn't have been unexpected, given the restlessness of the nights that had gone before. 'Like a log. You?'

'Same.'

Hmm. He didn't look as if he had, she thought, assessing him carefully as he took the seat opposite her and poured himself some coffee. Despite the tan, his face was slightly paler than usual, and drawn. Faint lines bracketed his mouth and the frown creasing his forehead looked as if it had been there a while. But his expression was unreadable and his eyes revealed nothing.

She wished she knew what he was thinking. It took no great leap of imagination to suppose this had to be hard on him. By his own admission, the discovery that he was adopted had turned his life on its head. She couldn't even begin to envisage what kind of upheaval it must have generated.

And now here they were in the country of his birth, the land of his heritage. Not only that, they were half an hour from the orphanage where he'd spent time before being taken to the US. It had all happened a long time ago, certainly, but surely it had to be having some kind of effect on him. He'd acted so swiftly on hearing the news and then moved so decisively. Those weren't the actions of a man who was largely indifferent. So could it be that deep down he was all over the place emotionally, and stoic detachment was his way of handling it?

'How are you feeling?' she asked, wondering

if there was any way she could help, if there was indeed something troubling him.

'About what?'

'Well, everything, really,' she said, watching him closely for a reaction or a sign, however minuscule. 'But principally, being here in Argentina.'

'I'm feeling fine. Why?'

'I was thinking that today's visit to the orphanage might be difficult for you.'

'Not in the slightest,' he said as he reached for a roll.

'Are you sure?'

'Yes. It'll be fine.'

Right. So that was two 'fine's in a row. In her experience, nothing suggested a problem more. 'What time shall we leave?'

'There's no need for you to come.'

So that wasn't happening. For one thing, she wasn't being cut out of the loop. For another, his shoulders were tight. His jaw now looked as if it was about to shatter. He was very much not 'fine'. There was no way she was letting him go through whatever he was going through alone. Her chest tightened and her throat ached at the mere thought of it and he'd had to deal with enough on his own.

'I disagree,' she said with a tiny jut of her chin as resolve surged inside her.

'Too bad.'

'This is my case too, Max. I've been working on it exclusively for eight months. I'm as invested as you are.'

His eyes met hers finally, incredulity shimmering in their indigo depths, along with a good deal of scepticism. 'You couldn't possibly be as invested as I am.'

Debatable, but also possibly an argument for another time. 'Consider me moral support then.'

'I don't need support,' he said flatly. 'Moral or otherwise.'

Yes, he did, despite the waves of rejection and denial radiating off him. She could understand why he might want to push her away. For him this had to be intensely personal. They weren't friends. They certainly weren't lovers. They were colleagues at most and she'd told him to back off. Why on earth *would* he want to share the experience with her?

But he could protest all he liked. Just because she'd put an end to the chemistry and the flirting, it didn't mean she didn't care. What if he *did* turn out to need the support? She was the only person to provide it right now and, in her admittedly biased opinion, she was also the best. A large part of her job was handling the fallout of her investigations with perceptiveness and sensitivity, and she excelled at reading emotionally fragile situations, instinctively knowing when to step in and when to stay back. She'd also learned to look beneath the surface, and beneath Max's, beneath the outward stoicism and steely control, she sensed great, seething turmoil.

'You have it, whether you want it or not.'

'You once asked me to back off, Alex,' he said warningly. 'Now I'm asking you to do the same.'

'This is different,' she said, having no intention of getting into a tit-for-tat. 'I'm worried about you, Max, and I have lots of experience in picking up pieces, should there be any. So I'm coming with you.' If he continued to reject her offer, then so be it, but if he said 'fine' again she'd know it was the right thing to do.

He let out a deep sigh of defeat and gave a shrug as if he couldn't care less. 'Fine.'

The drive to the Santa Catalina orphanage took longer than expected. Not only was the road riddled with potholes and strewn with rocks, they had to keep stopping for meandering alpaca. It was taking every drop of Max's concentration to avoid the hazards, yet with every passing kilometre his pulse thudded that little bit faster and his stomach churned that little bit harder.

Despite what he'd told Alex, in the hope she'd stop her damn prodding and leave him alone, he'd been feeling off-kilter ever since they'd landed. At first the unease had been vague, a mild cocktail of anticipation and uncertainty. But overnight the pounding of his head had intensified and a tight knot had lodged in his chest.

He didn't appreciate that he hadn't been as successful at hiding the mess of his emotions from Alex as he'd hoped, but he couldn't deny she'd been spot-on about the reasons for it. The minute he'd set foot on the land of his birth, he'd been rocked in a way he could never have anticipated. Arriving in La Posada, knowing that the orphanage he'd spent time in was so close, had compounded the unsettling sensation that his foundations were cracking.

But why any of that should be the case, he couldn't work out. Argentina was a country like any other. Largely destroyed in the earthquake, the orphanage was just a pile of stones. He'd read a report and seen a photo of the place in one of the attachments Alex had forwarded him. How traumatic could the reality actually be?

Nevertheless, he recognised that he was standing on shaky ground, metaphorically if not literally. He had been for days now. He'd held the chaos at bay by focusing on getting Alex into his bed, but, thanks to her determination to resist the attraction, that shield had shattered and, without it, havoc prevailed. The emotions he thought he'd got a handle on over a decade ago now crashed around inside him, fierce and volatile. If he didn't keep a tight grip on them, they could all too easily result in the hot mess of an eruption he'd once predicted, and he wanted no witnesses.

So why had he caved and allowed her to accompany him today? He could have simply taken off without her. He hadn't had to wait for her to meet him at the car. Yet his resolve, already weakened by the tempest whipping up a storm inside him, had crumbled to dust with petrifying speed.

Why did the idea of her support appeal so much? He'd survived perfectly well without it—or any support, for that matter—previously. The last thing he wanted was her picking up his pieces in the event there were any to pick up. And what did it matter if he couldn't recall the last time anyone had worried about him? He was totally used to being on his own and worrying about himself, well, *himself.*

For all he knew, Alex's concern and the support were just an excuse, and for her it was all about the job anyway. She'd made it blindingly clear how important the assignment was to her, so of course she wasn't going to give up the chance to find any more evidence for herself, or, if there wasn't any, closing down that line of enquiry once and for all. If he had any sense at all he'd be focusing on that instead of allowing himself to get side-tracked by contemplating other, more unsettlingly appealing motivations she might have, such as simply wanting to be there for him, which he knew, after their post-dinner conversation, couldn't be the case.

However, regardless of everything going on inside him, he was oddly relieved that she hadn't been deterred by his attempts to push her away. He was glad she was here, whatever her reasons. And because that was confusing as hell when she'd so flatly rejected him, and because he didn't have the wherewithal to analyse it right now, he thrust it from his mind and focused instead on navigating a patch of vegetation that had encroached onto a section of the road.

After consulting the map that the hotel receptionist had sketched out, Alex directed him off the main road and along a track lined with the remains of what looked like houses.

'It must have been quite an earthquake,' she said, gazing at the devastation all around.

'Seems risky, building a new town quite so close.'

'Better materials and modern methods, I suppose. There it is,' she said, pointing at a dilapidated building a couple of hundred metres ahead on the left and effectively cutting off his attempt at a distraction.

Max parked up, the hammering of his pulse and the thumping of his head more intense than ever, and got out. A dry, dusty wind was whistling down the abandoned streets and around the ruins. The only signs of life were a couple of goats, wandering about and nibbling on the odd wrecked tree. It was bleak and desolate and eerie, and there was a chill in the air despite the warmth of the midday sun.

Barely aware of Alex now, he walked on, as if being pulled in by some invisible force. The front door had long gone, as had the windows. Most of the walls had fallen in and there was no roof.

How on earth had he and his brothers wound up here? was the thought pummelling away at him as he moved from one destroyed space to another, numbly picking his way through the rubble. Who had left them here? Why? Had they been happy? Well-fed and cared for? How could they have been separated? What kind of adoption agency would have allowed such a thing?

In the absence of memories, speculation flooded through him, blurring his vision and quickening his breath. Babies. Kids. The noise, the bustle, the nuns. He could be standing on the very spot where he and his brothers had once slept...

But there were no clues here. This place had been stripped of anything useful or valuable long ago. The rusty filing cabinet that was bolted to what was left of a wall had already been emptied of documents by Alex's on-the-ground contact, who'd found his birth certificate and those of his brothers within. Nothing else remained.

He didn't know what he'd expected to find, he realised, his throat aching and his chest tight. Or why he'd come, when the place had been thoroughly searched already. The rashness of the decision, the uncertainty and the confusion indicated a weakness that he hated. If he'd somehow hoped to find a connection with his past, it had been a hugely self-indulgent move.

In fact, this whole experience was making him feel sick. His hands were clammy and his head was swimming, the nausea rolling through him threatening to overwhelm him.

The world seemed to be spinning around him and he could hardly breathe. The blood was draining from his head and the strength was leaching from his limbs.

What if he never got the answers he sought? What if neither he nor Alex ever uncovered the truth? How would he be able to get a grip on everything that was going on inside him and figure out what his life really meant? What if he never recovered a sense of peace? What if this chaos was for ever?

He needed to get out, away from the thoughts and the emotions ricocheting around him. His control was unravelling faster and more wildly than ever before, and it was terrifying. He couldn't handle any of this any longer. It brought back unwanted memories of vulnerability and desperation, and it was making him unhinged.

Forget wanting to find out who he might have once been. He didn't need to know that to work out who he was now. The future was his to decide. This trip had been a mistake. For a decade he'd been all about looking forwards with a single-minded focus that had not wavered once. So what the hell had he been *doing* this last week?

'Alex?' he yelled, summoning up some

strength from who knew where and striding off in the direction of the exit, the car, sanity.

'Over here,' came the response from somewhere to his left.

'We're leaving.'

# CHAPTER EIGHT

'ARE YOU ALL RIGHT?' said Alex, a little breathless as she half walked, half jogged to keep up with Max's long quick strides and a lot concerned with the way he appeared to have the hounds of hell at his feet.

'No, I'm not all right,' he muttered, a deep scowl darkening his face, his jaw clenched and his hands curled into fists.

'What's wrong?'

'I'm through with this.'

Her chest squeezed in a way that had nothing to do with the burn in her lungs. She shouldn't have left him alone, she thought, her throat tight and her pulse galloping. She'd wanted to give him space and privacy and so had taken herself off, which had clearly been an error of judgement, but at least she was here now, to help him navigate this stage of his journey.

'This has to have been a lot to deal with.'

'I don't just mean today,' he said curtly, unlocking the door of the car and yanking it open. 'I mean the entire bloody investigation.'

Alex opened her own door and clambered in, her mind reeling with shock. 'What?'

'I'm done.'

Having buckled up, he fired the engine, released the handbrake and hit the accelerator with such force that the wheels spun and kicked up a cloud of dust so large it completely obscured the ruined town that he seemed intent on putting as far behind him as possible.

'What are you talking about?'

'I'm leaving,' he said tightly, his gaze on the road, his fingers gripping the steering wheel as if his life depended on it. 'Going home.'

She clung to the door handle, for a moment too stunned for words. 'No, you can't do that,' she said once she'd regained the power of speech.

'Keep the plane. I'll make my own way back.'

What had happened? What was going on? 'But why?'

'Work.'

That made no sense. Hadn't he told her he was between contracts?

'You said all you needed to work was your laptop,' she said, thinking of the device he'd been so occupied with on yesterday's flight.

'You don't need me here.'

'I do.'

'In what possible way?'

Well, quite. She'd managed on her own for eight months. It was an entirely fair question. She didn't need him here, in truth. But her mind had gone blank. She couldn't think. All she knew was that she didn't want him to leave. She'd got used to having him around. They were supposed to be working *together*. Besides, he clearly wasn't in a good place at the moment and how was she supposed to keep an eye on him for Finn if Max went home on his own?

'I don't speak Spanish,' she said, her head spinning as she grappled for an excuse.

'You're competent and driven. You're more than capable of finishing up here. You'll manage.'

'I know, but this isn't right, Max.'

'It's my call.'

'I have a plan.'

A muscle hammered in his jaw. 'I'm sure it's great.'

It wasn't particularly, but at least it was something. 'Step one is checking out all the hospitals within a hundred-kilometre radius of here. Step two is taking a gamble on your biological parents living close by. It's you parading around town on the off-chance that someone might recognise you. That can't happen if you're not here.'

The brief glance he threw her way was incredulous. 'That won't happen even if I am.'

'It's worth a try.'

'It's even more of a long shot than a DNA match.'

'I am aware of that,' she said, determined to keep her cool so she could work out what to do. 'But I am also aware that the three of you reuniting after thirty years apart has little to do with me. Rico found out about Finn because of a photo he'd seen in the financial press, and you showed up because of the interview, which was originally suggested by Carla.' Rico's fiancée. 'Even the feelers we have out with the Swiss bank and the Argentinian government are yours. Nothing *I've* tried has worked and I'm not ready to give up.'

'Has it occurred to you that we might never discover the truth?'

'Yes, it has,' she said, her heart giving a quick lurch at the thought of defeat, of failure. 'But I can't dwell on that. I have to see it through.'

'I'm not stopping you.'

'You need to see it through too.'

'No, I really don't,' he said, his jaw tight. 'I'm done with digging around in the past. It can't be changed. I'm going to focus on the future.

That's how my brothers have handled things. They're all about looking forwards, not back.'

Yes, well, they had partners to help them and children in various stages of development to focus on. Max had no one. And while he might not think it at the moment, he needed to deal with this. The truth was what he sought. She wouldn't let him throw away the chance to find the answers because of what could quite possibly be a knee-jerk reaction to what had to be a very stressful set of circumstances. Not without further consideration anyway.

'They've had far longer to process things,' she said, her heart in her throat as the car swerved violently. 'And it wasn't easy for either of them at first.'

'Then all I need is time.'

He needed more than that. 'Pull over.'

'What?'

'Stop. Please. You're in no fit state to drive.'

'I'm fine.'

'You nearly hit an alpaca just now.'

'What alpaca?'

'Exactly.'

She could practically hear the grind of his teeth, but a moment later he'd pulled over, killed the engine and tossed her the key. They got out and swapped seats and Max did up his seatbelt, but Alex had other plans. She twisted to face him and it tore at her heart to see the torment he was trying so hard to contain.

'The key goes in the ignition, Alex.'

'Let's look at this calmly,' she replied, ignoring his sarcasm as much as the sizzling effect of his proximity on her.

'I am calm.'

No, he wasn't. He was anything but calm. The tension gripping his whole frame buffeted hers. There was a wildness to his movements and his words that suggested he was a man fast reaching the end of his tether.

'What's going on?'

'Stop trying to psychoanalyse me, and drive.'

'In a moment.'

'Am I going to have to get out and walk?'

'If that's what you need.'

'What I need is to get back to the hotel so I can start packing.'

That was the last thing he needed, in her opinion. But how was she going to keep him here? If he was determined to go, there was nothing she'd be able to do to stop him. Could she appeal to his better nature? Did he even have one? What incentive would work? He was so wound up. How could she get him to relax enough to be able to realise she was right?

But hang on...

'Why don't we take some time out?' she

said as the idea of relaxing triggered a memory from dinner at La Copa Alegre and inspiration struck.

He whipped round and stared at her as if she'd sprouted a second head. 'Some time out?'

'The last few days have been incredibly intense for me,' she told him, steeling herself against the blaze of astonishment and turmoil she could see in his eyes. 'I can't imagine what they've been like for you. I read that there are some salt flats not far from here, just across the border. They could be worth a look.'

'Are you mad?'

She'd never felt saner in her life. 'We'll go out there,' she said, more convinced it was the right thing to do with every passing second. 'After lunch. Check out the nature. Take advantage of the new moon and gaze at a few stars once the sun has set. There's even a luxury lodge. We could stay the night there and come back refreshed tomorrow.'

'*Refreshed?*'

His disbelief was fierce but she refused to quail. 'You did say I should take a break.'

'You don't need me for that.'

'And you don't need me for anything,' she said, reminding herself that this wasn't about her. This was about him. And even if it hadn't been, she ought to be glad he thought he didn't need her for anything because that was exactly what she wanted. 'I get it. But I won't let you mess this up, Max. You need to give it a chance. For the sake of your brothers but, more importantly, for yourself. I know what it's like to not know who you truly are, and I know how petrifying it can be to have to work that out. But I also know the relief that comes when you're through it. You'll regret it if you leave. Running away doesn't solve anything.' She let that sink in for a moment then leaned forward a fraction, keeping her gaze firmly fixed on his. Injecting as much persuasion into her tone as she could, she said, 'So let's be tourists for a while. We won't talk about the case. We'll just take the opportunity to relax and forget ourselves for once. We can start again tomorrow. It would be less than twenty-four hours. What do you think?'

Max didn't want to hang out in any salt flats and relax. He couldn't think of anything less appealing than doing the tourist thing and stargazing with a woman who'd so ruthlessly rejected him yet to whom he was still wildly attracted. He'd have to be some kind of masochist to agree to it when all he wanted to do, but couldn't, was reach out, pull her tight against him and run his hands all over her, before kissing her until neither of them could think straight.

He didn't want conversation of any kind with her. They'd talked plenty—too much, in fact— and they were already staying in a perfectly good, if basic, hotel in La Posada. And what did she know about relaxing anyway? Could she even do it? Not once in the brief but impactful time he'd known her had she shown any evidence of it. The kiss they'd shared, the one that she'd been able to dismiss so easily but still tormented him night and day, hadn't been in the slightest bit chilled. Even during dinner at La Copa Alegre her conversation had been laced with wariness, her body gripped with tension.

And what the hell gave her the right to tell him that he'd regret it if he left? he wondered, his stomach churning and his head pounding. She knew nothing about anything. He wasn't petrified. He wasn't running away. He'd just had enough. He was completely overwhelmed by everything that had happened recently, that was all, and God, he was tired. He'd barely slept recently. He'd hardly been able to breathe. He wanted to go home, crash out for a month and wake up to the realisation that the last week had been nothing but a bad dream.

But it wasn't. It was reality. His new reality, in fact, and much of it—namely the discovery of his brothers—he was delighted about. The rest of it, not so much, but, if he was being brutally honest, he probably wasn't going to be able to escape that by simply going home. No matter how much he tried to convince himself that the past was of no interest or importance to him, it was, and it would follow him wherever he went, evermore festering away inside him and corroding his identity and his self-worth the longer it went unaddressed.

He needed to track down his biological family in order to find out whether he'd been wanted. If he'd once mattered to someone, to anyone. It was only on meeting his brothers and feeling somehow anchored by them that he'd realised how adrift he'd always been, how unsure of his place in the world at large, knowing somewhere deep down inside that he was entirely on his own.

But now he had the chance to make sense of it all, so what choice did he have but to stay and see it through to the bitter end? Whatever the outcome, and he was aware that he might not get the results he so badly hoped for, at least then he'd know he'd given it everything. At least then he could process it and, somehow, move on.

Whether she knew it or not, Alex's point about not letting Finn and Rico down had struck him deep in the gut. He shouldn't need their approval, or anyone's, but he craved it nonetheless. He liked them, he valued the relationship they were developing, and he'd do nothing to jeopardise it. He'd told them he'd do what he could to get to the truth and, while he was all for breaking rules, he didn't break promises. How could he have forgotten that?

He hadn't been thinking straight for days now. Could it be that he wasn't thinking straight now? Could Alex be right and he *did* need a breather? The thought of handing over even the minutest modicum of control made him want to recoil in sheer horror, but perhaps he'd be wise to concede to her on this. The tumultuous news of his adoption and all it entailed sat like a rock on his chest, crushing him with its ever-increasing weight, and his judgement wasn't exactly firing on all cylinders at the moment.

And, in any case, this wasn't just about him. It was about Alex too. Her career and her future. He'd agreed that they'd work together and so far she'd kept her end of the bargain. In fact she'd gone beyond it. She hadn't let him push her away, no matter how hard he'd made it for her. She'd been resolute and unshakeable. He'd never had that kind of steadfast unconditional support. He didn't know quite what to do with it, but at the very least he owed it to her to stick around a little while longer.

Besides, maybe she *did* know how to relax. Despite the stress and turmoil storming his defences, he couldn't deny that he found the idea of it intriguing and alluring, a tiny beacon of light piercing the dark maelstrom of chaos. He'd failed to entice her into his bed, but if he could get her to lower her guard and ease up, he would at least be able to claw back some kind of pride.

'The salt flats it is.'

They set off after lunch and spent two hours driving along huge, wide, empty roads that bisected great swathes of desolate rocky landscape before reaching their destination. En route they passed cactus fields, a stretch of bubbling geysers and abandoned towns made entirely of salt. The jagged mountains that rose majestically in the distance were awe-inspiring. In every direction, as far as the eye could see, bright white salt sparkled in the sun, the light reflecting off it dazzling. They came across flocks of flamingos, wild vicuña and ruby-red lagoons. The sky was cloudless and the air clean and raw. It had to be one of the most isolated, most beautiful places on earth.

Heading out here had been the best idea

she had had in ages, Alex reflected as she and
Max sat on the viewing platform attached to
the one dome-shaped pod-like cabin that had
been available, watching the sun dip beneath
the horizon, having dined on a feast of yucca
soup followed by grilled *paiche* served with a
delicate risotto and then, to finish, an exquisite mousse of dark chocolate and eucalyptus.
She had to admit that she needed the break.
It felt so wonderful to throw off the shackles
of work for a while. To put aside her worries,
even temporarily, and lose herself in the won-
ders of the world.

As agreed, she and Max hadn't talked about
the case or family or anything, really, of a personal nature. Instead, the conversation had
meandered through a wide variety of largely
neutral subjects—travel, food, books. It had
hardly been scintillating but, even so, she
hadn't been able to get enough of it. She wanted
to know everything about him, and she didn't
even bother to try and convince herself that
her interest was professional. It wasn't. It was
entirely personal. Those complex layers of his
that she'd identified during the floating dinner,
that she'd caught a glimpse of at the orphanage,
drew her attention like the brightest of beacons
and were impossible to ignore.

But now, with the fire crackling in the pit that

stood in front of them, the conversation had petered out. Max seemed to be as lost in thought as she was and she wondered whether he too had been struck dumb by the mesmerising reflection of the sun on the mirror-like surface of the ground and the staggeringly beautiful streaks of reds and gold slashing across the vast blue sky or if he could possibly be thinking the same thing she was, namely the fireworks he'd mentioned.

Despite her best efforts, she hadn't been able to scrub them from her mind, but that was what came of spending so much time cooped up with him in a car, however large and luxurious. The distance between places here was immense. Five minutes was all it took for her to become achingly aware of him sitting beside her, his shoulder mere centimetres from hers, and then she found she spent the rest of whatever journey they were on trying not to lean into him and keeping her eyes on the scenery and not on his profile, which inevitably was agony.

And then there was the lodge. If she'd known it was billed as a honeymooners' paradise and that the half a dozen domes came with a king-size bed only she'd never have suggested staying the night. The air of romance was everywhere, from the double shower in the ensuite bathroom to the intimacy of the tables set for two in the dining room to the cosy sofa they were sitting on out here. Not only did she feel like a fraud, she couldn't stop thinking about how exciting their kiss had been, how desperately she wanted more and how nearby and enticing the bed was.

Max, on the other hand, clearly wasn't suffering from the same kind of struggles. He hadn't batted an eyelid about there only being one dome available. He'd dismissed her suggestion they drive back, saying it was too far, and told her he'd take the floor, as if it didn't bother him in the slightest that they'd have to share a room. He still hadn't touched her. His distance was polite. His smiles were entirely impersonal. She both envied and resented his ability to simply switch off the attraction. How did he do it? she wondered for what had to be the hundredth time in the last hour.

And what would it take to switch it back on again?

It was a question that shouldn't have been of the remotest interest but, despite everything, she badly wanted to know the answer. The longer he obeyed her request to back off, the more she wanted him to dishonour it. She desperately yearned for him to deploy that rebellious streak of his and break every single one of her rules, which made no sense at all.

Or did it?

As she gazed up at the vast canopy of stars that now spread out above them like a giant glittering blanket, her heart began to thump that little bit harder while her head began to spin that little bit faster. The sky was so big out here, the universe so huge. She could make out the Southern Cross and the Milky Way and suddenly she felt very small and very alone. At least Max had his brothers now. She had no one. No one on her side, no one to turn to for support.

She'd been so lonely for so long and just for one night, maybe a few more, she didn't want to be. She was so tired of keeping how she felt about Max at bay. Constantly fighting it when she was achingly aware of every movement he made, every breath he took, his scent, his warmth, the impact of his gaze on her, took more effort than she could possibly have imagined and she was running on fumes.

Why shouldn't she sleep with him? she thought, her mouth going dry and her entire body heating as the last of her defences bit the dust. Why shouldn't they have the fling he'd proposed the night she'd told him she would never act on the attraction they shared? It needn't be complicated. Sex with him wouldn't mean anything beyond a release of tension and, she hoped, outstanding, mind-blowing pleasure.

He'd certainly be a boost for her self-esteem, if the kiss was anything to go by, and God, she could do with one of those. How she hated the angst and insecurity she'd developed about her body, thanks to her ex. She wanted to feel good about herself, physically as well as professionally, and if Max was as skilled as he said he was she knew she'd feel amazing.

But what about her rules?

Well, those no longer seemed quite as important as they once had. As he kept reminding her, he wasn't a client. Neither of them was looking for anything long-term and, as he'd pointed out, no one else need ever know.

So what if she let a little bit of chaos into her life? She could handle it. She'd spent years building up her armour against precisely this sort of thing. She didn't need to worry about possible heartbreak and misery. There'd be no regrets. Things would never get that far. It wasn't as if she wanted a relationship with him. Or anyone, for that matter. Even if she could overcome the major trust issues her husband's many infidelities had engendered, the possibility of failure, the potential upheaval when it all went wrong was too distressing to contemplate and deeply unappealing. But a fling?

With Max? That she would welcome. That she wanted with an all-consuming hunger that was fast becoming unbearable.

So what was she going to do? Was she brave enough to find out whether, despite the discouraging signs, he still wanted her too? Was she prepared for the very real yet faintly sickening prospect that she'd killed the attraction he'd once had for her? If she had, could she somehow manage to rekindle it?

Whatever the outcome, she had to try, she thought, her heart hammering as desire and longing rushed through her blood. She had to know. Because she couldn't go on like this. She didn't want to for ever wonder, what if. She'd had enough of the loneliness and the constant battle to ignore how he made her feel. And, above all, despite what he might think of her, she wasn't a coward.

'Look,' said Alex, wonder tingeing her voice as she pointed up at the sky. 'A shooting star.'

In response, Max just grunted. He didn't trust himself to speak right now. If he opened his mouth, there was every possibility it would be to beg her to change her mind about sleeping with him, because he was finding it increasingly hard to remember her rules and respect her wishes.

With hindsight, he should never have agreed to this whole ridiculous taking a break thing. What had he been thinking? Had he gone completely mad?

The afternoon had started off great. He'd never been to Bolivia. The landscape was stunning and fascinating. Alex was an amusing and interesting travelling companion, and with the investigation and the drama of the last few days firmly, if temporarily, put to one side he'd felt the chaos recede and a modicum of calm descend. It might have taken every ounce of strength he possessed but he'd ignored her proximity, and dismissed the fanciful idea that he could listen to her talk about nothing for ever, and had instead forced himself to concentrate on nature in all its vast and varied glory.

Things had started to fall apart for him when they'd arrived at the lodge and there'd only been one dome available to book. It had been too late to head back, he'd realised, deep unease setting in as the consequences dawned. The roads were unlit and wildlife with a death wish had a tendency to appear out of nowhere.

He'd briefly toyed with the idea of leaving Alex to occupy the dome while he slept in the car, despite the temperature dropping to subzero overnight. But he'd pulled himself together and reminded himself that his control wasn't that unreliable. He didn't have to face hypothermia. Alex could have the bed. He'd take the floor. She'd viewed that as an acceptable compromise and, quite honestly, how hard could it be?

Then he'd walked into the sumptuously furnished, seductively lit room, which was mostly bed and very little floor, and realised he was in for a night of pure, agonising hell.

'And there goes another one,' she said, yanking him back to the deck and the dazzling display of stars. 'You're meant to make a wish.'

That was a joke. The only thing he wanted right now wasn't going to happen, and the frustration was excruciating.

'Yeah, well, you were meant to be relaxing.'

'I am.'

No, she wasn't. She was huddled up at her end of the sofa, as far from him as she could get, practically clinging to the arm of it as if it were a lifebelt.

'I don't bite,' he muttered, loathing the fact that she didn't trust him.

'That's a shame.'

What the hell did she mean by that? he wondered, whipping his head round to find her watching him in a way that had his pulse suddenly racing. She'd loosened her death grip on the sofa and turned to face him, but why was she looking at him like that, sort of nervous yet hopeful? What was going on?

He was about to ask precisely that when she suddenly reached up and back, pulled off the band holding her hair back and, to his utter shock, shook out her hair. It fell in great, soft, dark brown waves around her shoulders, the tendrils framing her face shining in the light that came from the firepit, and it was every bit as exciting as he'd imagined.

'What are you doing?' he said, shock and desire turning his voice into almost a growl.

'I thought I would let my hair down.'

'It's beautiful,' he said before he could stop himself.

'Thank you.'

'All of you is beautiful.'

'Do you really think so?'

How could she possibly doubt it? Her smile, her eyes, everything about her, was lovely and he liked it all. He also liked their conversation, their differences and their similarities, not to mention her interest in him and the support she offered, but he couldn't go there, not even in his head. All that mattered, all that ever mattered when it came to women, this woman in particular, was the physical. 'Yes.'

She took a deep breath and leaned forward an inch, dizzying him with her scent and confusing him beyond belief, because what was she doing? 'You're the most attractive man I've ever met,' she said, the words coming out of her mouth in a rush. 'And the most dangerous.'

His heart gave a great lurch. 'In what way?'

'You make me want to break my own rules.'

Yeah, well, he knew that. But he'd failed. And he'd had enough of this. He was tired and turned on and in for eight hours of agony.

'We should call it a night,' he said gruffly. 'You in the bed. Me on the floor.'

Her gaze dropped to his mouth and the chilly air between them thickened with heat and tension. 'Is that really what you want?'

'Not by a long shot,' he said, the truth drug he appeared to have taken continuing its effect.

'Neither do I.'

He went very still, his gaze locking onto hers, his heart hammering as her intentions became clear, but he wasn't taking anything for granted. Not this time. 'What are you saying?'

'I want us in the bed together.'

God. 'You know where that will end up.'

'I know where I'd like it to end up,' she said, the desire and heat shimmering in her eyes stealing the breath from his lungs. 'I want you, Max. So much I'm going out of my mind. And I'm sick of trying to convince myself otherwise.'

Not giving in to the need drumming through him and reaching for her was taking every drop of control he possessed. His head was spinning. He was so hard he hurt. But he couldn't get this wrong. He didn't think he could take yet another rejection.

'You have rules.'

'They don't seem very important at the moment.'

'Prove it.'

# CHAPTER NINE

ALEX DIDN'T EVEN HESITATE. Max had flung open
the door she'd feared might be permanently
shut and she was going to head on through it
before she thought better of it. Excitement and
anticipation rushed through her, obliterating
the nerves and the doubt. In a flash she tossed
aside the blanket, and with one quick move
she was astride him, sitting in his lap, wrapping her arms around his neck and crushing
her mouth to his.

And oh, the *relief* when he instantly started
kissing her back, clamping his hands to her hips
to hold her in place while the kiss burned hot-
ter than the fire in the pit. Tongues tangled and
teeth clashed and when he ground her pelvis
against his, the rock-hard length of his erection
rubbing her where she ached for him so desperately, she actually whimpered.

That seemed to trigger his inner caveman because suddenly he tried to take control of the

kiss, but she used the advantage of her weight on and above him to push him back and increased the pressure because *she* was in charge right now. She had something to prove and she wasn't going to stop until she absolutely had to, so it went on and on, battering every one of her senses with the most delicious of assaults.

He filled her vision. He tasted of chocolate and whisky, dark and wicked. His touch set her alight and his scent dizzied her head. The desire that was sweeping through her was intense and undeniable, which was absolutely fine because she didn't want to deny any of this any more.

'Is that enough proof for you?' she said huskily when they finally broke for breath, noting with satisfaction that his eyes were glazed and a flush had hit his cheekbones.

'Are you sure about this?' he muttered, his voice spine-tinglingly low and gravelly.

'I've never been surer about anything.'

'You're not going to tell me it's a mistake or a conflict of interest?'

'No,' she said with a tiny shake of her head and a faint smile. 'Well, it's probably both, but I don't care.'

'Good.'

Without breaking contact, Max surged to his feet, his arms like steel bands around her back. She wrapped her legs around his waist and tightened her arms around his neck, and felt as light as a feather as he strode into the dome. He kicked the door shut and then fell with her onto the bed in a tangle of limbs before rolling her onto her back and pinning her to the mattress with *his* weight.

He didn't seem to have a problem with her attributes, judging by the hardness of his erection and the fierce intensity of his gaze that was locked to hers. He wouldn't care that her boobs were on the small side and she didn't have much in the way of hips. This was going to be everything she'd hoped for, she could tell.

And then she stopped thinking altogether because his head came down and his mouth landed on hers and once again she was nothing but a molten mass of need.

'I've wanted you since the moment we met,' he muttered against her jaw while he slid his hand beneath her clothes and up her side, making her shiver and shake.

'Really?' she breathed raggedly, clutching at his shoulders and wishing he wasn't wearing so many layers.

'I took one look at you in your tight skirt and neat top and I wanted to strip them off you then and there.'

'Likewise. Only in your case it was your worn jeans and crumpled shirt.'

'It made no sense.'

'I know. We're so unalike.'

'You can't imagine the agony I've endured.'

'I do have some idea,' she panted as he reared up to whip the clothes off his upper body. 'That kiss... I haven't been able to stop thinking about it, and that's been driving me nuts.'

Having hurled his clothes onto the floor, he set about hers. 'Your willpower is both awe-inspiring and frustrating as hell,' he muttered, removing her layers with flattering speed and throwing them in the general direction of his.

He undid her bra with impressive dexterity and tossed that to one side too. Her spine seemed to have dissolved because all she could do beneath the heat of his gaze was lie back, as if granting him permission to look, which he did for one heart-stopping moment, and then touch, which, to her relief, he decided to do too.

When he bent his head to her breast and swept his tongue over her nipple she nearly jack-knifed off the bed. He held her down and did it again and she moaned. After what felt like far too short a time, he transferred his attention to her other breast, whipping up such staggering sensations inside her that she could scarcely breathe, and she jammed her fingers in his hair to keep him there for ever.

But Max obviously had other ideas and, true

to form, he simply did what he wanted. Just when she thought she couldn't stand the electric shocks stabbing through her any longer, he moved lower, sliding his mouth down her stomach, the hint of stubble setting her achingly sensitive skin aflame.

When he reached the waistband of her trousers and pants, she instinctively lifted her hips and he eased them down and off. Then he settled back between her legs, holding her thighs apart, and put his mouth to where she was so hot and needy.

Her entire world centred on what he was doing to her and, at the sparks zinging through her, her head fell back while her fingers tightened in his hair. The tension was unbearable, the pleasure so intense she felt as though she were on a roller coaster, going faster and faster and higher and higher. He slid two long, strong fingers inside her and she moaned and gasped. And then he did something clever with them and quite suddenly that roller coaster left the rails and soared into the ether and she broke apart into a million tiny glittering pieces, wave after wave of ecstasy washing over her.

'I knew you'd be good at this,' she managed once the world had stopped spinning and she'd got her breath back.

'Alex, sweetheart, we've barely begun.'

He levered himself off her, his face dark and intense and his jaw so tight it could have been hewn from granite, and he jerked away to locate his wallet. Having found what he was looking for, he stripped off his jeans and shorts and ripped open the foil packet. Her breath caught as she watched him roll the condom onto his impressively long and thick erection with hands that seemed to be shaking, and her entire body trembled.

And then he was back with her, parting her knees and positioning himself before thrusting inside her, filling and stretching her so sensationally that she thought she might pass out with the indescribable pleasure of it.

When he began to move, she lost the ability to think altogether. She moaned and he kissed her hard. She clutched at his shoulders, feeling the flex of his muscles beneath her fingers and revelling in the masculine strength and power of his body. Her hips rose and fell instinctively to meet his movements and the pressure inside her swelled unbearably.

'Don't hold back,' she breathed on a sob, and it was like putting a match to a touch paper.

He moved harder and faster, his increasingly wild, fierce thrusts driving her higher and higher, their kisses becoming frantic and desperate until, without warning, she shattered again, the waves of pleasure hitting with such intensity that she cried out. Max followed her over the edge moments later, lodging hard and deep and groaning as he pulsated inside her before collapsing on top of her, his chest heaving and his entire body shaking.

For several long moments they lay there recovering, and then Max eased out of her and shifted onto his side.

'So,' she said with a giddy grin once she'd got her breath back. 'Fireworks.'

His gaze, as he looked down at her, was glittering and wild. 'Told you.'

'I saw stars.'

'That'll be the glass roof.'

'Not just the glass roof. You certainly know how to give an ego a boost.'

'Was yours in need of one?'

God, yes. 'When someone cheats on you repeatedly you find yourself…doubting your attractions.'

He frowned at that. 'You have many, as I think I just made pretty obvious,' he said, reaching out and running a hand slowly over her, making her sensitive skin shiver and her breasts tighten. 'But if you're still not convinced, I'd be more than happy to prove it again.'

'You know what?' she said huskily as fresh desire began to thud through her. 'I'm not sure I am.'

Yesterday, the overnight timeout suggested by Alex had felt to Max like aeons. At two in the morning, however, after the events of the last six or so hours, it didn't seem like nearly enough.

He'd never had sex like it, he thought, wide awake and staring up at the billions of stars through the roof made up of glass equilateral triangles while beside him Alex slept. She'd been insatiable and he'd been beyond desperate and they'd already got through half the box of condoms located in the drawer of the night stand, thoughtfully supplied by the lodge that clearly catered to honeymooners.

The edge of sexual tension and frustration he'd been living with since he'd met her had gone and, whatever the reason for her volte face, he couldn't be more satisfied with the way things had turned out. He'd known she'd be unable to resist in the end. It had taken longer than he'd anticipated but if there was one thing he *could* be sure of at the moment it was the power of chemistry.

He had to hand it to her, though. There was definitely something to be said for taking a break from reality, especially when that reality sucked. He felt he could breathe out here. Some of the chaos had calmed. Getting the answers he needed was still a top priority, despite the blip at the orphanage, but this little bubble that he and Alex were in at the moment didn't suck at all and, if he was being brutally honest, he wasn't quite ready for it to burst.

She'd suggested they head back to La Posada today to continue with her plan, which, frankly, didn't seem a particularly solid one, but what was the rush? There was plenty more to see and do here, and not just inside their dome. What would be the harm in staying another day or two?

It wasn't as if the investigation was moving apace and required their immediate attention, and it wasn't as if he hadn't chilled out with women before in a heavy-on-the-sex, light-on-the-conversation kind of way. None of them had been anything like Alex, it was true, but that didn't mean anything. All this was, was sex. Spectacular, head-wrecking sex, but just sex, nonetheless.

And sticking around a bit longer would do her good too, he thought as she turned in her sleep and sort of snuggled against him, which he found he didn't mind at all. Everyone needed a holiday, however brief, and by her own admission she hadn't taken one in years. He understood why she had an issue with letting her hair down, but she ought to do it more. Because he had to admit he liked the relaxed version of Alex, with her guard lowered and her inhibitions history. He liked her a lot.

Well, wasn't she full of good ideas at the moment, Alex thought with a wide satisfied grin as she sprawled across the bed and ogled Max, who was standing at the coffee machine wearing nothing but an open shirt and underwear, his hair damp from the shower.

Last night, and this morning, had been unbelievable, better than her wildest dreams, and God knew she'd had a few of those. The things he'd done to her... The things she'd done to him... Her confidence, so badly knocked by her lousy ex, was back with a vengeance and her self-esteem was higher than it had been for years. Max didn't seem to have an issue with any part of her body. In fact, he couldn't seem to get enough of it, and he'd made her feel like a goddess.

Taking up the challenge of proving that her rules no longer mattered had been a risk, but it had paid off in spades, and as she watched him stick a pod in the coffee machine, close the lid and stand back to let the machine do its thing, she wondered if maybe she ought to be a bit braver in other areas too. Maybe she ought to have it out with her family once and for all, and tell them exactly how she felt about the way she'd been brought up, how damaging it had been. It wouldn't change anything when the chasm between them now was wider and deeper than the Grand Canyon and equally unbridgeable, but at least then she'd have closure and the grip the past had on her would ease.

She knew now that she had what it took to be a success. As Max had pointed out yesterday when they'd been talking about work in a very vague sort of way, given the confidentiality that governed both their fields, she was still in business after five years, which was no mean feat when most start-ups failed within the first twelve months, and word-of-mouth recommendations were still coming in.

If this trip was the end of the road with regard to the investigation—and she had to face the fact that it could well be, because not only had Max heard back from his contacts, who'd come up with nothing, she didn't want him breaking the law and hacking into whatever systems he'd have to when he'd put such things behind him—would that really be the disaster she feared so much?

OK, so perhaps her track record would be

broken and her expansion plans might have to be put on hold, but what was the hurry? Wasn't it a bit pathetic to still be trying to prove something to people who couldn't care less? After all these years? During dinner at the floating bar, Max had suggested she just let it go and perhaps it really was as simple as that.

It would be no reflection on her if this investigation ended now. She'd done everything she could. She badly wanted Max to have the answers he sought for his own peace of mind, but in reality there were no avenues left to pursue. The three brothers had found each other after thirty years apart and were intent on forging a relationship going forward, and that was huge.

So wouldn't everyone be better off by simply moving on? In her considerable experience, not to mention her own *personal* experience, answers didn't always fix things. Look at all the investigations she'd run. Look at the mess of her marriage. Sometimes, success resulted in more unhappiness, more uncertainty and often innumerable other problems. Even if they did by some miracle get a breakthrough, it could well be the case that the truth was harrowing, more so than anyone could have imagined, and hadn't Finn, Rico and Max suffered enough? Didn't they need some sort of closure too?

Max handing her a cup of coffee snapped

her out of her thoughts, and as her gaze fixed on his bare chest, which she'd explored at great length and now knew in exquisite detail, she flushed with heat.

'What is it with you and buttons?' she said huskily, taking a sip and feeling the welcome hit of caffeine suffuse her blood.

'What do you mean?'

'You have a habit of forgetting to do them up.'

'No, I don't.'

Her eyebrows lifted. 'You mean it's deliberate?'

'It might be,' he said with the hint of a grin as he grabbed a coffee of his own and stretched out on the bed beside her.

'At dinner the other night too?'

'I don't know what you mean.'

He knew exactly what she meant. 'It wasn't that warm and there were mosquitoes. You had an ulterior motive.'

'I didn't think you'd noticed,' he said, shooting her a look of pure wickedness.

'I noticed.' Oh, how she'd noticed.

'And it bothered you.'

'I didn't think it was very professional.'

'Perhaps this is simply how I roll on holiday.'

'You were showing off.'

'I was getting desperate.'

At the thought of how much he'd wanted

her, desire flooded every inch of her body. 'It worked.'

'Ever play poker?'

'No. Why?'

'You'd be very good at it. No one would ever be able to tell what you were thinking.'

'Can you tell what I'm thinking now?'

'You're thinking what I'm thinking,' he said, his gaze dropping to her mouth, and it was so tempting to lean in for a kiss that would blow her mind and lead to another hour of outstanding pleasure, but it was getting late and check out was looming.

'Sadly, I don't believe I am. I was thinking we should be getting going and heading back,' she said with real regret because, even if they carried on sleeping together back in La Posada, there was something magical and special about this place.

'I disagree.'

'Oh?'

'I think we could do with more refreshing.'

Her heart began to hammer. 'What do you suggest?'

'Another couple of nights here.'

Her willpower was no match for the excitement beginning to ripple through her. If she were stronger she'd insist on leaving now, as had been the plan. But being out here, just the two of them with no cares, no work between them, was intoxicating. There was something about the freshness of the air and the vastness of the scenery that made everything else seem very insignificant. Max had eased up yesterday afternoon while they'd been exploring the landscape and she longed to see more of the man behind the assignment, to burrow further beneath those layers of his. Besides, after eight months, what was another couple of days?

'I could get behind that.'

'And then we head back to La Posada. Where the investigation will resume and this,' he said, indicating the both of them, 'will continue.'

'Until either we find the answers we seek or we decide to call it quits,' she said, for some reason feeling it needed confirmation.

'Exactly.' His expression sobered then and his smile faded. 'You should know, Alex, I don't do long-term. I don't do relationships.'

She understood where he was coming from but she needed no warning. She was entirely on the same page. She wasn't in danger of being swept up in the romance of the place and mistaking this for something it wasn't, no matter how many of his layers she managed to peel back. People didn't change, even if they promised over and over again to try, and in any case she didn't want him to.

'Neither do I.'

'Because?'

'Oh, you know,' she said lightly. 'A number of trust issues, thanks to a cheating ex. Not wanting to experience the monumental chaos of a breakup ever again. That kind of thing. You?'

'I witnessed the fallout of a disintegrating marriage,' he said, a shadow flitting across his face. 'Nothing would ever persuade me to go there. And, as I may have mentioned once or twice, these days I prefer my life free from chaos too.'

'Have you ever had a relationship?'

'Not since I went on the straight and narrow.'

'Why not?'

'I don't need the hassle. One night, one week, maybe two, suits me fine.'

'Me too.' Although she could count on one hand the number of dates that had ended up in the bedroom since her divorce and have fingers left over.

'A woman after my own heart.'

'Your heart is of no interest to me,' she said, even as hers gave a quick lurch. 'Nobody's is.'

'You don't believe in love?'

'It's not that I don't believe in it,' she said, thinking with a shudder of the potential pain and devastation a badly broken heart could cause. Hers had merely been dented by her ex, but even that had been difficult enough to recover from. 'On a theoretical level I can understand that true love exists, but the only kind I've ever experienced is conditional.'

'I haven't experienced any kind. What my parents felt for me was not love.'

No, it most certainly wasn't.

'Girlfriends?'

'They're never around long enough.'

'Deliberately?'

'It's just the way things pan out.'

Hmm. That didn't exactly answer the question.

'My family has always made it perfectly clear that unless I conform to their standards they want nothing to do with me,' she said. 'I know now that that's not a price I'm willing to pay.'

'Nor me.'

'Just as well that we're in this just for the sex then, isn't it?'

His eyes glittered, the look in them turning predatory, and as he took her cup off her and set it and his own on the night stand, his intention clear, desire began to sweep through her. 'I couldn't agree more.'

\* \* \*

By the following morning, Max and Alex had taken a trip in a hot-air balloon, had a picnic lunch on a shimmering sea of white and bathed naked in hot springs. Once again, the day had been warm and sunny, the night cold, clear and starry. And, once again, the minute the door of the dome closed behind them after dinner, clothes were shed and hands met skin and the temperature hit boiling point.

Unlike the day before, however, the talk had been anything but small. A thousand feet above the ground, catching Max at a moment his defences had been blown away by the sheer magnitude of the view, she'd drilled down into the nitty-gritty of his upbringing and rewarded him with details of her own. Over lunch he'd found himself telling her about why the need to find his biological family burned so much more intensely in him than in his brothers, how badly his self-worth needed him to have been wanted by somebody, and she'd reciprocated by confessing how she'd hated the insecure, needy woman she'd become after she'd found out about her husband's cheating, which had made him want to hunt the man down and throttle him.

The glimpses Max had caught of the woman behind the rules were fascinating. Who'd have thought Alex had such a dirty laugh? If some-one had told him the day they'd met that she couldn't pass a bottle of glittery nail varnish in a shop without buying it and that her collection was now in the hundreds he'd have scoffed in disbelief.

But then who'd have thought he'd find her beams of appreciation so addictive? Who'd have thought he'd do pretty much anything to elicit one of her blinding smiles of approval, whether it was simply building and lighting a fire in the pit, helping her climb into the hot-air balloon or closing down the hot springs site so they could have privacy?

She was like a drug running through his veins and making him feel invincible, and while part of him was all for the high, an-other part of him was troubled by the growing sense that things were heading in a danger-ous direction. The connection between them didn't feel purely physical any longer. Feel-ings were developing, he could tell, and his subconscious shared that unease because in the middle of the night he'd woken abruptly from the most erotic yet unsettling dream of his life.

He'd been sitting in his study back home, staring at his screens and trying to figure out how to fix a piece of code that wasn't quite right. Alex had sidled in wearing nothing but a half open shirt and a smouldering smile and had then planted herself between him and his desk. From there she'd proceeded to blow his mind several times over and he hadn't even had to leave his chair.

But when, still trembling in his arms, dream Alex had held him tight while murmuring that she was there and everything was going to be all right, an odd chill had swept through the room, freezing the blood in his veins and sending icy shivers down his spine. The more she'd continued to whisper reassurances and soft words of support in his ear, the more he'd wanted to get up and run. But he couldn't because firstly she was sitting in his lap, pinning him to the chair, and secondly his arms were wrapped around her and wouldn't loosen, no matter how much he ordered them to.

Now, he was sitting on the terrace in front of their dome, watching the most stunning sunrise he'd ever seen while tapping his phone against his thigh and remembering how, at dinner last night, a warm light seemed to have taken up residence in her eyes and her smiles had been somehow different, although he couldn't put his finger on quite why, and that added to the apprehension because he didn't know what to make of them.

His foundations, already on shifting sands, seemed to be cracking. His stomach churned with a low-level sort of anxiety and his mind wouldn't rest. He felt as if he could skid off the rails at any moment and he didn't know how to stop it.

'What are you doing out here?'

At the sound of Alex's voice behind him, husky with sleep, the anxiety ratcheted up a notch.

'Watching the dawn.'

'Are you all right?'

Why did she keep asking him this, as if she cared? Why did he hope she did?

'Fine.'

'You look a little tense.'

'I've had a text from Rico.'

'Is everything OK?'

'It's our birthday next month,' he said, telling himself that this was what was bothering him, with its stirring-up of unwelcome memories of birthdays gone by. 'He wants to know whether I'd be up for a celebratory dinner.'

'And are you?'

He wouldn't miss it for the world. 'I guess. I haven't celebrated my birthday for years.'

She pulled the blanket around her tighter and

came to sit beside him, which simultaneously made him want to shift closer and leap to his feet. 'Why not?'

'When I was a kid, my mother chose my friends, what I wore, what I ate. That didn't let up on my birthday.'

'My birthdays weren't much fun either,' she said dryly. 'No one ever even remembered. At least you got presents.'

'Only because they could be repurposed as weapons. She used to use the threat of taking them away as a punishment for whatever I did wrong.'

Her eyes shimmered. 'What a bitch.'

'Yup.'

'You're so lucky to have found your brothers,' she added with a wistfulness that, for some bizarre reason, made his throat tighten.

'I know.' He'd filled her in on the conversations they'd had and how much meeting them had meant to him. Now he came to think of it, there'd been a wistful look on her face then too.

'You now have family that cares about you. That gets you. You have an instant connection with people you met a week ago. I've known my family for thirty-three years and have no emotional connection with them at all. I have no such connection with anyone.'

She had an emotional connection with him. The thought spun into his head before he made it spin right out again. That couldn't be the case. The only connection they shared was a physical one. All that was between them was sex. He wasn't the one for her, even if she had wanted something more. He wasn't the one for anyone. Ever.

But he didn't like the clench in his chest at the thought of her all alone in this world, and he liked even less the jealousy that speared through him at the thought of her with someone else.

The dream, still fresh in his mind, was unsettling. He couldn't work out what was going on and he didn't want to, so it was a good thing that just then her phone, which she'd brought out with her to take pictures of the dawn as she'd done the morning before, beeped to alert her of an incoming message.

She focused on the device for a second or two, hitting a button there, scrolling up and down there, and then she gasped, 'Oh, my God.'

'What?'

When she lifted her gaze from the screen and looked at him, her eyes were wide and stunned. 'Remember I told you Finn had sent his DNA off for analysis?'

As if he'd ever forget anything he'd learned about his new-found family. 'Yes.'

'So it turns out it wasn't such a long shot after all.'

He went very still at that and his heart gave a great crash against his ribs. 'What are you saying?'

'There's a match.'

# CHAPTER TEN

As Alex's pronouncement hit his brain, each word detonating on impact, time seemed to stop. Max's head emptied of everything but this one massive revelation and then began to spin as questions started hurtling around it. His pulse thundered, his stomach churned and he couldn't seem to make any of it stop.

The facts. That was what he had to focus on. The facts.

'Who is it?' he said, his voice sounding as though it came from far, far away, even to his own ears.

'I don't know,' she said, sounding as dazed as he felt. 'A woman. A Valentina Lopez. The message is in Spanish.'

She held out the phone and for one moment he just stared at it as if it were about to bite. Valentina Lopez? That name hadn't come up in any of Alex's research. So who could she be? He ought to be snatching the phone out of her hand to find out, and yet he hesitated. There was an odd unexpected security in uncertainty. Once he read the message there'd be no going back. He could be on the brink of finding out everything he needed to make sense of his life, his value and who he was, or he could be opening a whole new can of worms.

But then he pulled himself together. This was precisely why he'd made the snap decision to fly from the Caribbean to London in the first place. Why he'd taken up Rico's offer of his plane and agreed to work with Alex, who'd been right that morning she'd stopped him leaving. He had to investigate this. For his brothers and, more importantly, for himself.

Bracing himself, he took her phone and glanced down at the screen. The details were blurry so he blinked, gave his head a quick shake and forced himself to focus.

'It would appear we have a first cousin,' he said a moment later, his limbs suddenly so weak he was glad he was sitting down. 'She's twenty-five. She's a marketing assistant and lives in Salta.'

'Oh, my God,' Alex breathed. 'That's five hundred kilometres south of La Posada. Does she say anything else?'

'That she'd like to meet.'

'Do you think she might know something?'

'I have no idea.'

'What are we going to do?'

As with so much that had happened over the last week, Max didn't have a clue. That he had more blood relatives was blowing his mind. His parents had both been only children, his grandparents long dead, so it had always been just them. But if he had a cousin here then he had an aunt and uncle and who knew how many more. He might have biological parents and grandparents. More siblings. An instant family, with the relationships and history and everything that entailed, things he'd never had. Or he might not. The chaos that had receded over the last couple of days was back with a roar, expanding and intensifying with every passing second, and it was making it impossible to think.

Or maybe that was Alex, who was sitting looking at him with a combination of wariness, hope and excitement, who still managed to stir up desire in him, even now, with this, and who, he realised with a jolt, confused the hell out of him.

What on earth had he been *doing* lately? he wondered wildly as he tapped out a reply, which took an age since his fingers were shaking so much he kept hitting the wrong letters. What had he been thinking?

All the things he'd told her... His angst over

his parents, the doubts he had about who he was and the reasons behind his drive to get to the truth... None of that was in the public domain. None of that she'd needed to know for the case. And what about the compromises he'd made, the lengths he'd gone to to please her, all so she would think more of him, better of him? He'd vowed never to change, to never again mould himself into being something someone else wanted, but that was exactly what he'd been doing.

For some reason his guard hadn't just lowered, it had disappeared altogether, and he felt as though he were on the edge of a precipice and about to hurl himself off it. She hadn't robbed him of the control and power he valued so highly and needed so much. He'd handed both over to her on a platter, without blinking an eye. He'd allowed her to break all the rules he hadn't even known he had. She'd pierced his armour. He was beginning to feel things he didn't want to feel, couldn't allow himself to feel, didn't deserve to feel.

He should never have allowed it to happen, he thought as panic began to set in. Hubris had been his enemy once again; in his arrogance he'd assumed he'd have this fling with Alex firmly under his control. But he'd been weak and foolish in his need for her and she'd sneaked beneath his defences. He'd become too involved. Their affair was supposed to have been a purely physical thing. It was never meant to have involved the discussion of innermost thoughts and emotions.

He shouldn't have indulged himself by analysing how alike they were, or wondered how the hell she couldn't see it, he realised, his throat tight and his head pounding as he hit the send button on his reply to Valentina Lopez. He shouldn't have granted her access to so many fragments of himself that she'd seen the whole.

But it wasn't too late to put a stop to it. To get some breathing space and perspective and regroup. He was going to Salta on his own. He was more than capable of handling whatever he found there alone. He'd spent thirty-odd years doing precisely that. He didn't want Alex there for any fallout. She'd already seen far too much of him and the thought of exposing any more of his vulnerabilities to her made him feel physically sick. It was now a question of survival.

'Well, I don't know about you,' he said bluntly, throwing up a shield of steel behind which he could restore his strength and fortify his defences, just the way he had as a kid whenever his mom had been particularly vicious or his father particularly uninterested, 'but *I'll* be leaving for Salta just as soon as possible.'

* * *

What the hell?

Stunned and confused, for one heart-thump-
ing moment Alex just sat there watching as
Max leapt to his feet and strode back into the
dome. One minute she'd been desperately hoping that he would invite her to his birthday dinner—which was insane when what they were
doing together firstly stayed in Argentina and
secondly definitely did *not* involve birthday
dinners—the next she'd been receiving a text
from Becky with the instruction Check your
emails!!!!!!, which she'd done and received a
shock that had knocked her for six. As if all
that wasn't enough to make her reel, Max's
blunt declaration that he was flying solo on
this whipped the air from her lungs and the
strength from her limbs.

But, whatever was behind it, it wasn't happening. They were beyond unilateral decision-
making. He had to be in shock. She'd noticed
that his fingers had trembled as he tapped out a
reply and the tension in his jaw. That was what
this was about, she was sure, and as a result he
needed her more than ever.

Filling fast with energy and determination,
Alex sprang into action and ran after him.
'Wait,' she said, faintly alarmed by the frenzy

with which he was gathering up his things and tossing them into his bag.

'What?' he snapped distractedly.

'Don't you mean *we* will leave as soon as possible?'

He didn't even look at her. He looked as if he was somewhere else entirely and her chest tightened with sympathy and alarm.

'No,' he said flatly. 'I mean "I".'

He sounded resolute and tension radiated off him like some kind of force field designed to keep her out. And as it dawned on her that he was not going to yield on this, was not going to talk to her about what he was feeling, hurt sliced through her.

'You want to cut me out of the loop now?' After everything they'd talked about? Everything they'd done?'

'It's nothing personal.'

The sting of that lodged deep in her chest and twisted. 'It is to me, Max,' she said, her throat tight, her voice cracking. It was deeply personal for a whole host of reasons she couldn't begin to unravel right now. 'This is *my* success,' she said, going for the simplest. 'I've waited eight months for a breakthrough like this. I need to be part of it.'

'It's *my* family. There's no point in you coming. You don't speak Spanish. You literally wouldn't understand.'

Another arrow pierced her heart, dipped in envy for the family, the connections, the love and acceptance he might find, and yet more pain. No, she didn't speak Spanish, but she could be there, in the background if necessary. She *would* understand. She could see what he was going through. She wanted to help him. But he wasn't letting her and that was more agonising than she could ever have imagined.

'I'd like to be there for you.'

'I don't need you to be there for me, Alex,' he said, his horribly and bewilderingly blank gaze finally meeting hers. 'I don't *want* you to be there for me. That isn't what this is. You knew the score. You *agreed* with the score.'

Yes, she had, but still. Wow. Just wow. It was as if he'd punched her in the stomach and sliced her heart in two. Her head was spinning and she couldn't breathe.

'We'll head back to La Posada now,' he said, tossing her bag on the bed and then striding into the bathroom. 'I'll drop you off at the hotel and then go on to the airport. I'll be back this evening and fill you in on the details then. Get packing.'

Max wouldn't be filling her in on the details this evening, or at any other time, Alex thought

dully as the powerful four-by-four ate up first
the Bolivian and then the Argentinian kilometres. She wasn't sticking around when she
clearly wasn't wanted. What did he take her
for? Some kind of sap he could use when it
suited him and discard when it didn't? Well,
that wasn't her.

She understood that the news that he had
a cousin—and therefore quite possibly more
relatives—must have come as an almighty
shock, but how could he dismiss her so brutally? Didn't she deserve more than that?

If she was being completely honest, the thing
between them had never been purely physical.
She'd been fascinated by him from the moment
they'd met and not just because of his devastating good looks. Somewhere along the line she'd
started thinking that maybe it was the same for
him. The things he'd told her had been freely
shared. She hadn't had to prise anything out of
him. She'd sensed his trust in her in his touch,
in the strength of his need for her.

Yet the security she'd been starting to feel
with him had been entirely false. One huge
toss of the sea and Max had retreated behind
his feet-thick walls, keeping her well and truly
out, more determinedly, more successfully than
before, and now everything was falling down
around her like a house of cards.

How could she have been such a fool? What on earth had made her think her support, her help, would count for anything? He'd never asked for it. He clearly didn't want it. And why would he when he'd never had either before, and had presumably adapted to that? Where had that arrogance of hers come from?

This was precisely why she didn't get involved, she reminded herself, the blood in her veins chilling at the thought of how close a shave she'd had. This was why she had rules. To protect herself from hurt. To ward off weakness. To prevent the kind of emotional turmoil that could destroy her focus and threaten her future. She ought to be grateful that Max had revealed his true self before she'd tossed aside what remained of her rules and found herself in too deep. Before she wound up trying to find ways to prolong the investigation and therefore their affair too, believing that it could turn into something it wasn't.

As soon as he dropped her at La Posada and left, she'd make her way home. Her work here was done. Once she was back in London, free of Max's impact and the cruelty of his whims, she'd focus on the fact that, after all these months of nothing, her long shot had paid off. She'd had the breakthrough she'd so badly needed. In terms of progress, she'd gone from zero to a hundred. Because of a recommendation *she'd* made. Once the implications had fully registered she'd be on cloud nine. She was sure she would.

To hell with what Max discovered in Salta. If she wanted to know she'd find out from Finn. She would not wonder how he got on or how he dealt with whatever it was that Valentina Lopez had to say. She would not regret that she couldn't be there to share the joy or the sorrow he might feel. She would not allow the pain of his rejection to linger or indulge the many what-ifs she could feel crowding at the edges of her mind.

In fact, she wouldn't think of him at all.

Max arrived back in La Posada at midnight, wrecked and battered by the events of the day, to discover that Alex had checked out. She'd left a brief note at Reception, informing him that she was closing down the investigation and going home and wishing him luck for the future, before signing off with her full name and professional title.

And that was absolutely fine, he told himself, his chest aching and his stomach churning as he strode into his room, kicked the door shut and cracked open the bottle of bourbon he'd procured from the bar on his way up, the words of her bald little note ricocheting around his head. Better that she wasn't around to see him like this, actually, and what had he expected anyway?

He'd had plenty of time to reflect on this morning's conversation. He hadn't handled the news of the match well, he knew now. In his mind's eye he could still see the hurt on Alex's face when he'd told her he was going to Salta alone, could still hear her gasp of shock when he'd told her why. That he'd been both knocked for six by the news that he had a cousin and thrown into a spin by various realisations about the nature of their affair was no excuse.

He'd planned on apologising and explaining, as well as confessing that he deeply regretted rejecting her support because all too soon he'd realised he could have done with her there, even though he wasn't entirely sure why. He'd have got on his knees to beg her forgiveness, if it had come to that. He'd have done whatever it took to calm the storm that was raging through him.

But none of that was necessary now, he reflected numbly, splashing bourbon into a glass and swallowing it in one. There'd be no grovelling, no recounting of the meeting he'd had with his cousin and no forgiveness and acceptance. No arms around him when he broke down over the fact that his biological mother had died six years ago and, his father had been a one-night stand she'd had when she was sixteen, and no soothing insight into how he might go about dealing with the heart-breaking fact that he would never know if he was like either of them or who he truly was.

But at least there was also no risk of him crashing through his shield of steel and begging Alex to agree to continue their fling even after the case closed, which was not only impractical when they lived half a world apart and unprecedented when he rarely reversed a decision once made, but also so very, very dangerous.

He wasn't good enough for her, he told himself, pouring himself another glass of liquor and again downing the contents. He wasn't good enough for anyone. How could he have forgotten that? Wanting to be wanted by her would lead to nothing but misery and disillusionment. Even if this morning had gone differently and by some miracle she'd agreed, how long would it be before he screwed up so badly that her approval and appreciation turned to disappointment and regret?

No. As he'd always known, he was far better off free from the emotional havoc of a relationship that he'd inevitably mess up through ignorance and inexperience. He neither wanted nor deserved the responsibility of Alex's happiness and well-being. He wouldn't know how to take care of them. He could scarcely believe he'd even contemplated it. Hell, he didn't even know who he was. The confused, unwanted, unloved kid? The cocky, rebellious hacker? The cool-headed cyber security expert? Or a man being torn apart by pointless feelings for a woman he could never have?

He'd survive. He always did. And he had his brothers now. He'd take the bundle of unopened letters Valentina had given him to England. He'd read them with Finn and Rico instead of with Alex. It was much more appropriate that way anyway.

He had no doubt that tomorrow he'd realise that things had turned out for the best today. He'd treated Alex appallingly and the regret and shame scything through him were nothing more than he deserved. He'd been wise to put a stop to their affair before it had got out of hand and he'd done even more damage. He didn't think he could bear it if he made her unhappy, which he inevitably would.

He picked up the bottle for the third time and figured that since the bourbon was doing such a good job of dulling the pain he might as well finish it off. In the morning, with hindsight, he'd see that he'd had the luckiest of escapes and, more importantly, so had she.

* * *

But if he'd had such a lucky escape, thought Max three tumultuous days later as he sat with his brothers in Finn's drawing room in Oxfordshire, the letters strewn across the vast coffee table that sat between two enormous sofas, why was Alex all he could think about? Why did the fact that she'd sent her invoice to Finn the day she'd got home, as if she hadn't been able to wait another minute to sever the connection they'd once had, cut him up so painfully?

He'd assumed, an inch from the bottom of the bottle, he'd have no trouble wiping her from his head. He'd told himself that he had more than enough to worry about and did not need either the confusion she wreaked or the hassle she caused. He'd deal with what was going on inside him somehow. He'd done it before. He could do it again. She was out of his life and it was a relief.

But, if that was the case, why was he still feeling so out of sorts?

Outwardly, he was just about holding it together, but inside he was falling apart. Every time a memory from the time he and Alex had spent together slammed unbidden into his head, the impact of it nearly wiped out his knees. When he recalled the way she'd smiled at him, warmth spread through him like a blanket seep-

ing into every corner of him, even those parts
that had always been so cold and empty, before
it was whipped away by regret.

He was untethered, adrift, and he itched to
return to his old ways. He wanted to break laws
and hack into a system or two, just to claw back
some kind of control and power over what was
happening to him. He wanted to immerse himself in the dark web and find out what his former colleagues were up to and maybe lend a
hand. It was only the thought of Alex's disapproval that stopped him and that was baffling,
since her opinion of him was neither here nor
there any more.

It wasn't as if he didn't have anything else
to occupy his mind. Once he'd sobered up he'd
gone home, where he'd spent two days translating the letters their mother had written, and
what a weekend that had been.

The letters, which ran to dozens of pages
each, detailed a history of her life and as much
of theirs as she'd known. They were filled with
explanations and reasons and the hopes she'd
had at first of finding her sons and then, when
that had looked less and less likely, the dreams
she'd had for them. Her anger, her sadness, her
love poured from the lines, and reading them,
analysing them as he'd translated them, had
completely wrecked him.

It seemed to be wrecking his brothers too. For two hours they'd been studying the letters, largely in silence, and jaws were tight and brows were furrowed. The struggle for self-control seemed to be as tough for them as it had been for him.

'Bit dusty in here,' said Finn gruffly, clearing his throat as he put down the final page, the one in which their mother's heartbreak at knowing she was going to her grave without ever finding them had ripped Max to shreds.

'I appear to have something in my eye,' said Rico, looking as if swallowing was hard.

Finn rubbed his face and got to his feet. 'I think I'll go and find Georgie.'

Rico shoved his hands through his hair and did the same. 'I'm just going to call Carla.'

They exited the room, leaving Max alone with nothing more than a pounding head and a racing pulse. His chest ached. His vision blurred. He could hardly breathe with emotions that were crushing him on all sides, one in particular scorching through him like lightning.

It was envy, he realised with a jolt as the room began to spin. He envied his brothers. For the relationships they had and the women they loved. How did they do it? He wished he knew. Because, deep down, he didn't want to be alone. He wanted Alex, in the way Finn had

Georgie and Rico had Carla. Not only to help him navigate the choppy waters he was in, but to sail along with him even when they weren't choppy. In other words, all the time.

Which meant what? That he'd been the biggest fool on the planet to turn her away? Well, that seemed pretty much spot-on. Despite his attempts to convince himself otherwise, Alex *was* different to the other women he'd hooked up with over the years. Quite apart from the fact that what they'd been doing was far more than 'hooking up', they'd travelled similar paths. They understood each other. Until he'd been spooked into falling back into bad habits and internalising his fears, everything had been going great.

So could he have pushed her away deliberately, sabotaging something good before it blew up in his face? Had it been his way of maintaining control over a situation that was fast slipping out of his grip? It wasn't beyond the realms of possibility. But what if it didn't blow up in his face? What if he'd thrown away the best thing that had ever happened to him because of some ridiculous concern that he might not survive it?

He had to take responsibility for his behaviour, he realised suddenly as he sprang to his feet and began to pace the length of the drawing room. His hang-ups about the past might be valid, but his response to what happened now was his own. He had a choice, and he could either continue to allow it to eat him up with bitterness and resentment or he could let it go.

He was fed up with dwelling on the past. Shouldn't he take a leaf out of his brothers' book and start looking forwards rather than back? It would be charting new territory and that was scary as hell, but that was no excuse not to do it. That smacked of cowardice.

Could the future hold Alex? He desperately wanted it to, because he could see her in it. He wanted her in it. Was he in love with her? How would he know? Where was a flowchart when he needed one? But *something* had to account for the gaping hole in his chest and the tightness in his throat. The ache in his heart and the spinning of his head whenever he thought of her, which was pretty much all the damn time.

He had to be in love with her, he thought, going dizzy at the idea of it. He probably had been from the moment they'd met. That was why he'd found it so much fun to provoke her. That was why he'd been so determined to make her his. Why he craved her smiles and wanted to make her happy.

Their mother's letters proved that he and his brothers had once upon a time been loved. Very much. He'd mattered and been wanted. And now he realised that he wanted to matter to Alex, as much as she mattered to him.

And all those worries of his? Pathetic. He hadn't changed. He hadn't moulded himself into anyone. He'd made no sacrifices. She'd demanded nothing of him. The compromises he'd made had made him happy too. He had nothing to fear from love or a relationship. It didn't have to be toxic or manipulative.

Who he'd been was of no importance. What was important was the sort of man he wanted to be, and that was a man who deserved her, and if she had expectations of him, well, he wanted to spend the rest of his life attempting to meet them.

This morning Finn had asked him if there was anyone he wanted to invite to their birthday dinner on Saturday. He'd flatly said no, but here, now, he'd changed his mind. He wanted to invite Alex. He wanted a second chance. He could only hope it wasn't too late.

# CHAPTER ELEVEN

WHEN ALEX HAD arrived back on UK soil, she'd hit the ground running. Finn had settled her invoice with much appreciated efficiency and she'd wasted no time in paying off her debts before hiring a recruitment consultant and calling up a commercial estate agency.

In the midst of the flurry of activity she'd paid her family a visit, which had been a tense and unpleasant hour, not least because her elder brother had put in a request for ten grand and then spat at her feet when she'd refused. In that moment, any qualms she might have had about cutting them out of her life for good had evaporated, and once she'd got everything she wanted to say to them off her chest she'd left with no looking back and no regrets. She was wholly on her own now, but she was independent and strong, utterly content with who she was and her place in the world.

True to his word, Finn was already recommending her agency, and Becky, who'd done a great job of holding the fort while she'd been away and whom she was on the point of promoting, was taking more calls than she could handle. The plans for expansion were once again within touching distance and the new kit Alex had ordered was scheduled to arrive imminently. The future looked bright and brilliant and she was marching straight into it.

She didn't have time to think about Max, nor did she care to. She'd been so upset, so angry at the abrupt, careless way he'd dismissed her and, for some unfathomable reason, so damn sad, but by the time she'd landed in London after a lengthy journey that involved a number of changes and a lot of analysis, she'd been totally over it. And him. She couldn't believe that at one point she'd actually been hoping their affair might turn into something more. Anyone who could be that cruel didn't deserve her and wasn't worth her head space, no matter how many times he'd rocked her world.

And that was why, when the invitation to the triplets' black-tie thirty-second birthday celebrations at Rico's house in Venice had dropped into her inbox, Alex had seen no reason not to accept. She hadn't dressed up in months. She'd never been to Venice. She might even make a long weekend of it. Besides, she'd like to see Finn and Rico again and meet Georgie and Carla and it wasn't as if she was going to go all dewy-eyed over Max. That was the very *last* thing that was going to happen. Thank God she hadn't done anything stupid like gone and fallen in love with him. That really would have been recklessly insane.

If she'd made the guest list, she was, no doubt, one of a hundred guests, so she'd probably hardly even see him. And in the unlikely event she did, well, her unflappable facade was in place and these days it was impregnable. There'd be no shock, no thundering rush of lust, just polite professionalism and cool distance.

So what if she'd bought a new dress? She could hardly wear a trouser suit to a black-tie dinner. Her hair was loose tonight but that was because the style suited her outfit, not because Max liked it like that. The fact that she'd brought him a present had nothing to do with wanting to show him they could be given freely, without any strings attached. It was merely polite. She'd brought gifts for Finn and Rico too, although the books she'd selected for them were far less personal than the tiny bag of Bolivian salt she'd had sent over at vast expense for him. And if her heart was pounding so hard she feared it was in danger of escaping her chest…

well, that was entirely down to the exhilaration of the boat ride across the lagoon.

But when Alex's water taxi approached the jetty and she saw Max standing there, tall, solid and so handsome he took her breath away, frowning out across the water as if looking for her, she realised, with a nosedive of her heart, she'd been kidding herself.

Everything she thought she'd successfully buried shot to the surface, all the hurt and misery she'd felt on the plane home, and she knew, with a sinking of her spirits, that she was no more over him than she could fly to the moon.

How on earth had she managed to ignore the X-rated dreams she'd had, which woke her up on a regular basis in a tangle of sheets and a puddle of lust, her heart aching with regret and sorrow?

How many times had she had to stop herself calling him up to tell him how well her business was going and to find out what he was up to?

How much had she wished he'd been there to hold her after she'd cut her family out of her life, which had been hard, even if completely the right thing to do?

Taking a couple of deep shaky breaths, Alex ordered her galloping pulse to slow and pushed the memories and the flush of heat that came with them aside. It was only natural that her subconscious would remember the best sex she'd ever had and miss it. It meant nothing. She could handle it. And how could she have missed *him* when he'd been so horrible? Her plans for the future were of no interest to him and he wouldn't have been there to hold her anyway. That wasn't what their affair had been about and she mustn't forget that.

'Hi,' he said with the ghost of a smile that annoyingly melted her stupid soppy heart.

'You look awful.' His face was gaunt, she noted as she alighted. There were bags under his eyes, his cheekbones were sharp and the black suit he was wearing fitted a little more loosely than she suspected it should or indeed than she'd once imagined.

'You look beautiful.'

Well. She wasn't going to be distracted by that, no matter how much of a flutter it sparked in her stomach. She was still so angry. 'Thank you.'

He thrust his hands in the pockets of his trousers and she refused to notice how lovingly the fine fabric pulled across the powerful muscles of his thighs. Nor would she think about how much she'd missed wrapping her arms around his broad, strong shoulders, or how heavenly he smelled.

'How have you been?'

'Good.' He didn't look it. He looked as if he'd been to hell and back, and yet there was something remarkably calm in his indigo gaze, something sort of settled, which she just couldn't put her finger on. 'You?'

'Very well,' she replied, intent on keeping her tone impersonal. 'Busy.'

'Work going well?'

'Work is going very well, thank you,' she said coolly.

'I'm glad you're here.'

'I can't imagine why.'

'You left without saying goodbye.'

He'd given her no option and what did he care anyway?

'The case was closed, Max. My work was done. Once you'd gone to Salta there was no need for me to stay.'

He tilted his head, his gaze turning quizzical. 'Don't you want to know what happened?'

She did. She badly did. She deliberately hadn't asked Finn. She'd worried she wouldn't be able to stop herself from asking about Max too, which was pathetic when this case had taken up nearly nine months of her life.

'All right, fine,' she said with a casual shrug, as if it were neither here nor there. 'What happened?'

'I met with Valentina,' he said as they started

walking up the jetty to the magnificent villa she could see peeking through the towering cypress trees.

The early autumn sun was low in the sky and the heat of the day still lingered. That was why she was so warm. It had nothing to do with the man walking with her, so close that he was taking up all her air, so close that she'd barely have to move her hand to be able to hold his. She had to focus and stay strong if she stood any chance of getting through this evening which she was beginning to regret with every passing second.

'Did she know anything?'

'Not a lot. She never met our mother, whose name, by the way, was Silvia Solana, contrary to what appears on our original birth certificates.'

'Was?'

'She died in Buenos Aires six years ago. Pancreatic cancer.'

She tried not to care but it was impossible when her chest ached for him. He had to have been *so* disappointed. 'I'm so sorry.'

'It's fine.'

'How can it be?'

'She left us letters.'

'Letters?'

'Twenty-six of them. She wrote to us once a year on our birthday and then one last one a few weeks before she died. In them she explains everything.'

'What happened?'

'She had a one-night stand with a guy she met in a bar when she was sixteen. She didn't know who he was and she never saw him again.'

'What was she doing in a bar at the age of sixteen?'

'Rebelling.'

'Like mother, like son.'

He cast her a quick startled glance and then grinned, and he looked so carefree that she found she could hardly breathe. 'I guess so,' he said. 'Perceptive as always.'

He made it sound as if he knew her, which he didn't or he'd never have treated her so badly, but, before she could tell him that, he continued, 'Her parents were deeply religious and when they discovered she was pregnant they sent her to a convent. We were removed from her by the nuns when we were two months old. She was never told where we were taken or what ultimately happened to us. She escaped the convent, went to Buenos Aires to find work and never spoke to her parents again. When they died, she established contact with her sister, but by then she was ill and didn't have much time left.'

'That's so sad.'

'She never stopped looking for us.'

'She must have loved you all very much.'

'She did.'

Alex cleared her throat to dislodge the knot that had formed there against her will. 'Do you have other relatives?'

'We have aunts and uncles and cousins galore. Some in Salta, some in Buenos Aires. One cousin lives in New York, oddly enough.'

'Will you visit them?'

'Some time.'

'That would be good.'

'Would you like to read the letters?'

God, yes. But the case was closed. They were done. 'I've moved on to other things.'

'Have you?'

'Very much so.'

'I'm sorry I didn't take you to Salta with me, Alex. I needed you there.'

She steeled her heart not to melt. His apology came far too late. 'Don't worry about it,' she said with an airiness that she didn't feel at all. 'It's all water under the bridge. No hard feelings. We agreed to a short-term thing that was going to last just as long as the investigation and it ended. It's completely fine.'

'Is it?'

Something in his voice made her meet his

gaze and her pulse skipped a beat at the dark intensity that shimmered within. It wasn't fine, she thought with a sudden surge of alarm. It wasn't fine at all. 'Absolutely.'

'What if I told you I loved you?'

The world stopped for a second and then began to spin, but she couldn't let herself go there. She was in such a good place at the moment and she'd worked hard for it. The risk of upending everything for a man who played fast and loose with her emotions was too great. 'I'd say we've known each other for less than two weeks and ask what you were on.'

'I know it's been quick but I *am* in love with you, Alex. I think I have been since the moment we met.'

'You could have fooled me.'

'The only person I've been fooling is myself.'

She badly needed a drink and to mingle, to be able to remove herself from his presence in order to be able to think straight, and they'd reached the pretty terrace now, which overlooked the lagoon and was decorated with strings of light. But where was the party? Why was the table set for six?

'Where's everyone else?' she asked, confused and alarmed by the absence of other people.

'Finn and Georgie are putting their son to

bed. Rico and Carla are in the kitchen doing something clever with pasta.'

And that was it? This wasn't a party. This was an intimate dinner. A family dinner. What did that mean? She couldn't work it out. All she knew was that Max had whipped the rug from under her feet yet again and coming here had been a mistake.

'I'm sorry,' she said as panic swept through her like the wildest of fires. 'I can't do this. I should go.'

Of all the responses Max had expected to his apologies and his declaration of love, Alex spinning on her very sexy heel was not one of them. Yet she was charging back down the steps towards the jetty and he was so stunned it was a full ten seconds before he sprang into action.

'Stop,' he said, even though, this being an island and her water taxi having left some time ago, she couldn't actually go anywhere.

'No.'

He caught up with her and put a hand on her arm which she threw off, but at least she stopped and turned to face him, even if the torment on her face sliced straight through his heart. 'What's wrong?'

'This is.'

'In what way?'

'We had an agreement,' she said wretchedly.

'I know.'

'You don't do love.'

'It turns out I do, with you.'

'Then how could you have pushed me away like that?' Her eyes filled with sadness and he felt physically sick at the knowledge that he'd put it there.

'I'm so sorry I did that,' he said, his chest aching with regret. 'You'll never know how sorry. I guess I was trying to protect myself. I learned early on in life to suppress my emotions. The only way to survive was not to care and so I didn't. I grew up believing I was worthless and unwanted, which was compounded by the discovery that I was adopted, and that's a hard habit to break.'

'You hurt me badly.'

The ache turned into pain of the sort he'd never felt before. 'I know and that guts me. Not that it's any excuse, but I was struggling to work out who I am.'

'You should have just asked. I know who you are.'

'You're the only person in the world who does,' he said, not taking his eyes off her for even a second, willing her to believe him because his entire future depended on it. 'You came along and crashed through my defences, Alex, and it was terrifying at first and now it isn't at all. You knowing me and me knowing you makes me incredibly happy. I love you and I'd like to spend the rest of my life proving it to you.' He took a deep breath, his entire world now reduced to this woman and what she said next. 'The only question I have is, how do you feel about me?'

Alex didn't know. Max had stirred up so many emotions inside her and she couldn't unravel any of them. But he was waiting for an answer and, with the way his gaze bored into hers, it mattered. A lot.

'Volatile,' she said, wishing she was better at explaining it.

He jerked back as if she'd struck him and she wanted to hug the shock out of him, but if she did that she might not be able to stop and they'd have resolved nothing. 'Volatile?'

'Like I'm on the top of the world one minute and at the bottom of a pit the next. It's not the way I want to be. It's not the life I want to live. I need stability and security. I always have.'

'I'll give it to you.'

No doubt he thought he could, but it was impossible. That wasn't who he was. 'How?' she said desperately, all pretence of control gone.

'You are chaos and unpredictability. You don't want to change who you are any more than I want to change who I am, and that's fine because I wouldn't want you to.'

'It's far too late for that,' he said, his gaze on hers steady and sure. 'I already have changed and I'm OK with it. I'm done with the chaos. I figure it's a choice and I choose, well, not that. I choose you. I've always feared the idea of being responsible for someone else's feelings. But I want to be responsible for yours. Trust me with them, Alex. Take a risk with me. You won't regret it.'

Wouldn't she? How could he be so sure? How could anyone? He was so calm, while she was the one who felt wild and out of control, and yet the longer she stared into his eyes, the more she could feel the wildness ease. It was as if they'd swapped roles, as if she'd rubbed off on him and he'd rubbed off on her.

Could she do it? That was the thought ricocheting around her head, making her breath catch and her heart race. Could she take the risk? Did she even want to?

Yes, yes and, God, yes.

Because she was in love with him too, she realised as the walls she'd built around her heart on the plane home crumbled to dust. Madly and irreversibly. She'd been so miserable these past couple of days, so sad. Just being here with him, colours were brighter, sounds were sharper. When he pushed her buttons she loved it. She never felt more alive than when he was challenging and provoking her. He was the polar opposite of everything she'd ever thought she wanted but she'd been wrong. They were like two sides of the same coin.

'I've missed you,' she said, her voice shaking from the force of the emotions rushing through her.

'I've missed you too.'

'I cut all ties with my family.'

'That was brave.'

'It had to be done, even if I am now all alone. I could give you tips, if you want.'

'You aren't alone, Alex. You have me. If you want me. You need never be alone again.'

She did want him, desperately, but... 'What if it all goes wrong?'

'It won't.'

'You don't know that. It did for me before.'

'I do know that,' he said with quiet certainty that filled her with confidence and brushed away the doubts. 'I won't allow it. I don't want you to be anyone other than who you are, Alex. Why would I when you are absolutely brilliant?'

'You are *not* worthless,' she said, her throat thick.

'I know. Silvia's letters prove it. I love you and I will always be there for you, the way you've been there for me.'

She had to trust him. She wanted to trust him. All she had to do was take a risk, and it wasn't even that much of a risk. This might have been quick, but she'd never been surer of anything in her life, and they could work out the logistics later.

Her heart was pounding and her eyes were swimming as she took a step forwards, but nothing was going to stop her telling him how she felt now.

'I love you too,' she said, winding her arms around his neck, her heart so filled with happiness it felt too big for her chest.

He pulled her close and she lifted her head as he lowered his, and their mouths met in a kiss that was hot and tender and went on and on until the sun dipped beneath the horizon.

'Happy birthday,' she murmured raggedly when he finally lifted his mouth from hers.

The smile he gave her was blinding. 'It's a *very* happy birthday.'

# EPILOGUE

*Christmas Day, three months later*

THE NORDIC FIR standing in Finn and Georgie's drawing room in their sprawling mansion situated in the Oxfordshire countryside was so tall it nearly touched the ceiling. Strings of fairy lights were draped over thick wide-spreading branches from which gold and silver baubles hung, and tinsel sparkled in the bright winter sunlight.

Outside in the snow, under a cloudless blue sky, two-and-a-half-year-old Josh was building a snowman with his mother, Georgie, and his aunt, Carla. Alex was searching for sticks, presumably to be turned into its arms. Inside, the rich aroma of roasting turkey and stuffing filled the house and carols rang out from speakers hidden in the ceiling.

This year the dining room table was set for seven. Next year, wherever they chose to spend it—London or Oxfordshire, Venice or the Caribbean—there'd be more. Georgie and Finn were expecting a daughter via surrogate in May. Carla was due in August, and only this morning Alex had told Max that come September they too would be welcoming the patter of tiny feet.

Before the roaring fire, the brothers stood side by side, each nursing a glass of Scotch as they gazed out of the window at the activity outside.

'I'd like to make a toast,' said Max, raising his glass and thinking how unbelievably lucky he was, how unbelievably lucky all three of them were, to have found each other and have the love of incredible women.

'To the best Christmas in thirty-two years?' said Rico.

'To many more in the future?' said Finn.

'To family.'

\* \* \* \* \*

*Swept away by* The Billionaire without Rules?
*Don't forget to check out the previous
instalments in the
Lost Sons of Argentina trilogy*

**The Secrets She Must Tell**
**Invitation from the Venetian Billionaire**
*And don't miss these other Lucy King stories!*

**The Reunion Lie**
**One Night with Her Ex**
**A Scandal Made in London**

*Available now!*

*Summer's End,*
*Love's Beginning*

# *Summer's End, Love's Beginning*

**Veronica Denham**

*Rhapsody Prelude Romances*

First published 1989
© Veronica Denham 1989
First published in this edition 1990
Published by Geddes & Grosset Ltd
New Lanark
Scotland

ISBN 1 85534 102 6

Printed and bound in the United States of America

# 1

*"Opatija*

*Dearest Raddy,*

*As you may see from the card I enclose, I am now almost at the end of my long trek around the Istrian peninsula. Another few days and the job will be done and I shall be flying home. Expect me sometime next Sunday afternoon with my photos and postcards for a cup of tea – unless I get sent to Dubrovnik, or one of the excursion boats sinks.*

*"I can't tell you how much I have enjoyed myself, though I have told you before how I find your country utterly beautiful and enthralling . . ."*

. . . Interrupted by one of the reception clerks, the tall, well-proportioned brunette in her early twenties cast her glowing face toward him, causing his middle-aged heart to do a sudden flip and his eyes to become wistful as he guided her toward the private telephone in the manager's office.

"Christine . . ." the imperious voice of her boss in London crackled over the line. ". . . We're in a mess. Personnel has gone crazy and ordered the Kranjska Gora representative to go to Bohinj for the rest of the summer. Forthwith. At this stage in the season. Just when we'd got the concession in the big hotel there working smoothly. And now Mitja Minic has turned up breathing hell fire. Threatened to kick us out. You know the scene. Forthwith. You'll have to sort it out . . ."

"Don't tell me," Christine interrupted resignedly, for she had not the remotest idea either who Mitja Minic was or what exactly to sort out. "Forthwith?" she added teasingly.

"You've got it, but it's no joking matter," he replied darkly.

"Who, exactly, is Mitja Minic?" she asked.

"He's the owner of the Hotel Vitranc. I gather he comes and goes a bit. Unfortunately he's arrived at the worst possible moment."

"Personnel might have sent a replacement immediately," Christine agreed ruefully, knowing Mr Barker's opinion of that department. "I suppose there is going to be one, eventually?"

"Naturally, but not for some days."

"Do you know anything else about Mr Minic?"

"Only that he's a bachelor and something of a sportsman, with business interests."

Christine envisaged a short, stocky Yugoslav, typical of so many she'd met, unflappable, well-organized, easy to cajole into good humor. "I guess I'll be able to soothe his ruffled feelings," she said.

"That's precisely why I'm sending you." Mr Barker had placed the greatest confidence in his young assistant from the moment she had walked into his office some nine months previously. "And while you're about it, you might as well finish the local excursion report which was never completed last year."

"It'll be a bit difficult, under the circumstances, surely?" she objected.

"Why? One mountain's very much like another, don't you think? So you'll do it?"

Christine hesitated, surprisingly for her. Then she sighed audibly and replied, "I'll get up there as soon as I can and assess the situation," procrastinating. "At least I should be able to hold the fort for a few days. Report back when the new rep is installed."

". . . *The unexpected did happen after all, Raddy.*" Christine concluded the letter. "*I'm sure you'll forgive me for not tearing this up and starting again. So, I'm off to the mountains, which is a heavenly prospect in this heat. And I promise to come and see you as soon as I return.*'

She smiled tenderly as she addressed the envelope. She had always been grateful to Raddy for his kindness to her as a child. She had always wanted to be more than just a typist. Those evenings when Raddy had persuaded her gently to her books had given her a good start in life. Usually she throve on a challenge . . . then, throwing off her inexplicable misgivings, she fetched her files and began to consult transfer times to the mountains.

The journey between Opatija and the mountains was made by coach, and it was incredibly tedious. Not even some spectacular scenery as the coach swung up and out of a cold, mist-draped valley into the early morning sunshine of a range of high hills compensated for the sticky and exhausted state the travelers were in as they tumbled into their mountain hotel some ten hours later. Christine was traveling light, so she stood back to allow the heap of baggage and its owners to be dispersed around the hotel, large, modern, spacious and comfortable at first sight.

She was expected: it seemed politic not to impose on the management too soon. She wondered how they coped without a rep and if Mr Minic was around to view the chaos disparagingly. Except that there was no real chaos; everything appeared ordered, organized. Then a disembodied voice announced in excellent English, "Welcome to the mountains, ladies and gentlemen, I will meet all of you tomorrow after breakfast to discuss all that there is to do in the mountains. Until then, supper awaits you, and good night."

It couldn't be! Christine became aware that Mitja Minic's eyes had swept over her and rejected her as the one he was seeking at the instant she matched the voice with the man in the dim foyer lights. But this was no middle-aged sporting bachelor with business interests who happened also to own the Hotel Vitranc. This was not what she had expected, this tall young man exuding energy and vitality, with eyes that smoldered even at a distance of thirty feet.

She continued to register shock while he approached individually a couple of middle-aged women, obviously seeking exactly the female counterpart of what she had expected to find. Eventually his glance returned to her – there was no one else left – and with a slight frown between those dark eyes that, yes, she had been right, she thought idiotically, *did* smolder, he strode up to her.

"Don't tell me you're Miss Howard!" he declared witheringly.

Christine was above average height, her large-boned frame generously covered. Even so, Mitja Minic towered over her by a head and well-set shoulders. She had not sought a welcome. She had not anticipated blatant antagonism. She nodded briefly, unsure how to phrase a reply that would not exacerbate a situation that was difficult enough already.

"Oh God," he said wearily, and in his own language. "They might at least have spared me a schoolgirl."

That did it. "I have had a long day, *Gospodine* Minic," Christine replied icily. "Perhaps we could save the recriminations until tomorrow?"

He was thrown momentarily by her fluent Serbo-Croat (a legacy from Raddy), then he grinned, picked up her bag as if it weighed no more than the proverbial feather, and announced over his shoulder, "I'll even act the porter and show you to your room as the boys are still busy. It's a small single in the staff corridor. I'm at the end of it. but I'd prefer to get the – recriminations – over with. We'll meet in the coffee bar when you've eaten. Perhaps then," grimly, "you'll be good enough to explain precisely what this charade is all about."

She followed him meekly and in silence – there was not a lot else she could do – and managed a thank you in the same icily polite tone, but as the door closed firmly behind Mitja Minic she sat down abruptly on the bed. This was far worse than anything she had imagined! Her knees were decidedly wobbly and her pulse accelerated. Sheer panic. Absurd to panic. She was only doing her job, soothing the ruffled feathers of a disgruntled hotel owner. But what a man! And she had to acknowledge he was justifiably disgruntled. Mr Barker would have known how to set about soothing him, she thought wistfully. So how was she going to cope? No use, plainly, appealing to his better nature, or prevaricating . . .

"I regret very much the necessity which brings me here," she ended candidly, over coffee in the bar, later. "I can only repeat that it seemed imperative to Head Office to move Igor as they did. I do assure you that the man replacing him will be very efficient," and under cover of the marble-topped table she crossed her fingers and prayed she was not deceiving him.

"He'd better be," came the forthright answer. "If this is the way the firm deals with its new clients, heaven help the established ones," he declared harshly. "I tell you plainly, I'll not stand for it, and I've already written to London to declare the contract broken, as from yesterday. If your firm wishes to renew it for next season it has to show a sight more good faith than it has done up to now."

Christine swallowed, "I . . . *Gospodine* Minic, that is why I'm here, in part," she temporized, recalling her other brief from Mr Barker. "I intend to do all I can to help until Dragomir Caric arrives after the weekend."

"You can bet you will," he answered gratingly, his eyes flashing with a hard light, "beginning tomorrow, with an hour morning and evening sorting out excursion tickets for one thing."

She knew nothing about the local arrangements, but, "Of course, *Gospodine*."

Suddenly his fury abated, as if at last he accepted that the cause of it was not the girl in front of him. "I believe we could both use a *veniak*," he stated.

It appeared instantly, as if the bartender had been awaiting a sign, before Christine could explain she disliked firewater of any description. Then it seemed churlish to decline, besides which, false courage though it might induce, she needed something to get her through this interview. "Thank you, *Gospodine*," she said.

"Mitja."

She looked a question.

"Mitja," he repeated. "You do, after all, represent Head Office," he pointed out impatiently.

She recovered. "Of course, Mitja. My name is Christine."

"I know." She gulped the *veniak*. It was a mistake and she choked as the fiery local brandy hit the back of her throat, and she coughed to conceal it. Mitja noticed that, too, and smiled sardonically. "You don't have to drink it," he pointed out.

"Maybe I need it, as you said," and she smiled disarmingly. "My job is not always of the easiest."

It was not really meant as an appeal. She was not sure how he took the remark but for a while he regarded her searchingly and when she returned his gaze unflinchingly (that was probably the brandy), he shrugged once more and answered, "Very well. Now tell me the other reason why you are here."

She did, concentrating on the report which had to be completed. "I know nothing about mountains, or excursions into them," she confessed, "but it'll be such a relief to report on something other than boat trips. I want to try everything."

"You want to climb a mountain?" There was the sound of such eagerness in his voice that Christine remembered this was a sportsman – how could she have forgotten? "Not exactly climb," she told him cautiously. "What does your hotel recommend to inexperienced tourists, Mitja?"

Boyishly enthusiastic now, he opened the briefcase which lay on the chair beside him and took out various papers. "It is all here, in detail. All the coach trips. As for the walking, there is anything from flat walking along the valley floor to paths at two thousand, five hundred metres. Easy routes for strollers to . . ."

"I think I'd better stick to the easy routes," she declared emphatically. Anything more and he would see through her in minutes.

"As you wish. In that case, there is a walk I intended doing tomorrow from the Italian border. We suggest the bus, for the unadventurous, but there is a well-defined route marked on the map through a couple of villages. We will do it together, and the day after you can do the trip to Bohinj and Bled. Bohinj is where I own a sports center. Where I should be now," he said darkly.

"Ah. Th-thank you."

"Perhaps not your fault. So. After we have met the new people we shall take the bus to the border tomorrow morning and walk from there." He got up. "If you will excuse me. Good night, Christine."

Christine gathered together her scattered wits and had just enough presence of mind to thank him for her coffee before he had gone. He was formidable! Quite the most formidable assignment she had been given. She didn't think she had ever met a man quite like him before; a man whose natural authority expected, and obviously got, the best from those who worked for him. No wonder he had been so furious about the breakdown in communications with Head Office. She would hate to be on the receiving end of his temper directed deliberately at herself. And yet, his smile when he used it (she had seen it in action at the reception desk) was singularly sweet, his lips were sensitive and sensual at the same time. She wondered . . . no she didn't! Christine went cold all over as she realized just where her errant imagination was leading her and clamped down on it, hard. This was a job, not an outing.

Clad in tan corduroy breeches, green socks and walking-boots, Mitja, when they met in the foyer after the meeting, looked even more intimidating than in the guise of the casually dressed hotel owner whose aim in life was the well-being of his guests. Christine was aware immediately of the inadequacy of her own apparel, cotton trousers, a T-shirt and trainers. So was he.

"Oh lord," he sighed. "Haven't you brought anything suitable for walking in the mountains?"

"No," she shook her head.

"Not even a sweater and an anorak?"

"Of course I have those," and she indicated the bag slung over her shoulder, "but I left London prepared only for the coast."

"Those trousers aren't substantial enough."

She had known that, but her present unease stemmed from the way his dark eyes were sweeping over her long shapely legs, and despite her resolution of the previous evening, for a crazy moment she could not help wondering if her sinews would have melted totally had she been wearing one of her skimpy swimsuits instead of modest cotton that was baggy and revealed little of her shape beneath. "Never mind," he continued without a pause so that she thought he had probably not guessed where her stupid senses were leading her. "We're not going high. We'll just see if we can hire you a pair of boots, shall we?"

His smile was disarming. Christine thought he concealed his irritation admirably, and she was humbly thankful that he could not see into her mind for she did not think she could bear his contempt at what he would read there, and she sat and fought with herself silently as he chose and fitted her carefully into two pairs of thick socks and shabby but comfortable walking-boots. She succeeded. Coolly confident, once they were actually walking, that her aberrant senses were once more perfectly under control, Christine commented on the beautiful day, not too hot and with the faintest of breezes, the blue sky showing only traces of cloud. "It'll rain mid-afternoon," Mitja predicted. "Mountains can be very treacherous."

"I don't mind," she answered happily, and she looked so alive, seemed to fit so well into his lovely scenery, despite the cotton trousers, that the last of his misgivings about her fled and his answering grin was warm with approval. As always, the very nearness of his mountains had acted as a salve.

The bus had taken them to the last village in Yugoslavia. It was a pretty place with flower-filled balconies dripping with carnations, and tubs around the front doors brimming over with geraniums. They made an early stop, at a rest house where they ordered coffee and chocolate cake. "Packed lunches may be adequate for most people," Mitja declared, a large piece of cake on his fork, "I need more calories," and this time Christine dared to chuckle out loud. "It is lucky that everywhere in the Julian Alps there are rest huts like this," he replied composedly.

The constraint Christine could not help but feel in his compelling presence disappeared along with the chocolate cake, and they began talking as if they had known each other for years. Christine, having been brought up in the company of boys of different ages and varying dispositions, was not naturally shy, but she had been intimidated by Mitja. Now all that worried her was his sheer athleticism.

He sensed that too, for he asked, pausing in his stride after one steep stretch, "Not going too fast for you, am I?"

"Uh . . . not really," she smiled back, pink-cheeked, but not completely breathless.

"Just the guinea pig I wanted in other words."

"Thank you!"

"I expect a lot of my walkers have sedentary occupations, like yours. Tell me about it."

She told him about her job and he told her about his mountains, how their mood could change with frightening rapidity; how he loved them in all their moods and, all the time, he matched his pace to her slower one, shortening the stride of his long legs so that she should feel no discomfort.

Once he asked her if her parents minded that she was away from them for so long. "I live on my own," she replied, without rancor. "My parents died when I was thirteen." It was not quite the time for confidences – to explain how her parents had run a Children's Home and how, afterwards, Josip and Isobel Radivojevic who had helped them, had taken over both the job and herself. Josip, Raddy, was Yugoslav-born, Isobel a Cockney, and it had seemed the most natural thing in the world, after the initial shock, to transfer her affections to them.

They picnicked in a sunlit meadow and it was quiet and peaceful and companionable. "Just as I've always imagined the mountains," Christine sighed rapturously. "Do you spend much of your time walking, Mitja, or do your business interests take you to the cities?"

"My business interests, as you call them," he told her, "are entirely to do with sport. I have a sports center in Bohinj – skiing in the winter, walking and climbing in the summer. The Vitranc is a new venture for me." Rather to his surprise Mitja found himself telling her how the Vitranc had belonged to his English mother who had been caught in Yugoslavia by World War II and had married and remained there until her death the previous year. "I was never very interested in the hotel trade," he confessed. "In her latter years she had a manager, a splendid man whom we trusted implicitly, but once she had gone he decided the time had come for him to retire. That is why I have had to take over. I opted for the concession with your company because it seemed the sensible thing to do . . . and now you can see why I am so furious at the complete mess that has resulted . . ." He stopped. "That was unfair of me. I never intended to let business intrude on our outing. Sorry," and he touched her hand casually in apology.

Christine caught her breath suddenly, her eyes locked inexplicably with his as though held there by the magnetism of his gaze. Then she turned away and stretched out on the soft grass feeling as if she had run a hundred yards. He—it—this situation was the most extraordinary thing she had come across, she thought in confusion once more. Why, when always before she had been totally invulnerable? She closed her eyes, for self-protection, hoping he would think it was against the glare. "Tell me about your mother," she asked him.

"She fell in love with a Yugoslav – my father – married him and stayed on here after he died. The Vitranc was her development of a small, family-run affair. I'll bore you with the story the next time you come to visit. You must come back to Kranjska Gora," he said lightly, after a pause. It emerged mechanically, spoken as he had said it so often before to tourists who might, or might not, return. Then, as his gaze took in the girl as she lay supine in the sun beside him, her eyes closed and a smile on her soft lips, as he focused on her clearly, an expression . . . almost of surprise came into his eyes and he seemed to be seeing her for the very first time. Without thinking, he leant over her, touching his lips to hers in a gentle kiss.

It was the very last thing Christine expected, the pressure of Mitja's lips on hers. Her eyelids opened abruptly, a glimmer of righteous indignation flashing from the brown velvet depths they had concealed. Almost at once she recalled how she had felt earlier under his scrutiny, and the indignation turned to apprehension, but he was already sitting back on his heels grinning, yet with so rueful an expression on his face that she had to smile. She had not really meant it as an open invitation – or had she? She would not have been a woman if she had been anything but disappointed if Mitja had not immediately kissed her again.

This time the kiss was different. The touch of his lips was neither tentative nor apologetic. His mouth moved over hers with an expertise of long practise that threatened another bout of indignation. Only for a second; it became too enjoyable for indignation all too quickly, and as it teetered on the brink of becoming far too enjoyable for safety, Mitja raised his head, his mouth releasing hers with a deliberate slowness that said, without words, that he would have liked to continue, but thought maybe the time was not right.

Christine's eyes met his with equal, and unwavering, honesty. She had never been kissed like that before, and knew that it showed. The experience had been shattering, the kiss had begun to stir her in a way that was dangerously unfamiliar, the kiss or the man – or both – sending a shiver down her spine, setting her nerve endings tingling and making her want to arch her body to meet his in a way that could only be described as deliciously wanton. Again, with an effort, Christine turned away, a blush rising because he could read that, knew he had overwhelmed her . . . had known that from the first. The blush brought back reason. Reason stilled her reeling senses that clamored for her to sway back into his arms, forcing her instead to listen to the coldly rational voice of her mind that could still say Mitja and she were like ships that passed in the night, and she was not the sort of girl who indulged in passionate, brief encounters.

He thought he could read her still. His hand, used to acquiescence, went out to caress her cheek, lift her chin unresistingly so that he could claim her lips once more, but suddenly she jerked away. "Please don't!" she cried, her eyes enormous, mutinous.

"Why not?" he asked indulgently. "You're not going to tell me you didn't enjoy that?"

Christine did not even think of prevaricating. "Of course not," she admitted. "I think I could get to enjoy that sort of kissing a lot too much," and as his hand returned to her hot face she went on urgently, "but I'm here to do a job . . . p-please, Mitja!"

He moved away. "And I'm part of that job?" He seemed amused rather than angered by her rejection. "And you are a nice girl, Miss Christine Howard. No wonder you were sent to soothe my ruffled feelings. I hope you'll come again," and he found himself holding his breath for her answer, not quite sure how, exactly, he had meant that suggestion, how much he meant it now.

"Oh, I shall," she replied fervently, and gave herself a mental shake afterward, for though she might well come back to this man's country because of her work, there was little likelihood of her ever coming back to him, but Mitja felt almost light-headed with relief, as if a huge obstacle in his path had been surmounted.

He concealed it, though, grunting by way of a response, and turned away from her, busying himself with his rucksack. Satisfied with it, or his self-control, he got to his feet. "Come on," he smiled, "it's time to go."

# 2

The easy companionship of the remainder of that walk lasted as they recrossed the valley floor and climbed into the foothills toward the Austrian border, and while they drank beer in the square back in Kranjska Gora, listening to a band of youthful musicians in local costume as they played Strauss. Then suddenly Mitja announced, "Your coach leaves tomorrow morning promptly at eight-thirty. Now I have to go and work," and with a curiously formal bow, he was gone.

So should she, Christine thought, embarrassed because she should have remembered there were excursion tickets to sell. Yet later, as she tidied away the paraphernalia of business, her parting with Mitja gave her a pang. It could have been nothing she said, or omitted to do . . . surely, that sent him away so abruptly? She had felt tired, but elated, after the walk. Now she was bone-achingly weary, and vaguely miserable. She pulled herself together, chided herself for behaving like a teenager in the throes of her first infatuation, and thought determinedly only of piping hot bathwater and dinner to come.

The next day the lake at Bled was entrancing, the waterfall at Bohinj worth the 564 steps (just) and the cable car trip suitably thrilling. Mitja had been proved right about value for money.

Mitja, to her delight, was waiting outside the

Vitranc when the coach drew up, and as Christine stepped off it her smile mirrored his own of eager welcome – only his welcome was not for her. She realized all at once that the pretty girl in jeans in front of her had definitely not been on the coach all day. Now, with a cry of delight, the girl dropped her bag and ran into Mitja's arms. There was a brief hug and without casting a backward glance at the more than interested spectators the two, their arms still around each other, strolled in the direction of the staff wing.

How could she have been so stupid as to have thought him unattached, Christine castigated herself. Bachelor he might be, here was a very obvious tie. No wonder Mitja had been so furious about having to come to the rescue of the hotel in Kranjska Gora with that waiting for him in Bohinj!

For the second time in twenty-four hours, Christine set aside all her illusions and as she prepared for her stint in the foyer she allowed her mind to dwell only on the pleasure of a hot bath, clean clothes and dinner to come.

It was getting late. No one had seen any sign of Mitja since he had walked away from the coach several hours previously. Christine drummed her fingers impatiently on the marble top of her coffee table in the bar. No one had seen anything of the girl he had greeted so rapturously, either. In the ordinary way of things she would not have thought twice about this, but Mitja had promised to arrange her next day's outing and she had no idea whether to prepare for a shopping expedition, a trip into the mountains by coach or another walk. It was too bad of him.

She bore the inaction while she drank her third cup of coffee then, with a very determined air, she approached the desk. "I wish to see *Gospodine* Minic," she said stiffly.

"I do not think he is available tonight," came the answer, "but if it is important I will call his room." Christine nodded, stifling a pang of conscience. Her ears caught the sound of Mitja's voice, crisp and clear, as the receptionist held the receiver tucked clumsily into her neck.

". . . And I am not in the least interested in any confounded guest's problems, requests or demands until seven-thirty tomorrow morning. Have I made myself clear!"

She did not wait to hear the apologetic, red-faced translation, "*Gospodine* Minic says he's so sorry but . . ." Wasn't he interested? Well, she would just have to change his mind for him!

Mitja's door was flung open at her second sharp knock. "I thought I left a message that I did not wish to be disturbed tonight," he declared angrily. "Must I . . . oh, it's you. What do you want?"

"I'm not a confounded guest," she retorted, equally angrily, "nor am I one of your employees! You told me you'd see me this evening."

"So you did hear that, did you?" He laughed. "All right. I had forgotten. So you'd better come in, Miss Christine Howard," and he held the door wide open for her.

As she had expected, this was a family suite containing a small living-room, a shower room, one large bedroom and a tiny single. The door to the double room was open showing the beds made up with clean, fluffy white duvets. Propped against the pillows of one of them was a girl. The girl. Suddenly Christine's righteous anger evaporated, leaving her cold and empty.

"Hallo," the girl said. Her dark hair was caught up on the top of her head. "Come and join us," she said, and patted the bed beside her. The movement dislodged her curls and a long lock slipped on to her shoulder. She put up a slim hand to catch the errant clip which had restrained her hair and the huge, pale blue terry toweling robe she was wearing fell open to reveal a long length of bare, brown thigh as the sleeve slid back to the top of her bare, brown shoulder.

She might as well be wearing . . . she *was* wearing nothing underneath. Christine caught her breath. "Oh," she said, "I didn't . . . I mean . . . Oh!" In her consternation she flushed, and scarlet and agitated she turned and fled from the room as if the hounds of hell were pursuing her.

Safe in her own room, the door locked, and under her own, cozy duvet, Christine's agitation gradually subsided to be replaced by intense embarrassment. It had been entirely her own fault, a tactless *bêtise*. It should have been plain that an attractive man like Mitja must have hordes of young women chasing after him. Why should she be so surprised at being faced with an example, a gorgeous example, so soon? Except that he might have warned her; he might have kept her in the corridor, could have remembered he had promised to see her that evening. He need not have thrown open his door and invited her in. And what had she meant by her "Come and join us"? Come and join us, indeed! What did they take her for! Chagrined and furious, Christine tossed and turned for half the night.

She breakfasted at 7 a.m., still embarrassed by the prospect of encountering Mitja. She had decided in the night that she would brazen her way on to the High Peaks tour and stay out of his way for the whole day. By the evening it was to be hoped her equilibrium would be restored.

Mitja forestalled her by coming into the dining-room while she was still eating. Christine had assumed he would be breakfasting with his mistress, but a prickling of her senses announced his presence seconds before her eyes swiveled involuntarily to the doorway. Hastily she lowered her gaze, praying he had not seen her. Too late. Without hurrying, Mitja collected his food from the buffet and strode deliberately over to her table where a nervous young waiter set a place for him clumsily.

"Your mind has an unpleasant turn to it," Mitja said conversationally, seating himself beside her and depositing two eggs, several slices of sausage and three bread rolls on to the table then ordering his coffee with a reassuring smile at the boy who departed with a relieved grin.

"Because I realized too late why I should not have disturbed you last night? . . . For which I apologize, of course, if belatedly," she returned, more composedly than she had dared hope. "Are you really going to eat all that?" she asked aghast.

"Yes. Because you should not have come to any such conclusion," he replied, opening a roll and buttering it lavishly.

"Oh, come on!" Christine exclaimed. "I'm not

a child. I apologize for disturbing you, again . . . both of you."

"You were shocked rigid. I have never seen a more prudish display in my life."

"My morals have nothing whatsoever to do with you," she declared hotly.

"Nor mine with you." They glared at each other fiercely for a full minute while Christine bit back the retort she had almost uttered, that it didn't matter to her in the least where he spent his nights, or whom he took to his bed.

Mitja's eyes gleamed with unholy joy as if he were waiting for her to make a remark of appalling taste and knew exactly how to counter it. When she did not he laughed shortly. "Alex said you wouldn't sleep. You've bags under your eyes."

"So have you," she hissed nastily, but her gaze dropped under his cold stare. To her horror tears prickled behind her eyelids, tears of hurt which she was too overwrought to analyze, childish tears which stung her into self-mastery.

Mitja shrugged indifferently. "Alex wanted me to come after you last night," he told her.

"Whatever for!" Christine cried.

"I said you deserved to stew in your own juice until this evening. We compromised."

"I don't understand."

"Of course you don't. Alex is my sister. You now have exactly three minutes to catch the coach," he said, with evil satisfaction at having routed her. "It won't wait, you know."

She fled.

The High Peaks trip was all that Mitja had promised, glorious views of ridge after ridge,

peak after peak, light and shadow never the same
for more than a moment as the clouds scudded
past. The tree-covered lower slopes, dark and
mysterious, the distant valleys brought her comforted spirit back to mundane, human matters.
After the morning's encounter, Mitja and she
were quits. All that was left was to apologize to
Alex.

Alex was waiting for her, sitting on the wall
outside the hotel. "Come and have an aperitif
with me," she invited, "there's a band playing in
the square this evening."

"I saw it just now. Alex, I'm sorry . . ."

"It was all my brother's fault. He should have
explained when I arrived. I'd no idea you were
on that coach."

They strolled off toward the square, both liking
what they saw in the other. "So you see, I
decided I might as well come and join Mitja here
instead of staying on my own in Bohinj," Alex
concluded her tale as they sat in a bar in the
square in the last of the evening sun.

Mitja and Alex had lived alone together since
their mother died. Alex was now nineteen to
Mitja's thirty-one and it was clear she regarded
him as a father figure. She kept house for him,
she said, evasive as to any other activities. It
was getting chilly. "Christine, we're eating in the
small restaurant tonight. Will you join us?" as
they rose to go.

"Thank you very much . . . only . . . Mitja and
I didn't exactly part friends this morning," she
confessed.

"Don't you worry about my brother," Alex
answered promptly. "It was Mitja's suggestion."

An olive branch: Christine glowed, dispro-
portionately happy that he must have forgiven
her. It was quiet in the foyer and few people to
see, so the thought came, and persisted, that
she might be falling a little in love with Mitja. It
wouldn't last, of course. As soon as she was
home again and she was no longer disturbed by
his compelling personality her mind would
return to its customary unemotional state. Just as
well Dragomir was arriving tomorrow. Soon she
could leave. A corner of her mouth lifted ruefully.
Perhaps it would have been safer had Alex been
mistress rather than sister!

They all spent a very pleasant evening together,
and during it they decided how Christine should
spend her Saturday in the furtherance of her
report – taking the chair lift up the mountain for
the panoramic view at the top. "I'll come with
you," Mitja suggested casually. "The walk will
only take us forty minutes or so each way."

"Don't you believe it," said Alex feelingly,
though she was looking slightly startled by his
offer and she glanced with speculation toward
Christine.

Mitja intercepted the look. "Come on, you two,
didn't someone say something about bowling?"
and swept them into the basement for a game.

Apart from a family group, the bowling alley
was free. The three of them played for some time,
with increasing hilarity, Mitja and Alex bickering
amicably as to which of them was the more pro-
ficient cheat. Christine, unused to such a degree
of sibling rivalry, began to feel quite dazed. Sud-

denly Mitja announced, "I declare Christine the winner."

"Well, of all the . . . why!" demanded his sister.

"You know," he answered. Then, "Doesn't the winner always buy the coffee?"

Christine laughed. "Coffee it is, then."

"Not for me, thanks," Alex said. "I think I'm going to have to go to bed."

Christine glanced at her inquiringly. Under the tan, Alex did seem a little pale. She turned toward Mitja who shook his head imperceptibly.

After they had said good night to Alex, Christine, with shy insistence, added a *veniak* to her coffee forfeit and the two of them sat companionably in a corner of the bar. "Just sufficiently out of the way to avoid all but the most persistent seeker-after-advice," Mitja grinned. "Thank heavens Dragomir starts on Monday. This part of a hotelier's life is definitely not for me. Christine, I'm sorry we had to pack in the bowling so suddenly. Alex-Alex isn't – hasn't been well. She's not allowed to overdo things."

"I thought she looked a little tired," Christine said gently, but she saw in his face that he didn't want to talk about it so she changed the subject. "Don't you have very much to do with your clients in Bohinj?" she asked.

"Not a lot. Maybe I should do more. I deal mostly with the overall planning. I do make time for myself on the mountains, though. It's a good life. Perhaps a little solitary . . . except for Alex." There was a pause which Christine found she could not fill. Then Mitja seemed to force himself back to the present. "But you, Christine . . . how is it you speak my language so well, and do the

British always give positions of responsibility to
one so young?"

This time Christine explained, about Raddy
and the Children's Home, and Mr Barker and
Head Office. Then she stopped suddenly, slightly
shocked at the ease with which she had made
her revelations to a complete stranger, almost a
stranger.

"So you have ambitions?" was his only comment. "That is good. I rather gathered you had no
brothers or sisters," he finished with a twinkle.
"Together Alex and I can be a little formidable."
She rather thought that applied to Mitja alone.
There was another pause. "Does a husband and
children fit in your scheme of things?" he asked
casually.

She blushed faintly. "Eventually," she replied
hesitantly, "but not for years," she said stoutly,
and Mitja laughed. It came to her all at once that
marriage, a deep relationship with a man, could
be an experience to long for, and treasure when
it came. Did men ever come to that conclusion
too? She supposed they must.

"Don't forget your anorak tomorrow," was all
Mitja said, though. "It can be treacherous in the
mountains."

The chair lift to the top of Mt Vitranc dog-legged
upward, the single chairs clunking along the
wires in an eerie silence as the valley opened out
underneath. Half-way up there was a wooden
rest house gaily painted in red and green, pretty
with pink and white phlox in its tiny garden. At
the top there was another one, starker because
of its height, but here they stopped for beef stew

and dumplings, talking about whatever came into their heads. "It's clouding over," Mitja observed as they finished. "Time we made a move."

Christine glanced at the tiny white wisps forming, shrugged, but followed him at once.

It took them twice the forty minutes to the panoramic view and back. Like all novices to the mountains, Christine had failed to see from the map that there was a 200-metre difference between the chair lift and the view which the closeness of the contour lines should have told her, and by the time they reached the top of the chair lift again the sky had darkened. "It's not going to rain, is it?" she asked uncertainly.

"Probably," Mitja frowned. "Better put on your waterproof just in case."

They had just begun the second leg of their descent when the first drop fell. It was a deluge within seconds. Then it began to thunder, ominous grumblings that rolled out and over the mountains and rumbled across the valley. Christine had never been afraid of storms but, exposed in the middle of this one, to all intents alone, the drenching rain soaking through every seam and running in rivulets into her lap, her cotton trousers wrapping themselves coldly and soddenly around her legs as she sat in the chair vulnerably shelterless, she began to wonder apprehensively how close the lightning was . . . did they stop the chairs in a storm? . . . And she began to shiver helplessly.

Then it happened. Within sight of the hut that housed the lift machinery, it happened. "Mitja!" Christine screamed as, to her horror, her chair began slipping on the thick cable.

"Mitja!" she screamed again.

It was instinctive, she told everyone afterward. As her chair cannoned into his she braced her feet in her solid walking boots and aimed them at the back support. Afterward she blamed herself. "I knew I was too big to roll myself into a ball. I kept thinking about shattered kneecaps if I did nothing. I was so frightened of hitting Mitja in the back . . . of seeing him fall out . . ."

Alerted by her screams, Mitja had had time to see his danger, but at the moment of impact there was the sickening sound of bone cracking, and he knew the sight of her slumped forward would live with him forever.

There were onlookers below. Their reaction was instantaneous and purposeful. "Mitja?" Christine mumbled as help reached her. She did not hear the answer. As they lifted her to the ground and her weight rested for a second on her feet another agonizing spasm of pain shot through her body. She screamed again. This time, mercifully, she fainted.

The blackness was warm and safe. She came to in a whiteness that echoed and hurt. "Mitja?" she whispered. "Where are you?"

"Ssh. It's all right. I'm here."

Whose was the voice? "Raddy? It hurts, Raddy," she muttered through a tongue that had grown thick and fibrous. It did not seem to be Raddy's solid figure, though it must be Raddy, she thought. He was the only man she knew whose dear familiarity could make her feel secure no matter what had happened. "Dear Raddy," she sighed, her eyes closing despite herself.

The hand that brushed the hair from her forehead was cool and gentle, though it trembled slightly. "Hush," said the disembodied voice. "I should have taken more care of you. Sleep now, and when you wake there will be no more pain. Sleep, my Christine." Then an arm slid under her shoulder and she was drawn toward a muscular chest in a wordless embrace, but the sleep the voice promised overtook her before she had time to ask how Raddy came to be there.

She awoke to sunlight and she was thirsty and there was a white-clad middle-aged woman there to administer water. They might at least have removed my boots, Christine thought crossly as she lay back again and felt the restriction on her feet, but the words would not emerge.

"I do think you might have taken off my boots," she complained when she opened her eyes again. This time the light was electric and the nurse bending over her was young and pretty.

The nurse laughed as she attended to Christine's immediate needs. "We had to cut them off. You're in plaster, that's why you're uncomfortable. Now you lie still and I'll fetch the doctor. We were expecting you to wake this evening."

She was asleep before he arrived. She was so *tired*. But at least she was alive. Was Mitja?

Christine fretted all the next morning until her visitor entered. It was Mitja himself. "Hallo," she said uncertainly. Then her lip quivered perceptibly.

The cage over Christine's feet left little room on the bed, besides, he was afraid of hurting her. Mitja knelt by her, taking her hand in his. "Hey. What's this all about?" he asked gently as the tears began to seep from under her lashes. "Christine? *Christine!*" and releasing one of her hands he tried to wipe the tears from her cheeks with his palm. His gentleness only caused her tears to flow faster. "Now my hand is as wet as your face," he smiled, as he reached over to the towel hanging on a rail and patted her dry with it. She sniffed, and he gave her a tissue. "So, what is this all about?"

"I thought I'd killed you," she replied, shuddering.

"Killed *me*? You could have been maimed for life!" he said insistently, a white line of tension around his mouth. He made a visible effort for self-control and continued more quietly, "As it is, you've one broken ankle and a couple of broken bones in the other foot. As if that isn't enough! I still can't believe it happened." Then he took her hands again and held them strongly, warmly, in his. "These two days have been dreadful. Did you know you'd been out for two days?" When she shook her head wonderingly he went on, "You caught some sort of chill. The hospital wants you to stay here for a day or so. After that you can trust us to look after you. You do understand that, don't you, Christine?"

"Two days? Head Office . . ." she was suddenly frightened, bewildered, filled with uncertainty.

"Mr Barker knows all about it. I spoke to him myself. I said you'd ring him when you'd left hospital. All you have to worry about, Christine, is concentrating on getting your strength back. We will take care of you, Alex and I. I promise."

# 3

Christine did little but sleep and eat for the next few days but, in bed in the hotel once more, she awoke fully to the enormity of her position. She was now almost totally incapacitated. Despite the walking plaster casts on both feet she was not supposed to put too much weight on either foot yet she found the crutches she had been lent both heavy and difficult to manipulate. She would be in this state, unable to work, for another five weeks.

A wave of uncharacteristic panic swept over her, starting in the pit of her stomach, rolling up across her chest and exploding in beads of sweat that bedewed her upper lip coldly and left the palms of her hands clammy. *What was she going to do!*

The door opened and Mitja came in. "Didn't you hear me knock?" he asked, then he looked more closely at the girl on the bed, wide round eyes, a flush on her cheeks, staring at him as if she had never seen him in her life before. "What is it, Christine!" And at once he was sitting on her bed, clasping her in his arms as she wept into his shoulder.

His obvious concern was too much for her; Christine clutched his broad shoulders frantically, as if she were drowning and he her only means of rescue, and she sobbed as if her heart were breaking. But it was not; and the heat of her tears soon melted the cold knot of panic that had been the cause of her distress, and she became acutely aware of whose shirt she was wetting, and gradually she grew calmer.

He held her close for a little longer, then he put her away from him and asked solicitously, "Does it hurt so very much, Christine?"

She sniffed, blew her nose and smiled a watery smile. "I always dissolve into tears in front of you, don't I? It isn't really me at all. I was just being silly and sorry for myself," she answered honestly.

"So, tell me all about it," he encouraged her.

"I said I was stupid. I suddenly got panicky over how I was going to manage on my own for the next few weeks, and then you came in, and . . ." she blushed. How naïve she sounded, as if she were asking like a child, to be held, and a memory, a feeling that it had happened somewhere before, came fleetingly into her mind.

"I cannot understand," Mitja scolded her gently, causing the memory to disappear, "how you could have forgotten what I told you in the hospital, that Alex and I would take care of you."

"And you have done, but I have to take thought of tomorrow," she said bravely. And I didn't much like what I saw, hung between them.

Mitja had just taken her hand again when the door opened a second time and now it was Alex framed in the entrance. "There you are!" she exclaimed. "Mitja, I've been looking all over for you."

"I just came for Christine's things."

"My things?" asked Christine.

"A new arrangement," said Alex airily. "You are going to move into the double room in our suite with me," she said, "so that if you need anything in the night I shall be there."

"The London Office knows all about your accident, and has agreed that there'll be insurance money since you were injured doing your job," said Mitja. "There is room here for you as long as you need it." He spoke hurriedly, seeing a mistiness in Christine's eyes as she listened to brother and sister. It threatened to spill down her cheeks and she brushed her hand over her eyes. "No more tears, please!" and he groaned in such a way that she had to smile a watery smile.

"So you can take your weight off Christine's poor feet and move some of her stuff now," Alex told him cheerfully.

"Right. You deal with the drawers. I'll take the things on hangers, and . . ." when the job was done, ". . . I trust you're not going to be childish again," he said to Christine, with mock severity. "I have to leave you now, but I'll be in to see you this evening, and I'll expect to find you a lot more cheerful."

"I'm not a foolish child," Christine said haughtily, "I am a woman, even if I was weak enough to make a fuss just now."

"Yes," he answered consideringly. "I had noticed," and there was that in his voice which made her eyes widen and a flush spread across her cheeks.

Then Alex noticed that her eyes were too bright against her flushed face and she asked Mitja anxiously, "Are you able to carry her to the other bed? She really ought to be resting or she'll be feverish again."

Mitja lifted Christine in his arms, duvet and all, and because it was the most comfortable thing to do she buried her hot face in his shoulder while he carried her the few short yards. Even in her weakened state he had the power to make her aware of him intensely – especially in her weakened state. Christine shivered, and it was not because she was cold this time.

Alex, all concern, drew the drapes and smoothed the duvet cover. "Try and sleep for a little," she urged. "I'll be back later," and Christine turned her burning cheek to the pillow, and slept instantly.

A few days after Christine had been installed in the Minics' suite, Mitja declared his intention of going first to Zagreb then to Bohinj for a few days. "I never thought I'd be away for so long as it is," he said ruefully. "There are several things that need my attention. No, it's not your fault, goose," he emphasized softly but firmly as Christine looked at him crestfallen. "If I had really been needed in Bohinj I should have gone sooner. I thought I was needed here more."

He had been, but in a way she was glad when he had gone. His presence was too much, at times, too exhilarating, too disturbing by far. After a time, though, she noticed a tendency in herself to fret, to quibble over the slowness of her treatment, to find food tasteless . . . until she realized she was missing him.

And there was another worry. This time it was not herself, but Alex.

". . . I'm telling you because I just want to see it
written down, I suppose, Raddy," she found herself
confessing. "I am very worried about Alex, and I
don't know why. I suppose it is something to do with
the illness Mitja mentioned. I do wish he would come
back . . .

"Mr Barker has been wonderful. He says I can stay
here to convalesce in return for typing his report which
he'll fly out to me. That means I can do something in
return for all the Minics have done for me, by keeping
Alex company, if nothing else.

"In the meantime I sit and look out at the mountains
and daydream and try to commit to memory how
beautiful it all is so that I can put my enchantment
into words for you when I return. For it is enchanted,
and I hate the thought of leaving."

Mitja arrived. He took one look at his sister's face
and exploded. "How could you be so foolish as
to try to conceal a thing like this!" he declared
witheringly. "You realize you may have lost valuable time by delaying the treatment, don't you!"
His expression was set and angry, but underneath it Christine thought she detected something else, fear.

"Don't be cross," Alex pleaded. "You had
enough to think about, and I thought it would
pass. Besides, you know how I hate it," and she
picked up the hand that rested on the arm of her
chair and kissed it lightly on the back, by way of
apology.

"Silly girl," he said fondly, "as if anything
could be more important to me than your welfare.
I'll get on to the doctors immediately," but as he
turned away once again Christine saw the

shadow cross his face. For a heart-stopping moment she imagined her lips on his hand, her hand caressing that frown away . . . only there was nothing sisterly about her desire to be in Alex's place.

Mitja: Christine had sworn to Raddy that it was the place that so enchanted her, the place from which she would be so loath to tear herself when the time came. How much was it the place, how much the man whose face was the last thing her mind's eye saw as she dropped into sleep and the first image her consciousness formed when she woke?

When had been the moment that this man had – had what? Impossible, still, to put into words, even to listen to what her heart was telling her. So Christine told herself firmly as the day progressed and she sat outside in the afternoon sun. There had been no man in her life quite like this one.

He was tall, wide of shoulder, slim of hip – but so were many men in this part of the world. His hair was a glossy black, his lips could smile a smile of singular sweetness. His eyes . . . Christine fell to dreaming of the liquid brown pools that were his eyes . . . and jumped like a startled rabbit when a man's hand was placed on her shoulder and ran down her bare arms to her elbow. His hands. *Could* she have summoned him by the intensity of her thoughts?

"Don't tell me you were dreaming of someone else!" he declared mockingly. "By your expression I was sure you were exercising your magnetism and willing me to your side."

"I was gazing at the mountains and day-dreaming. I like looking at the mountains," and her face dared him to contradict her.

"I'm glad they have the power to move," he replied softly, his eyes locked with hers. "There are many they frighten, others they leave untouched. Those who love them are a special breed."

"They would frighten me, too, if I were at their mercy," she responded. "They *did* frighten me," she added, remembering all too clearly how she had reacted to the storm the day of the accident.

"They scare me also, sometimes," he confessed soberly, "but I would not live far from them."

"Well, I do not have to leave them yet," she said lightly, to ease the moment. Then she said, "Did you want something, Mitja?"

"I came for you," he answered laughing. "Did you not notice, in your contemplation of my mountains, how chilly it is becoming? I do not think you would want to delay your departure for an attack of pneumonia."

She laughed too, and she got to her feet. That was the easy part. "So, hand me my crutches, please," she said, "and I'll come in."

"I think not," he replied. "They are ugly, clumsy things."

"But I cannot do without them," she protested, still laughing.

"Then I will be your crutch. Come, lean on me," and he placed her hand on his shoulder, his arm around her waist.

But their progress was slow. He was too tall for her to lean her weight on him comfortably and after a few steps he gave a low exclamation, turned and swung her into his arms. "There. Much better!" he declared.

It was, but she was too aware of his nearness, of his arms around her body, his breath stirring the hair on her forehead, the quickening beat of her heart that he *must* feel against the steady thud, thud of his own.

It was not far. He seemed strangely breathless for a fit man, though, as he dumped her unceremoniously in the chair by the window. "You look flustered," commented Alex with sisterly candor from the bed where she had been resting on Mitja's orders. "Whatever were you carrying Christine for?"

"I thought it would be a good idea as she looked cold outside, but those plaster boots must weigh a ton – or else it's all that good Slovenian food we've been stuffing her with," and he grinned wickedly.

"Thanks. It was your idea," said Christine dryly, though it was all she could do to still the trembling of her limbs. She remembered the time he had carried her to her bed, wrapped up in the duvet. Then she had hidden her flushed face in his shoulder knowing he thought her feverish. This time there had been no excuse, yet still she had pressed her body to his, delighting in the feel of her breasts crushed against the solidity of his masculine frame. So why had she done it, instead of remaining tautly rigid as any self-respecting woman would have done?

"It's an idea I might find an excuse for repeating, when you're out of plaster," Mitja murmured, leaning toward her so that Alex could not catch what he was saying. Her eyes flew to his face, stricken, and she saw in it that he knew that what she had done had been deliberate, and that it pleased him, and she was rendered speechless. "And now I suppose I'd better go and retrieve those wooden monstrosities," Mitja was saying as he left the room.

"What was all that about?" Alex asked curiously.

"You're supposed to be resting," Christine replied evasively.

Alex, who was not stupid, giggled.

Christine dined alone with Mitja that night for Alex was too tired to get dressed. Not alone – for the chef wanted an opinion of a new dish and the head waiter was obsequious. "You mustn't fret about Alex," said Mitja, when at last they were left in peace.

She sensed that this time he wanted to talk about her so she asked quietly, "Tell me about her?"

"Did she tell you we have an appointment at the hospital in Ljubljana? It's a leukemia. She's been in remission for three years now. We were warned this could happen at any time. It doesn't mean she – she's going to die, you know."

Christine leant across the table and smoothed away the lines that had appeared on his forehead with his words. She said nothing; her fingers were gently caressing as her heart turned over. He had been trying to comfort *her*. Her action was totally unexpected, to them both. Mitja fought his own, equally inexplicable yearning to catch her to him in public. Then, "Thank you," he said simply. "I guess you were the best thing that could have happened to either of us, right now.

So, let's take Alex a glass of red wine. She'll drink it if we call it a tonic." His hand was warm, his touch warm on her skin, and he did not release her until long after she was on her feet. "I suppose you had better use the crutches this time," he said, handing them to her. "I'd offer to carry you again," and he grinned, "but I need a hand for the wine," as she stood there with her crutches under her armpits, acutely conscious of his words, of his nearness, and of the feel of his fingers which continued to tingle on her skin.

Suddenly it became important that she should seek the protection of Alex – even an Alex in bed – and Christine turned and put on her best speed to reach the safety of the bedroom.

"Stop scurrying," Mitja protested mildly from behind her. "Anyone would think you were trying to get away from me."

"How absurd," she countered. "I couldn't anyway," she pointed out with a deliberately dramatic gesture with a crutch. They had reached the bedroom door. Mitja was close behind her.

"No," he agreed with quiet intensity. "You've no escape this time."

It was the way he said it that set her heart pounding wildly. The corridor was deserted. Alex was in bed with her transistor tuned loudly to pop music. Christine stood there, mesmerized, and watched him put down the wine and lay the glasses beside it. She made no protest when he took her crutches from her nor when his arms closed around her, gently but firmly, as much preventing her from overbalancing on her plasters as evading him, nor as his face descended slowly, slowly, until his lips covered hers. He had given her every opportunity to move away, call out, but both knew she wouldn't, that there was, as he said, no escape.

What was this chemistry between a man and a woman that could leave her cold nine times out of ten yet stop her heart quite without warning? Not that she had been kissed by nine men, nor half that number, Christine thought incoherently when he took his lips from hers and gazed deep into her eyes for a long moment. Yet she had accepted moonlit kisses, friendly kisses, farewell kisses, avoided more, and had quite believed the whole thing an overrated pastime. Then thought fled as his strong mouth claimed hers a second time. She stood there, not answering the demand of his expertise, but enjoying the strange, new sensations of arousal. Not for long: soon she was totally incapable of withholding a response, and moved her lips under his as he dictated while she relaxed into his embrace.

Mitja knew it, held her closer momentarily, then released her without haste. There was a wary expression in his eyes as if he had got more than he bargained for, again. Christine could not look him in the face as she stood before him, helpless without her crutches. How strange, how revealing, how nice a gesture of affection could be. Yet that was definitely not the word for it, though it warmed her to think there might be some affection for her in him. Though her experience with men was minimal, Christine was capable of recognizing that Mitja was attracted to her, her mind beginning to whirl as a firm hand under her chin forced her, inexorably, to lift her face to his once more.

Once again there was the anticipatory tingle of blood singing through her veins as his mouth closed over hers and Christine knew with every fiber of her being that she was incapable of tearing herself away from his embrace as one hand splayed against her waist, pressing her into his hard body, the other sweeping up from the curve of her hip to close over a full, round breast. Even through layers of wool she could feel the heat of the palm of his hand tease an instant aching response from what he fondled that was reflected in the pit of her stomach.

Locked in blissful surrender of her will to his, Christine was oblivious of the time and the place, but the transistor had been turned off and still the time was not now. Mitja's hold on her slackened imperceptibly and gradually she came to her senses. No, affection was not the word, was her first coherent thought as her eyes fastened on his face, but too soon he had bent to retrieve what lay on the floor.

"Yours, I think," he said, with a quirk of a smile on the lips she would never forget, as she would never forget anything about him, the bones of his face, the way the hair grew on the nape of his neck, crisp yet soft and which clung to her fingers exactly as her fingers and palms knew how to cling to him, and her body was learning how to mold itself to his. Then, protectively closely, almost affectionately, Mitja walked behind her into the bedroom where he set down the wine and helped her into her chair.

She wished he would not always be so thoughtful; he hypnotized her, often made her do, and say, stupid things, imagine situations which could never be other than dreams. How he disturbed her, with his penetrating gaze, his proximity, his touch that lingered like a burn long after he had left her side, and his kisses. Did he, had he disconcerted her deliberately, she wondered as she had before? Was he playing with her? She gritted her teeth as she watched him set down her crutches by her chair. Only one more week and her plasters would be off. Two more, and she would be back home; three more, and she could tell Raddy blithely of the gorgeous Yugoslav who had quite caused her heart to flutter, for a while.

"Wine for me?" inquired Alex.

"That's right," answered Mitja. "I thought you deserved it as you've been so good about resting." He handed the second glass to Christine. She took it and their fingers touched, and once again the electricity they generated between them ran up her arm so that she exclaimed involuntarily and her eyes flew to his face once more.

His look betrayed nothing, until she saw the slight smile. Oh, he was aware how her heart fluttered like a bird on the wind; but the bird was wild and free, and wanted to remain so. It would take all the skill of a master to ensnare it, and she dared him, inwardly, to use all his wiles on her.

Mitja drove Alex to the specialists in Ljubljana. It was a long day which Christine occupied by helping Dragomir who, though not exactly a ball of fire, was competent and had a nice manner with the guests. It was late when brother and sister returned and she heard what the doctors had decreed.

"I have to try rest and various drugs for three weeks," Alex told Christine gloomily. "After that, it's the usual therapy. Ugh. Then we wait and see. There's another problem," she said hesitantly, "which I don't think Mitja anticipated. Last time I had treatment I was living here, at the Vitranc. The house in Bohinj is isolated, and with Mitja spending so much time away, I . . ."

"I think that'll be no problem at all," Mitja said carefully, interrupting her. "Igor Fattuta is perfectly capable of holding the fort at the sports center, especially if I go down there once a week. It's the Vitranc where the difficulties lie."

"I thought you preferred to live in Bohinj," Alex interrupted in her turn, guessing what was coming.

"I do," he shrugged. "But if I stay in Kranjska Gora for a few months I thought it might be nicer if we rented a house."

"A house . . . here?"

"Edita mentioned something the other morning about finding tenants for the winter." Edita cleaned their suite and had become a friend to the girls, fetching and carrying trays of food uncomplainingly. "The house on offer belongs to her widowed aunt. How would it be if we took it until you're better?"

"Could you bear to be in one place for as long as that? Why, it might take a year!" Alex exclaimed anxiously. "I know you think the skiing at Bohinj is better, for a start."

"I could be proved wrong," Mitja said. "Besides, it's time this hotel really established itself as a top winter resort, and it might as well be now as later. You see, Christine," he said, "my sister thinks I'm a nomad, not able to settle in one place for more than five minutes without getting restless."

"Is she right?" asked Christine, as if it really were her business or mattered to her.

"It's people who are important, not places," he answered seriously, his eyes fixed on hers as though it was very much on his mind that she should understand this, though for the life of him he could not think why. The girl was attractive, he had known that all along, but so were many others. She stirred his senses, but so had many others; and if there were an indefinable something about her that gave her an exclusiveness he had not attached to any other girl, she was a foreigner, in the very nature of things alien. Attractive aliens boded no good for a man. A man could desire without desiring permanence, and he groaned inwardly because she had speaking eyes that were telling him that she had always known that people mattered more than places, that desire might be unknown to her but that she was more than willing to be tutored by him.

By you, only you, Christine's eyes replied, and she was too innocent to realize how her gaze spoke volumes to the man of experience who dared not let his iron control slip for, after all, she would be gone so soon.

"So," he continued determinedly, "I will still be in the mountains, in Kranjska Gora, won't I? Which is no small thing. And the mountains will help to make Alex better, of that I am sure. And if I can also knock the Vitranc into shape that will be good, too," and Mitja smiled at Alex, content that his sacrifice, if it were one, at least met with her approval. "So Bohinj can wait. I'll see Edita in the morning and find out more about the house. Then we'll settle ourselves in for the winter."

It sounded marvelous, Christine thought, for them. She wondered wryly where she herself would be, when winter came.

# 4

"The house is ours for as long as we need it,"
Mitja told Christine the following evening, "and
Edita's aunt will remain there herself and look
after us. I hope the arrangement works," he
added doubtfully. "I suppose I can always escape
to the Vitranc, if necessary, but I don't know
about Alex. Mrs Martinovic, I think, is what you
might describe, politely, as a nosy busybody who
is going to take us over. Of course, I realize that
she's a lonely woman and that she believes she
is doing us a favor, but it will take getting used
to, having a very interested third party at home
the whole time."

"You wouldn't say that if the so-called third
party was your wife," Christine observed, chuck-
ling because she couldn't see any local woman
actually taking over either of the Minics.
"Besides, surely Mrs Martinovic will allow you
your privacy?"

"There'd be no comparison if I were married,"
Mitja declared, leaning negligently against the
bar where they were having a drink. "I would
expect my wife to share my interest in my work."

"No. You couldn't call a wife a third party,"
Christine observed soberly, not looking at him.

"I could call her a lot of things, but not that,"
Mitja agreed softly, and still Christine could not
meet his eyes. There was a constrained silence

47

between them. Christine bit her lip. She was on the point of asking what sort of a woman Mitja envisaged in his house as his wife: but that was the sort of question you only asked if you knew someone very well – or if you really wanted to hear the answer, and all of a sudden, with a fervor that startled her, Christine did not want to know what sort of a woman Mitja would take to wife. She had drained her glass and set it down on the bar counter with a little thud before she dared look at Mitja again. He was regarding her with an odd, quizzical expression. "That was a funny remark to make," he said at last.

"What was?" she asked nervously, wondering – oh horrors! – for an awful moment if she could possibly have voiced any of her thoughts.

"About me having a wife."

"It meant nothing," she hastened to assure him. "I might just as easily have made the remark about Alex, having a husband, that is. She's old enough."

"So?" he prompted.

"You're not going to suggest that's too young!"

"I hope very much, for Alex's sake, that one day there will be a husband for her," he remarked quietly, and immediately Christine was mortified. He shook his head, understanding how easy it was for an outsider to forget the disease which might, or might not, be arrested. "I'm not sure about you," he went on easily. "Are you thinking about marriage, Christine?" he asked then, casually, though there was an unnatural tension in his broad back which the dimness of the lights concealed.

"Certainly not," she answered instantly.

"That's what I thought," and he nodded as if with satisfaction. Then he asked abruptly, "Do you perhaps have a particular desire for a particular place in which to settle, Christine?"

"A place!" she exclaimed, mystified.

"London, or some small town, a place by the sea . . . English people like places by the sea, I'm told . . . anywhere?"

"No," she replied, without even bothering to consider the matter, "given the right – right circumstances, I could be happy anywhere." An imperceptible tremor ran through her body. She had all but said, "*the right man*," and the image that the words had invoked had been the face of the man opposite her. What was happening to her self-control that she could think so?

He seemed not to have noticed anything for he answered, "It is as well. I could not be happy away from the mountains," an enigmatic reply that almost sounded like a warning.

The day came when Christine's plasters were cut off; and her heady delight at the promised freedom turned to chagrin as she realized she almost needed to be taught to walk again.

Mitja, who had found the time to take her to the hospital, was kind, but firm. "Massage and a lot of gentle exercise, and your legs will be as good as new," he assured her. "I'll give you the massage myself – if you'll trust me to do it properly?"

"I . . ." Of course she trusted him. It was herself she was not so sure about. "I . . ."

"Mitja does know about massage. It's all right," said Alex earnestly.

He had made his offer cunningly, Christine thought, in the presence of his sister, knowing she could hardly refuse. "It'll save you a wait at the hospital," he added, not a flicker crossing his face.

"Th-thank you," she stuttered.

"A couple of sessions each day, beginning now," he insisted, rolling up the sleeves of his sweater. "Go and take off your tights, Christine. It'll be easier if I don't have to work against nylon." His expression was impassive, his tone quite impersonal, but oh, how could she bear it! Those fingers, the palms of his hands against her bare flesh. "Hurry up!" A note of impatience crept into Mitja's voice.

"Yes, go on, Christine. You might as well begin straight away, as Mitja says," Alex remarked encouragingly. For a dreadful moment Christine actually believed Alex was doing this deliberately, pandering to her brother – but one glance at that pale face and she was full of contrition. How could Alex be expected to understand the exquisite agony of what was to follow? She sat in the chair, tense, her hands clenched into tight fists by her sides, hidden by her woolen skirt from Mitja's sister.

"Relax," Mitja murmured, his eyes as warm as his fingers as they rested on her. "I shall only hurt you if you tense up." Not hidden from him.

How could she bear it, the feel of those long, tensile fingers stroking her thin legs, kneading the wasted muscles, seeking out the pain and the tension in her? Soothing . . . she remembered another time his hands had stroked, though it had not been there, and she gasped and almost cried out.

"Relax, Christine," he repeated softly. "Just lie back and let me do the thinking."

It took enormous effort, to lie back, unclench her fists and let the warmth and the pleasure steal over her. But she did, and for a brief spell her limbs became quite pliant under his fingers. They moved rhythmically and very soon her muscles responded to the heat the friction generated. If it had been anyone other than Mitja massaging her legs, kneading the muscles from calf to toe, Christine thought the sensation might well have sent her to sleep, so soothing it was. This was different. This heat was something else entirely. It was vibrant. It brought her to a new, sensual awareness that challenged her to admit her womanhood and enjoy it. It – *he* – succeeded. Mitja's hands moved where they needed to; his eyes, now on hers, now on her body, told her where they ought to be. Little beads of sweat broke out on her upper lip and she licked them away with the point of her tongue, tasting her own saltiness as a new and exciting thing, dizzy suddenly with the beginnings of an awareness of what a mature sexual response might be.

His hands left her: the spell was broken. It was over too soon.

"Tomorrow," he said, his eyes and his lips smiling as if he knew he had given her pleasure.

"If you can spare the time," she faltered.

"Of course I can." Suddenly he was impatient. Didn't the girl realize there was pleasure in it for him too, touching her? "Of course I can," he repeated more gently. "For as long as you are here."

It was that which brought the ache back, knowing it had to end. What was the use? Why bother, when there was no future in it? But Alex was there . . . and she had to pretend nothing was amiss. Mitja was right, though, and within a couple of days Christine's legs had ceased to feel like brittle sticks with thin jointed appendages lent her by a total stranger, and she became more able to enjoy stoically the bitter sweetness of Mitja's supple fingers as they continued to knead and stroke her, thinking fixedly of the time when she would walk with grace again.

Even Alex was impressed by Mitja's attentions. "I suppose he feels slightly responsible," she said ingenuously. "You can't finish your convalescence until you can walk properly, can you? So I imagine he's giving you all this time so that you can return home the sooner. That is, unless . . ." and her voice tailed off and she regarded Christine with her head on one side.

"Oh, I'm sure you're right," Christine answered blandly.

"Mm . . . I wonder. We're going to miss you."

Toward the end of that final week, Mitja asked Christine to act as go-between over the arrangements to be made with Mrs Martinovic. Her own departure and their move coincided. "Your walk could take you over to her house each day, couldn't it? I should be grateful, for I really haven't the time, and the phone hasn't been installed yet."

The house was one of a row in a narrow street that became the road to Jesna. The row was old;

the small, narrow houses opened off the road with a tiny, narrow garden at the rear. Christine was enchanted by it, especially with the few pieces of ancient, well-cared-for furniture which Mrs Martinovic dismissed airily as being as old as the house itself. "Edita's husband will move any of it that needs to be shifted," Mrs Martinovic declared, with cheerful optimism.

Mrs Martinovic was practical, motherly; her eyes gleamed sentimentally when she spoke of the English mother, the father long since dead whom she had known as a child in the village. "It is a pity they are alone. Even a distant relation can be a comfort at a time like this," she declared. Christine thought Alex would bloom under her caring, if the treatment was a success. Resolutely she suppressed the pang of envy that it was not for herself that the careful preparations were being made.

". . . Sorry?" she said, as she realized Mrs Martinovic was regarding her with bright-eyed interest.

"I merely asked how soon you would be back."

"In Kranjska Gora, do you mean?"

"It is a good-sized double bed, the one in the front room. Quite big enough for you to share with the poor Alex. I am sure she would be happy to see such a kind friend as you have been, as often as possible. And *Gospodine* Mitja must be so grateful for the load you have taken off his shoulders, being with her so much."

"I'm not looking for gratitude," Christine insisted stiffly. "I'm glad to do whatever I can. They have been looking after me, you remember,

since my accident. Anyway, I'm very fond of
Alex."

"Of course you are. And what a terrible thing,
that accident! Anyone could see you are genuinely fond of the girl, as I said, but kindness
deserves a reward, doesn't it? And I should enjoy
giving you the holiday they could not deny
you . . . please don't forget, now."

She was an old witch! Christine decided indignantly and cursed the flush that stained her
cheeks. Mrs Martinovic's knowing eyes did not
see her sharing Alex's bed at all, but filled it
with another figure whose masculinity was in no
doubt. "Kind friends do not always have the kind
of money to indulge in frequent travel," she
replied, "or the kind of job that pays that sort of
money," she added ruefully. "The Minics can
manage well enough without me."

But obviously if you could come once you could
come again, was in Mrs Martinovic's mind.
"There are holidays, and there is always the
skiing," and she returned to the long list of things
Christine had to check with Alex, sure that ways
would be found and her predictions come true.

Then it was Christine's last evening; her last
drink at the bar with a strangely abstracted Mitja
who would talk only of how best to settle Alex
into the house and who avoided meeting her
pain-filled gaze. Surely she had not been wrong;
surely he had been attracted to her, for a time?

Then it was her last morning: and Alex was
tearful and Christine longed suddenly for the
whole wretched business to be over, and
breathed a tremendous sigh of release and relief

as the coach doors closed with a pneumatic sigh
and they rolled away from the village.

Back in London it was wet and windy and the
sidewalks were slippery with fallen leaves the
color of bruised apple mud. Christine was faintly
amused how easily the threads were picked up.
Only the occasional, "You don't remember that?
– Oh, you were away . . ." reminded her that
she had left in early summer and now it was
autumn. That, and the periodic visits she had to
make to a physiotherapist to cure the stiffness
in her left ankle that the autumnal dampness
aggravated.

Raddy was never tired of hearing anecdotes
of her weeks in Yugoslavia so she visited him
frequently. He pored over her collection of postcards, especially the ones of the mountains, and
to her concern those of Kranjska Gora were dis-
played prominently on his mantelpiece and he
would pick them up and examine them minutely
several times a day.

Once he said, "There is a certain familiarity
about the village, that copper onion dome to the
church. It is as if I can see myself as a child,
gazing up at it, its brightness gleaming in the
sun against the blue sky and the white snow all
around."

She said slowly, anxious not to disillusion him
too abruptly, "Don't you think, maybe, it has
become familiar because of the number of times
you have looked at it?"

He smiled back at her indulgently because of
course she could not be expected to understand.
"I see you do not believe in coincidence," he

replied. "Yes, there must be a dozen such villages in the Julian Alps. It makes no difference," he shrugged.

"Raddy, I'm sorry. I didn't mean to be unkind about it," and she knelt beside him contritely.

"I know. But you see, I do believe in coincidence. And it does no harm to visualize it as I remember it, the village, and the people." He had left it as a child, his village, the name of which he could not recall, during World War II. He had been a displaced person for years and though he was a naturalized British citizen the loss of his birthright still hurt.

No, she could not disillusion Raddy deliberately for he, a widower now and increasingly lonely, needed something to hold on to. If it diverted him to believe he had been born in Kranjska Gora, to day-dream of a holiday he might take there one day, did it really matter that it left her heartsore and dismayed that, for once in her life a place mattered though she might never see it again?

Even without Raddy, Christine could not have ripped Kranjska Gora from her heart. Letters from Alex arrived with unfailing regularity:

*"In a way I am glad you are no longer here – glad all my friends are away at university. The treatment made me dreadfully sick, and grumpy – well, bad-tempered, actually – and shortly there will be a bone marrow transplant. Did I tell you before what a marvelous brother I have? It is Mitja who will cure me, if anyone can."*

She had not. It was like him, and for once, when Christine replied to divert Alex, there was an excuse to mention Mitja's name. Not that Alex

needed any excuse. She mentioned him
frequently.

"Mitja is busy. Already the hotel shows results,
Edita says when she visits me. He is also determined
not to let anything stop him from skiing after Christmas. I believe him. He is so strong willed . . ."

Unexpectedly she received a letter from Yugoslavia in an unfamiliar hand. It was from Mitja
himself.

"The news about Alex is encouraging," he wrote.
"She was very good, very brave, enduring what she
had to in hospital. However, I am worried, because
with the skiing season at its height when she is due
home, I will not be able to spend either as much time
with her as I would like, or as I think she should
have. Mrs Martinovic has been splendid but despite
appearances (Christine smiled), she is not robust and
Alex must have someone with her.

"It is a lot to ask, but I wondered, since Alex thinks
so highly of you, if you would be able to spare a week
or so at the end of the month . . ."

Even couched like that it was a bald request.
Surely there must be a girl-friend, a school friend
he could ask. Christine looked up from the letter,
a little piqued. Why ask her? He must realize she
could not take time off work just like that . . .
but there was a postscript over the page.

"I can't tell you how grateful I should be, especially
as I know how difficult these things are to arrange at
short notice and at busy times of the year — nor how
glad I will be to see you myself.

                                        M"

She read the letter, and the postscript, several
times, and put it away thoughtfully. Was it just
coincidence? She was beginning to have a healthy

regard for whatever it was, predestined, meant,
coincidence. There was Raddy, who had taught
her Serbo-Croat; there was the accident that had
prolonged her stay in Kranjska Gora. Now there
was an invitation to go back . . .

She was still humming "Never Mind the Whys
Nor Wherefores" when she went into Mr Barker's
office. It was settled quickly. She had a seat on
the plane to Ljubljana two days after Alex was
due out of hospital, two weeks holiday agreed by
the firm, there was a cable on its way to the
Minics telling them of her decision, and Mr
Barker was left with the suspicion at the back of
his mind that he just might be about to lose his
treasure after all.

There was snow on the ground at Ljubljana airport, the fir trees standing out like stark sentinels
on the approach run, a muddy slush on the
runway and town snow, nasty dirty stuff, piled
on the sidewalks in the valley. But as they
climbed higher into the mountains the air became
purer as the scenery grew prettier, like a thousand Christmas cards blended into one fairy-tale
landscape, silvery white and glistening.

Christine had managed to buy, at the last of
the sales, a good pair of fur-lined boots and a
red, fur-trimmed anorak, quilted and bulky
though light. In the centrally heated store it had
seemed almost absurd; now, despite the warmth
of the coach, she huddled into it, glad of its comfort and the warmth of a brushed cotton shirt and
pure wool sweater. She had also found a pair of
ski trousers in the same cherry red as the anorak
and red corduroys which she was wearing now.

Mitja was there, outside the hotel in Kranjska Gora, waiting for her, heart-stoppingly attractive in a sheepskin jacket thrown over a dark green pullover and brown corduroy trousers. "Christine!" he exclaimed. "Welcome back to Kranjska Gora." He swung her exuberantly off the bottom step of the coach and hugged her warmly before kissing her on both cheeks.

Christine was overwhelmed. She had speculated on the manner of their meeting – how not to? And she had wondered about the man she would be meeting again. Would he, in the winter, appear inflexible, like the high peaks that had loomed ever nearer the coach, dark and menacing in the twilight, as he had seemed to her occasionally, even in the summer? Or might it be that he had not changed, but that she had; that his image had detached itself from her heart as it had from her mind during those long weeks of waiting, grown fuzzy around the edges, as if her mind's eye had become short-sighted in the interval between fall and dead of winter? Would she think of him now as nothing more than a holiday Romeo?

He was all efficiency, as usual. Her case was extracted deftly from the mounting pile and within minutes he was striding off, his free arm draped loosely around her shoulders, keeping her close to his side.

"It is good to see you, Christine," he declared, a deep note of sincerity in his voice. "I can't tell you how delighted Alex will be when you walk in through the door. She has been counting the hours since your cable," and Christine, who had thrilled to the tone of his voice, stifled a sigh. Of course he was pleased to see her, for Alex's sake. She was being foolish again. He attached no more importance to their re-acquaintance than he would to meeting any girl able and willing to help his sister convalesce.

"You didn't mind my letter?" he was asking almost anxiously, somewhat to her amazement. "Afterward, after I had sent it, I thought you might be offended."

"Offended!" she exclaimed. "Of course not. After what you both did for me in the summer, how could I be anything but proud that you considered asking me to help you? Her glance forbade him to doubt for a moment her willingness to come. "And Alex," she added hastily. "How is she?" she inquired belatedly.

"The doctors are very pleased with her progress," Mitja answered, his arm tightening around Christine's shoulders. "Naturally she is very weak still, but you understand that, of course, and she is getting stronger every day. She only wants encouragement to get into the fresh air for a little exercise."

"How different it all looks!" Christine remarked, looking around in delight at the thickly piled snow that lay crisp and white against the houses and carpeted the open space where the mini-golf course had been constructed in the summer.

"Yes, I suppose it does," he replied, smiling at her excitement. Tendrils of freezing air curled up between them and at his smile Christine caught her breath painfully. She could not expect an easy two weeks in Kranjska Gora after all. She had not changed, that was now apparent. She was as susceptible to his every look, his every gesture, as before.

Time, though, had moved on since the summer as in her heart of hearts she had known it would. He was no longer attracted to her in the way he had been. Now he was completely impervious to her. There was nothing but indulgence in his look, a pleased awareness that she was happy to be there, a friendly, welcoming, *brotherly* attitude that did nothing for her morale except cause it to plummet. Almost Christine wished she had never come back.

# 5

The front door was flung open by Mrs Martinovic who had obviously been keeping watch for them. Christine was pulled into the glowing warmth of the house, stripped of her anorak and boots, exclaimed over, fussed over with spiced wine and little cakes, "To keep the cold out," and she could not but be glad that she had made the journey.

Alex was in a living-room upstairs. "I spend a lot of time up here," she said. "I can see the slopes and look down on the passers-by so I don't get a bit bored, but it will be so much better now you're here." Her eyes were shining with a loving welcome and there was a happy flush on her pale, thin face.

"Now that Christine is here you will be able to get a little exercise," Mitja said bracingly. "It was difficult before," he told Christine, "because Alex was afraid to go out on her own."

"And fresh air will help put some flesh back on those bones," Mrs Martinovic nodded, "so thin the poor thing has become."

"I think you look very well, considering all you've been through," said Christine, who was actually shocked by Alex's wasted appearance but would not have said so for the world.

They ate a solid, substantial stew – at least Mitja and Christine did, Alex picked at hers –

from trays carried upstairs by Mitja. "We live very simply." he warned Christine.

"You don't come back for lunch?" Christine asked him. He was different, she decided, or much had changed. In the summer she could not have envisaged Mitja living the informal existence of Mrs Martinovic's house, such a contrast to the hotel. She supposed it was Alex.

"I try to look in occasionally," he told her, "but I have to spend a lot of my time at the Vitranc. I discovered a number of deficiencies in its running by being on the spot, and I'm gradually reorganizing." Christine noticed the grim lines of determination around his mouth which hadn't been there before, and she wondered how many had found out how cleanly a new broom sweeps. Mrs Martinovic's house must be a welcome refuge at the end of the day.

"It's a long day, though," observed Alex wistfully. "I can't even seem to concentrate on reading any more."

"What about your skiing?" Christine asked Mitja.

"I do that first thing in the morning," he replied. "It's more convenient all round, and I can get in a good run if I'm first on the ski lift, apart from being back for breakfast before Alex wakes."

"Then for two weeks you won't notice Mitja's absence at all, I promise you," Christine said to Alex.

"But I don't want you to sit with me constantly," the girl objected with unexpected firmness. "In the early mornings you must get out on the slopes yourself."

"And that is definite," decreed Mitja.

"I've never skied before," Christine tried one, weak protest, "and what, exactly, do you mean by getting out on the slopes?" she finished cautiously.

"Just that," Mitja answered. "The nursery slopes for a couple of days, then down a mountain, with me."

"You sound a lot more confident of me than I am," Christine declared.

"Mitja is a marvelous teacher," Alex said, with sisterly pride in her brother's prowess.

"In that case I'm sure I shall be a star pupil," her eyes met Mitja's and she blushed. "At least, it won't be for want of trying if I'm not," she said, "just lack of natural talent." Oh darn it, she thought. Why does he make me talk and act like a smitten school-girl? It was so difficult to act, and talk, naturally, when you valued a person's opinion of you so much, when you longed for a glance of approval from him. And she did: from Mitja, more than she ever thought she would from anybody.

It wasn't mere attraction, something callow, shallow; but something far deeper and more enduring that she felt for this man, a feeling that she hardly dared put into thoughts, let alone words, to herself. She was in love. And what a time to find it out!

". . . tomorrow morning?" asked Mitja.

"Yes," she answered, and meant it, to any question he cared to ask.

The next morning Christine was out on the nursery slopes early for her first skiing lesson. Her boots and skis had been waiting by the front door for her, incredibly the boots a perfect fit, and skis just the right length.

"I remembered the size you needed for hiking boots," Mitja, debonair in navy with red chevrons, said smiling at her, "and I know exactly how tall you are," and he indicated a point just below his shoulder.

Christine's heart skipped a beat as she saw his smile. Surely a man did not remember insignificant things like that unless . . . and she yearned to reach out a hand to touch his dark, springy hair as, with care, he fastened her skis for her and guided her first tentative steps, his voice calmly encouraging as she slipped and slithered on the snow.

It was a beautiful morning: a cloudless sky with bright sunshine glistening on the snow, dark blue and purple shadows across the valley where the sun had yet to penetrate and where the pines loomed starkly. The nursery slope seemed to Christine more like a sheet of ice where the scores of beginners had made their way downhill gingerly and laboriously trudged, crabwise, back up again for yet another glorious, or ignominious, descent. For the first fifteen minutes it was all ignominy for Christine whose skis traveled everywhere she did not want them to go, usually separately, and deposited her in a far from graceful heap on her bottom. She was very glad there was no class to witness her inept first attempts, but Mitja did not once laugh at her efforts and coaxed and cajoled her toward her first downward run that ended with her still on her feet, her skis correctly aligned, and which earned her a pat on the back from him.

"Let's brush the worst of the snow off you before I go," said Mitja, and did so with gusto, the powdery stuff coming off in a small shower. "Beginners are really better in white," he grinned. "Cherry red shows just where you've fallen, even though it does match the lovely red of your cheeks." Then he added, "Well done," and dropped a kiss on the tip of her nose, and glided off toward the Vitranc.

Alex was sitting up in bed reading when Christine got back. "Would you like some of that delectable coffee Mrs Martinovic is making?" Christine asked.

"Why not?" Alex agreed. "Did you have fun?" she inquired. "You're positively glowing with health this morning," she said, without a trace of envy in her voice.

"Cherry red cheeks, I know," moaned Christine. "Mitja said I should have worn white, but how was I to know I'd spend most of my time on my bottom!"

"Did he? How very unflattering of him – or was he really showing his admiration? That color is gorgeous on you."

"Thank you. I think he felt it would have looked better unsullied by the snow I'd sat in."

"Did you? Sit in it often, I mean?"

"Frequently! But I think I was beginning to get the hang of it by the end of the lesson. But those nursery slopes!"

"I know," sighed Alex. "Like vertical sheets of glass when you're on skis."

"And actually only gentle inclines when you take them off," and they smiled companionably.

"I'm going to buy you a walking-stick," Christine said. "How about a gentle walk this afternoon if the sun is still shining, to try it out? We'll walk to the square, sit at one of the cafés and drink a celebratory glass of mulled wine."

Alex smiled involuntarily. "If you like," she said. "If you think I could manage it."

There was just the hint of a sparkle in her eyes at the prospect of a treat, Christine noted. "That's settled then. So now I'm going to leave you in peace while I go out and buy that stick and some postcards," she said, picking up the empty coffee mugs and thinking that too much excitement was probably as bad as too little. "And this afternoon, once we have reached our destination I shall tell you about my favorite man – the one I shall be sending my postcards to."

"Back in England?" her curiosity aroused.

"After we've had our walk."

The stick was a great success. Christine ordered the wine as she had promised. "Tomorrow it'll be coffee," she said. "Today is special."

Alex actually laughed,. "If you say so. And now I'm waiting, all agog as they say."

"What for? Ah, you remembered. Yes, let me tell you about Raddy . . ." and she did.

"I see," Alex smiled at the end of the recital. "Do you know, I thought you meant . . ."

"A boy-friend?"

"Well, yes. Of course I always . . . I mean, I thought you'd come back . . . I mean, most girls . . ."

"I came to see you," Christine answered gently, not pretending to misunderstand her.

"Thank you, but then, it's all right, isn't it? I mean, if Raddy's an old man."

Christine laughed. "Oh, I think you'll find Mitja continues to prefer the 'most girls.' " A figure across the square caught her eyes, a tall man in navy with red chevrons – but it was not Mitja after all – and she turned back to Alex, the smile on her soft mouth concealing her agitation. Her heart had leapt when she thought she recognized Mitja, its painful lurch becoming a flutter when she realized her mistake. How vulnerable her love made her.

Alex leant across and touched Christine's hand. "Thank you for coming, for whatever the reason. You are such a comfort. I do wish you were my sister," she said ingenuously.

"Yes, well, I'm not," replied Christine dryly, "so you'd better make the most of me while I'm here."

Mitja caught up with them a hundred yards from the house. "What a sight," he said, "two lovely ladies taking the air," and he bowed exaggeratedly.

"How could you tell we were ladies?" his sister demanded, giggling.

He outlined curves with his hands. "Not boys," he grinned a reply, "so I took a chance in accosting you. I knew, of course, that ladies would ignore me . . . ouch!" he yelped as Alex poked him with her walking-stick. "You could damage a man with that!"

"Christine's idea," said Alex. "Isn't she clever!"

"I'll have notice of that when I've examined my bruise. Come on, and we'll lean on each other," and he put his arm around Alex's waist, but his eyes regarded Christine warmly and the quick squeeze he gave her shoulder as he stood back to let her precede him into the house was full of silent approbation.

"My, that walk has done you good," Mrs Martinovic declared when she saw Alex's rosy cheeks. "What about a hot bath, Alex?"

"I'm starving," said Alex, surprised.

"Cakes and wine?" suggested Mrs Martinovic.

"Cakes and coffee, or I'll fall asleep."

"Cakes and wine," decided Mitja, "and if you do fall asleep we'll delay supper, just for tonight."

Supper, meat and dumplings, was served promptly after all. Alex ate all her meat and half of her dumpling, and followed it with a yogurt. After the meal they played cards for a while, the girls laughing and giggling over their hands until Mitja grew quite cross and threatened to send Christine home if she over-excited his sister. At once Alex sobered and a sheen of tears came into her eyes.

"Goose," Christine nudged her. "He's only joking. Can't you see? But bed, I think?"

She stayed where she was, reading in the living room, while Mitja helped Alex to bed, but he surprised her by returning almost immediately, coming back into the room and closing the door firmly behind him. "You marvelous girl," he declared. "I can't believe the change in Alex! What have you done to her?"

"N-nothing," answered Christine shyly, for his eyes on hers were full of gratitude and . . .

"Come here, Christine," he said quietly, compellingly, and when she rose slowly, drawn by the magnetism of the man, he took her by the hand and pulled her gently into his arms. Then he kissed her, butterfly kisses on the corner of her mouth that grew more insistent as he realized she was not pulling away from him. "Ah, Christine," he murmured, "how good it is to have you here again. I've missed you," he said, as though that had only just occurred to him. And this time his mouth came down firmly and warmly over hers, his fingers winding themselves in her luxuriant hair, and helplessly her soft lips parted in a sweet response that sent her senses reeling as it enticed him to an even more fervent embrace.

"I have to go out," he whispered reluctantly against her lips, his uneven breath mingling still with hers. "There's a minor crisis in the kitchen, or something. But, welcome back, Christine." There was a final, gentle pressure on her mouth . . . and then he had gone and she was left, stunned, and wondering where she went from here.

On her third morning Christine skied down the mountain with Mitja. "It wasn't as grand as it sounds," she confessed to Alex in the evening. "To start with, it was only half-way."

"Quite enough to begin with," commented Mitja.

"And the chair lift was a bit hairy."

"I'm sure no one would ever get me back on

one of those after the accident you had," Alex insisted.

"I wasn't afraid of that," Christine reassured them, "which surprised me, I confess. I was just too busy hanging on to my skis and worrying about how to get off at the top. And I did everything wrong," she admitted. "Most of the time I just shut my eyes and went."

"Women!" groaned Mitja. "I suppose that was why you kept bumping into me?"

"Oh no. That was deliberate. I was using you as a brake," she said cheekily. "A sort of emergency stop when nothing else worked. Still, it was fun. Can we do it again tomorrow, from the top!"

He smiled, then, at her exuberance. Then he shook his head regretfully. "I have to go to Bohinj, but I tell you what, the instructor at the Vitranc is doing the bottom chair lift with his class for the first time tomorrow. He'll take you, too, if you like, and the next time I go to the top I'll take you myself."

By the end of her first week, Christine knew she would never make more than an average skier, but she was satisfied with her progress and quite glowed with pride when Mitja told her she was good enough to spend the morning with him when unexpectedly he had one free.

"Wouldn't you rather do something more strenuous?" she asked doubtfully, feeling impelled to make the offer, though longing to go with him.

"Now would I have suggested taking you with me if I hadn't meant it?" he began with gentle exasperation, then his face softened. "Thank you for the thought, but I need some relaxation, occasionally, and this time I should prefer to relax with you."

It was one of those idyllic, unforgettable times, silent when they were silent save for the scrape of their skis in the compacted snow, sparkling and companionable. Toward the end of the morning Mitja faced Christine with a final, steep descent.

"Can I do that?" she asked in trepidation.

"Providing you traverse it as you've been doing," he said. "Follow me down, but don't take it too fast."

It was not until her final traverse that it threatened to go awry. Christine got on to the wrong ski, failed to complete her turn and found herself hurtling forward, downward. Her only way of stopping was to sit down, hard. She slithered to a halt, on her side.

When Mitja got to her he was breathing fast, a furious gleam in his eyes. "You silly fool!" he yelled. "Were you trying to kill yourself!" hauling her roughly to her feet.

"N-no," she protested, wobbly of voice and knees for she had frightened herself as much as him. "I started to do a turn, got on to the wrong foot, and then I couldn't remember what to do to stop so I had to sit down."

"It was my fault," he declared. "I shouldn't have left your side," he said, calmer now, a little, now that he could see she was not hurt, but his hands were still holding her upper arms firmly.

"I said it was my own fault, but I am all right," then to her consternation she burst into tears.

"Oh God," he groaned. "Don't cry, Christine." He sounded to her ears so infuriated, still, that she stopped instantly, appalled, like him, at how close she had come to hurting herself.

"But I didn't hurt myself," she insisted, and sniffed. He handed her his handkerchief, and while she blew her nose he dusted the snow off her. "I'm sorry," she gulped. "I didn't mean to scare you," and she held out his handkerchief.

"Oh God," he repeated, pulling her toward him. She came with a slither and a bump as their bodies made contact and her exclamation of surprise was drowned as his lips came down over hers.

She was too stunned, still, by her near accident to do anything but stand there, clutching him around the waist while he kissed her, his mouth probing her sweetness. Yet it was an angry kiss, that somehow told her even more positively than his words how frightened he had been for her safety. It punished her for scaring him and at the same time it was the kiss of a man made vulnerable; a kiss of searing passion as he claimed back what he thought he might have lost. It seemed to go on for ever. She wished it would go on for ever. Then Mitja groaned and lifted his head and, unclasping her hands, pushed her gently away. There was the same, dazed expression on both their faces as each tried to read the other, unsuccessfully, both of them wary of the raw emotion generated between them. He had never felt like this over a woman before, shaken, exasperated, relieved, all at once. This can't have anything to do with love, she thought. Love was supposed to be gentle, supportive, wasn't it? Not passionate and angry and demanding and—and hateful!

Then, "Come on, concentrate!" There was only amusement in Mitja's face as he picked up Christine's stick which she had dropped and turned her to start in the right direction.

"I don't think I can," she whispered, shattered, her legs like lead and her knees jelly, but not only from the mountain.

"Yes, you can. I'm right beside you," and he gave a nod of encouragement, and minutes later they were at the bottom of the slope. "There, I said you'd do it," and he gave her a quick, almost brotherly, hug as he took her skis from her. "Nothing to it. No harm done?"

"No harm done," she agreed shakily.

It was only a kiss, Christine said to herself over and over again that night. Like last time, only a kiss. Men kissed women without a thought . . . except that those times Mitja had kissed her it had not felt in the least brotherly. He had kissed her as if he would like to do a lot more, and each time her response was deeper, more helpless.

She should never have returned, Christine admitted to herself. Nothing would come of it except heartache for she could not bear that he only wanted an affair, though even that would be something . . . and she went hot all over in the darkness remembering his kiss and the strength of his body and how she had wanted to respond to him.

It was neither as simple – nor as complicated – as it sounded. With only three days of her two weeks left Christine was shocked to realize that Alex was suffering a relapse, a bout of weakness that left her depressed, tearful and over-anxious.

"Only to be expected," was the medical verdict, but Alex declined to leave the house, complained of insomnia and headaches and pecked at the food lovingly prepared to tempt her poor appetite.

Mrs Martinovic was in despair. Mitja was cross.

"I pushed her too fast," Christine wailed. "It's my fault."

"Nonsense!" they said together, Mitja a trifle more forcibly.

Christine could see the word "nurse" hovering around Mrs Martinovic's mind. "How would it be if I stayed on a little longer?" she suggested tentatively.

"It would certainly ease my mind," Mrs Martinovic replied at once.

"Out of the question," declared Mitja.

"Why?" demanded Christine. She had made her offer without thought: the more she considered it, the more it appealed to her. She *was* fond of Alex, would do anything to help the girl. She also dreaded the ending of her holiday, these blissful days of seeing Mitja daily – even in the company of others – listening to his voice, sometimes feeling his eyes on her, experiencing the occasional, purposeful touch of his hand as he demonstrated a skiing skill she was unable to master, or the occasional brush of his fingertips as he passed her a glass of wine or she proffered him a cup of coffee. And there was always the hope of more, of feeling his lips on hers again . . .

"I don't imagine you're entitled to an extension of your holiday," he answered coldly.

"What? Oh, no, I suppose not," she agreed, reluctantly.

"Then what do you think you would live on?" he asked irritably. "You certainly could not come and live in Yugoslavia without visible means of support to satisfy the authorities.

"Mitja, couldn't we give Christine a job?" Alex asked eagerly. "What about at the hotel? That would really solve all our problems."

"I think that would be a very bad idea," Mitja replied repressively. "If it comes to the time when you need constant care we should need someone with proper nursing experience. And it hasn't come to that."

"I have no nursing training," Christine said, equally coldly but quietly. For a moment hope had flared in her, to be douched as if with icy water.

"Oh, Mitja," sighed Alex. "It would be nice to have a companion." There was a world of pleading in her voice and his face softened magically, but there was nothing but granite hardness in it as he turned back to Christine.

"No, Alex," he said firmly. "It wouldn't work."

"I wouldn't want to work either in the hotel, or for you," Christine said indignantly. "I would only want to stay until Alex was better. What do you take me for!" she demanded.

"A rather generous idiot," Mitja replied, but softly. "Christine, you are kind, and generous, and I would like nothing better than to think it right to accept your offer on behalf of Alex, but for all sorts of reasons I must not. I don't expect you to understand."

She didn't. "If you say so," she shrugged. After all, he was right. She needed her job, if only because with it she could save – to return to Kranjska Gora and Alex. And Mitja.

There were the same doleful farewells all around. Mrs Martinovic was the only determinedly cheerful one and that was because she was firmly convinced that Christine would be back again shortly. "I read it in the tea leaves last night," she said flatly. "And they never lie."

Faced with such assurance, there was no answer except, "I shall miss you all," as she kissed the two women goodbye, and to Mitja the confession slipped out involuntarily, "I wish Mrs Martinovic was right."

In answer he held her hands tightly as he thanked her for her care of his sister, then as if he really could not help himself, he drew her to him and bending his head he claimed her mouth for the last time, kissing her as if he did not care for the interested spectators in the coach, as if he wanted to imprint on his memory the feel and the taste of her. "Dear, dear Christine," he whispered. "Fare well." He used the English expression, separating the syllables, and making it sound a blessing.

It was goodbye, nonetheless.

# 6

At Ljubljana airport there was a message for Christine. She was to stay put. Mr Barker would meet her there. *"Urgent staff problems,"* the message ended.

The matter took them four days. By the end of them Christine had come to a decision. "I want to remain in Yugoslavia," she told her boss.

"Tell me all about it," he encouraged her.

She did.

Mr Barker had been approached earlier by a publishing firm which needed a translator for a scientific journal. The work would be steady, if not particularly well paid, the articles would arrive fortnightly from Ljubljana university. "The point of it is, though, the publishers are willing for the translator to be paid in either country – just about a living wage."

"Oh, thank you!" she breathed fervently. "Thank you," and she reached up impulsively and kissed his cheek.

"The only other thing, Christine," he went on, trying not to seem moved, for he was genuinely fond of her, "I can't hold your job, so it has to work out as you hope."

*"So am I doing the right thing, Raddy? Heaven knows,"* she wrote, *"but I am still here. The only thing I'm sure about is that if I went back to London I should be closing a door that would never reopen –*

*if that doesn't sound too fanciful! The only way I shall
ever know if I can ever mean as much to Mitja as he
does to me is by remaining in Yugoslavia, as close as
possible to him. If I go away now, he will shut me out
of his heart for good. By returning to Kranjska Gora
now, there may be a chance for me."*

Christine returned to Kranjska Gora a week after
she had left it. Alex welcomed her a little tear-
fully, miffed at not being in on what she called
the great secret. She did not believe in coincidence, either. "You might have told us you were
intending to come back. I've been so miserable,"
was her complaint.

Mrs Martinovic, on the other hand, went
around with an "*I told you so*" expression on her
face for the whole day.

As twilight deepened Christine grew quiet with
trepidation. Mitja's reactions were what mattered. What would he say when he learnt what
she had done? Could he demand that she go
home?

His reaction was obviously on the minds of the
others, too, for both found themselves very busy
about the time Mitja was expected, Mrs Martinovic staying in her kitchen, Alex in the bathroom
washing her hair.

His first utterance was full of concern. "Christine! What has happened? Are you all right? Tell
me!" as he grasped her by the elbows, his dark
eyes searching her face minutely, anxiously.

She told him.

Afterward, long afterward, she was comforted
by those first words. At the time she heard only
his anger as he let go of her abruptly and

exclaimed roughly, ominously, "I hope to hell
you realize this is all your doing, and none of
mine!"

The first parcel containing articles to be translated
arrived a few days later, gratifyingly quickly, and
producing electric results. Alex became quite
respectful, quite overawed. Mrs Martinovic
declared, "Well then. Well, well. That does put a
different complexion on things, doesn't it?" Even
Mitja who had steadfastly refused to utter more
than commonplace politenesses thawed enough
to suggest she'd need a large table to work at.

Christine was vaguely amused, then, a quarter
of the way through her first paper, she felt a
sense of outrage. They hadn't believed her! They
hadn't believed she had the means of supporting
herself before she returned to Kranjska Gora.
Mitja thought she had disobeyed him deliberately
– probably he thought there would be difficulties
over work permits which he would have to sort
out. Probably they all thought she was throwing
herself at Mitja. Then common sense prevailed;
it was no worse than she might have expected.
It was what she deserved, for that was exactly
what she had done, come to throw herself at
Mitja. The only thing left now was to prove to
them that she was something worth picking up!
She laughed wryly, and, her equanimity somewhat restored, she reached out for her dictionary.

Mrs Martinovic decided to clean out a large
attic room for Christine's use (which the girl
insisted on adding to the board and lodgings she
would now be paying). It was not particularly
comfortable but it was quiet, and it had glorious

views of the mountains. Mitja helped her carry
up a table to work on and said he hoped she
wouldn't spend too much time day-dreaming.

"*I will lift up mine eyes unto the hills,*" she
quoted. "I'm very self-disciplined, Mitja," she
said, "despite appearances," she added boldly.
Then she said, "I'm sorry you mind about me
coming back." It was the first time they had been
alone, really alone. Both Mrs Martinovic and Alex
were shopping. "At the time," she continued,
"when the opportunity arose, I grabbed it."

His eyes narrowed. "I thought . . ." he began.

"Thought what?" she probed.

"That you had engineered it, the translating
job," he said. "That you knew all along you'd be
back soon."

"How could I do a thing like that! I mean, I
don't have contacts like that. It was Mr Barker
who told me about the publishers. I just jumped
at it. There wasn't the time to think, even." It
wouldn't have been necessary. She decided not
to add that she had done all her thinking long
before she encouraged Mr Barker to remember
that he had been approached.

"Obviously not," Mitja reflected dryly.

"I'm truly sorry," she said earnestly, "if you
believe I'm in the way. It was an impulse. I was
impetuous," she confessed.

He stirred uneasily. "I daresay you will do Alex
more good than anyone. I'll acknowledge that
the change in her since your return has been
remarkable. I only hope she maintains the
progress."

"So do I," Christine agreed fervently.

"So how about being honest with me, Christine? Why did you really come back?" he asked harshly.

"I told you . . ." she began hesitantly.

"No you didn't," he answered flatly. "You just gave me the public version."

"I don't understand," she said slowly.

"I think you do. If you didn't come here to chase a dream, a chimera . . . and nothing that happened between us gave you any reason to think there might be any permanent relationship between us . . . then I think you came back hoping for an affair." At the little intake of breath that betrayed agitation he glanced at her sardonically. She had gone quite white, he noticed, but then, anyone would once her scheming was revealed. "Not that I'm not flattered," he went on. "I admit I am attracted to you. You were well aware of that from the start, weren't you?" He waited for her to deny it. When she didn't, he shrugged. "You are an extremely desirable young woman," he said, and he made it sound like an insult. He compounded it by raking her body with his eyes, deliberately lingering where once his hands had caressed so that it seemed this time as if each item of her clothing were being removed by him piece by piece. To her dismay, even while her mind registered the cruelty, Christine felt every particle of her being leap to the call of those seeking eyes, her breasts swell as if to fill cupped hands outstretched to receive their fullness, her innermost core aching for the touch he denied her. Fiercely despising herself at that moment for a weakness that urged surrender under any terms, she fought for the self-control that would allow her mind to be mistress of her quivering senses.

"Mitja, I . . ." she began to protest.

He would not allow her to interrupt. The sound of her voice lashed him to fury. "Let me finish!" He caught hold of her wrist, crushing the bones with his strong, tensile fingers. "What we had . . . what started between us . . . was delightful. It had to end there, don't you see?" Color was stealing back into her cheeks, but she continued to regard him steadily. "We come from different worlds, you and I," he tried to explain, not trying to lessen the hurt, but make her understand. "When I am ready to settle down, it must be with a woman who understands my world, who is of my world. It has to be that way. Relationships are too fraught at the best of times for anything else to make sense, and I have always believed in the permanency of marriage." He paused, and she made futile efforts to escape his grasp, conscious all the time of the continuing and overwhelming desire to throw herself into his arms despite the hurt of rejection. His fingers were burning hot, his eyes bored into hers, stripping away the pretense that she had come back only for Alex's sake.

Christine swallowed with difficulty, the lump of humiliating rejection threatening to choke her. "Good heavens, Mitja," she croaked, and tried again. "Did you really think . . ."

"Yes," he said firmly, and her gaze fell from his. "But if you didn't come back for that reason then I think you are crazy enough to have come back for an affair."

Her mouth opened, and closed. What could she say that would not exacerbate the situation? "Always assuming there was the time and the opportunity," he shrugged, "in this household, do you think I could?" She frowned, not catching his drift. For the first time Mitja smiled. "Oh, Christine, of course I could! Don't you realize the number of times there were when I should have like nothing better than to have taken you to bed!" She had not. The notion startled her, that he could have felt like that and not acted upon it. "Well, one of us has to be sensible. Had to be sensible. I let you go. I was too fond of you to love you and then send you away, ruin your life for the sake of a transitory pleasure. So what am I supposed to do now?" When she said nothing, thinking that it didn't matter what he did so long as he didn't insist that she go home he continued, his voice hard once more, "Perhaps it would be a good idea if I were to make love to you, here and now. You wouldn't fight, would you, and then I think you would forget me all the sooner. One day you might even thank me for it."

What he said was shocking, yet Christine could not feel shocked. An affair? Would she settle for that? Probably, though not under those terms, expecting that she would be cured of an infatuation just by going to bed with him. "All right," she said at last. "I admit that what I did was stupid. Perhaps I'm not even clear about my own motives. They certainly don't seem as clear cut as you make them sound." On the other hand, she had not capitulated, yet.

"Then, go home, Christine," he said wearily. "Go home and consider your future sensibly."

She laughed lightly. "Didn't you know I have few hopes for the future?" she replied slowly, standing very still now, fighting with words since her body had, after all, failed her. What had she done! She had fallen in love with him, hoped that a similar emotion had grown within him to deepen the attraction, desire, for her that she had known was there. How cruel his words were.

She was defeated. She had burnt her boats, had nowhere to flee to, now that he had rejected her, at least, not until she could afford to go. Unconsciously Christine squared her shoulders. Mitja saw the expressions flit across her face: hope, despair, anger, fear, resignation, determination, and his admiration for her, never far from the surface, grew. Truly this was no ordinary woman. "People like me," Christine continued bravely, "the ones with no close-knit family ties, unlike you," she goaded him daringly, for what had she to lose? "We rarely do bother to plan for the future. The present is all we can hope for."

"What do you mean? That's nonsense," he declared roundly, diverted. "Everyone has to think of the future. If there was nothing to hope for, nothing to look forward to, the human race would go crazy. Christine," he hesitated, and without his volition, his thumb rubbed at the place where he had bruised her, as if in silent apology for words he would like to be able to take back. "Christine," he said, "do you really have nothing to look forward to, nothing, or nobody you see in the future?"

There was a look in his eyes, a new look that set her heart pounding, a look she scarcely dared to analyze. "I . . . Mitja . . ." she began uncertainly, but at the bottom of the stairwell came the sound of voices.

"Tell them now," from Alex. "Mitja. Christine," she called. "Come down, will you!"

Mitja looked at Christine, shrugged, let go her wrist and turned to the door. Christine sagged momentarily, then followed him.

"Of course it's out of the question," Mrs Martinovic was saying as they entered the living-room.

"I don't see why. Mrs Martinovic has to go away for a few days, Mitja," Alex said. "I found her in the kitchen weeping over a letter from her daughter, but it's all right. I've sorted things out."

"I was not weeping!"

"Well, agonizing over it. She really does have to go, Mitja."

"Of course she does, if you say so." There was a slight edge to Mitja's voice and a stiff look about his mouth as he stood by the window, his back to the mountains.

Mrs Martinovic clearly interpreted what she saw in Mitja's face as disapproval for she was exclaiming, "No, no. Indeed it is not necessary," as she sat down.

Christine had the oddest feeling that Mitja was not really listening, either to Mrs Martinovic or to Alex, but that his mind was still on his conversation with her, waiting for her answer. If she had had the time her reply would have been simple. "You. You are what I want in my life." But it was not an answer a woman could make unless she was very sure of the meaning of the question, not after the rejection that had come before. And there had been the interruption . . .

Mrs Martinovic was explaining, "My daughter has to go into hospital to have two wisdom teeth out. There are the babies to look after."

"Is that cause for weeping?" he asked, smiling gently at her. No one could stay abstracted for long in Mrs Martinovic's company.

She shook her head. "There is a sister-in-law . . . but she is very young, only twenty . . . it is such a responsibility, looking after two small children."

"Far too great a responsibility," agreed Mitja, and glanced quizzically at Christine.

"It's not that we don't need you, Mrs Martinovic," Alex said, "for we do, but I'm sure we can manage, for as long as it's necessary."

"I can manage very well," Christine said, "as long as you have no objection to English puddings."

"Well . . ." Mrs Martinovic replied doubtfully, "I would feel happier in my mind, but . . ."

"That's settled, then," Mitja said crisply.

"Why don't I come and help you pack," suggested Alex, "after supper, once you've phoned your daughter?"

Mrs Martinovic blew her nose delicately on a large handkerchief. "You are kind," she said, "all of you. I . . ." she seemed about to be overcome, but Alex diverted her attention with an armful of socks she picked up.

"After that," she declared, dumping them by her chair, "I have to make a start on Mitja's socks. Every one of these needs darning. Can you imagine! Besides, I loathe darning."

"If there's one thing Mrs Raddy taught me at the Children's Home, it was to darn great holes in boys' huge socks," Christine exclaimed, laughingly taking Alex's lead. "So, if they're worth salvaging and you have the wool, I'll start tonight."

"No, you won't," Mitja interrupted savagely.

"Why ever not?"

"You're not my wife . . ." he growled roughly, "or my sister," he added hastily.

"Nor your mistress, nor your slave," she said wickedly, "though since when any of those qualifications has been necessary to wield a darning needle defeats me."

"For goodness' sake throw the whole lot away and buy me new ones!' Mitja insisted forcefully. "This whole rigmarole is totally absurd, as you both well know."

"I've always darned your socks," objected Alex, beginning to look upset. "Why should I stop now?"

"Oh, be a martyr then, if that's what you want," snapped Mitja, uncharacteristically harassed.

"And I shall do half," Christine winked at Alex, "and you may thank me for doing my share by taking me with you one evening when you go into the village," she remarked sweetly, daringly, to Mitja. Alex giggled.

There was a moment's silence. "If you like," Mitja agreed, his tone not particularly agreeable so that Christine, who had caught Mrs Martinovic's eye at the wrong moment, choked, and Mrs Martinovic left the room hastily.

"You don't have to," Christine said meekly. "I

had intended doing it for free, you know," a
remark that left Mitja scowling at her back as she
also escaped into the kitchen.

Mrs Martinovic was still laughing. "You young
people do me so much good," she said at last. "I
bless the day Edita suggested you stayed here
with me for the winter."

"As long as we aren't too much bother – I am
not too much bother," she corrected herself.

"You just add a different dimension to it all,"
Mrs Martinovic replied, "which I watch with
interest," she added with a kindly smile at Christine's flush. "You'll learn there's some men you
have to fight for," she said, as she handed the
girl a pile of plates. "Mind you," she said darkly,
"there's some men you'd do better just to fight."

Listening to music that evening while she
darned a bright red stocking with almost no heel
to it, and Mrs Martinovic and Alex packed together, Christine thought back over what both
Mitja and Mrs Martinovic had said to her earlier.
She had been warned off by the one in no uncertain terms, hardly encouraged by the other. Yet
Mitja had misunderstood. She steeled her soul.
She was here, and here she would stay and Mitja
might as well get used to the idea.

Then, secretly she stored away in her mind,
like a squirrel his best nut, that when Mitja had
reminded her that she was not his wife, his
momentary pause suggested that he had bitten
back one word . . . *yet*.

There followed, for Christine, an exceptionally
busy time. If she had thought all would be peace
and tranquillity once they had packed Mrs Mar-

tinovic into the early morning bus, her do's and don'ts ringing in their ears until the doors closed (and mouthed at them as the bus drove off), she was very much mistaken.

It was on the second day that she was forced to wrestle with the intricacies of a recalcitrant stove that had gone out. "Drat the thing, Alex," she said crossly as the kitchen door opened behind her. "I'll never have a meal ready for tonight at this rate! Why won't it stay alight for me," and wearily she brushed the hair from her cheek, leaving a long, dark smear.

"You're probably overdoing the riddling." It wasn't Alex, but Mitja, who took the offending instrument from her grimy hand. "Let's have a look."

"What are you doing home?" she asked, startled into breathlessness. "You gave me a fright."

"Some papers I left behind this morning," he explained. "Now, how does this thing work?"

"Mrs Martinovic said to keep the damper either a quarter of the way out, or more than half. It sticks otherwise. It's obviously missing her delicate touch because it almost went out last night."

She watched him gradually coax a flame from the almost dead embers. It was a cozy, domestic scene. "I came down to make myself a cup of coffee," she said, "and start a casserole. Would you like a cup?" she asked him.

"On this?" he indicated the tepid stove with some amusement.

"The kettle's electric."

"So it is. Yes, please, then. Do you think the water'll be hot enough to remove coal dust?"

"Bath water. Oh lord!"

"Don't worry. The tank'll be hot enough by tonight. But I was thinking about now." He tested the tap water. "Just about."

She poured him some coffee while Mitja washed at the sink. Today he was casually dressed and he had rolled back the sleeves of his checked shirt to cope with the stove. She gazed almost hypnotized by the strong, slender wrists, the long fingers and well-manicured nails, until she realized he was staring at her. "I'm sorry," she apologized, sitting down.

"Whatever for?" he asked quizzically.

"Being a nuisance about it. The stove, I mean."

"Most stoves have their little ways," he shrugged. Christine, restless in his presence, got up and began sorting vegetables for her casserole. He watched her for a moment. "Do you do much cooking?" he asked her eventually.

"Not now. I helped Mrs Raddy for my last two years with them. She taught me a lot, but it isn't as much fun, cooking for one."

"I don't suppose it is," he replied neutrally, "but lots of girls nowadays, Alex included, haven't a clue about what happens in a kitchen. I'm glad you enjoy it."

"Why?" There she went again . . . and she groaned inwardly.

"Because otherwise I should be forced to endure bread and cheese," he grinned. "What are we having tonight, Christine?"

"Pork casserole, and a Sussex Pond pudding."

"A Sussex what?"

"A suet pudding with a heavenly lemony inside. The pork is one of Mrs Martinovic's recipes, the suet pudding is Mrs Raddy's, only of course she had to do everything in fours. I prefer not to have to cook in such quantities."

"No," he agreed, "you stick to being a family woman." He was laughing at her openly but it gave her a warm, happy feeling inside. He finished his coffee and got up, then he leant over and touched the smear on her cheek with the tip of his finger. "You could use some of that hot water yourself." Then he said, "I do appreciate what you are doing for us, you know, even if I don't say thank you very often." She began to demur but he continued, "It heaps coals of fire on me, especially after what I said to you when you came back so unexpectedly."

She said without expression, "I suppose that's one way of putting it."

"Yes. Well . . ." he had the grace to look uncomfortable. "In fact, I owe you an apology, it seems. I think I was taking far too much for granted. Anyway, I shouldn't have said what I did."

She lost the warm, happy feeling abruptly.

"So, let's just say I'm glad you're here and leave it at that, shall we? See you later," and he sauntered out of the kitchen as if he had said nothing of any moment.

# 7

Routine re-established itself: Mitja went away for a few days, returned preoccupied and uncommunicative. "Nothing strange about that," Alex commented, unperturbed. "He's got some sort of a deal going, if I know anything about my brother. He'll tell us soon enough."

He'd tell Alex certainly, Christine thought philosophically, never her, and never her first. She was wrong.

"Will you do me a favor?" Mitja had come into the kitchen while she was chopping vegetables for soup and he had asked his question almost brusquely.

"If I can," she looked up. "What is it?"

"I need someone to act as hostess at lunch today. Will you do it?"

"Of course," she answered simply, "but why me?"

"I need someone who isn't . . . involved," he said, his dark eyes boring into hers so that she could hardly concentrate on what he was saying. "Someone who isn't an employee . . . not Alex, who couldn't contain her curiosity."

"I'm not sure I will be able to contain mine," Christine admitted. "Mitja, you'll have to brief me a little better than that. For a start, is it formal?"

"You mean, do you wear a dress? Yes, please,"

he answered promptly. "As for a briefing, all I want to say at this stage is that it's business. They – there will be two men and a woman – will be interested to hear how you first got to know about the Vitranc. You may tell them anything they ask – just don't ask questions yourself. Is that clear enough?"

"It sounds simple," she replied, "and I really am happy to help, Mitja," she cocked her head on one side, "provided it's legal," she said, straight-faced.

For a moment his brows drew together ominously, then he grinned. "It's legal, Christine."

"And what do I tell Alex when I've prepared a sandwich for her?"

"Just say I'm taking you out to lunch. I'll pick you up at noon."

The dress, fortunately, presented no problems. A friend at Head Office had packed a suitcase of clothes for Christine, once she had decided to stay in Yugoslavia indefinitely, and the case had been flown out with a group staying in Kranjska Gora. Amongst its contents was a paisley wool dress in glowing colors. It was smart, but not too formal, and she both looked, and felt, good in it.

Alex presented none either. She was busy writing a letter and only raised an abstracted smile when Christine told her Mitja was taking her out to lunch. "Pretty dress, have fun," was all she said, though she did grin broadly once Christine's back was turned.

The two men spoke only Serbo-Croat, the woman, dowdy in gray tweed skirt, gray blouse and white cardigan, fractured English. They all kept to generalities during the meal: the beauties of Vienna which was a city Christine knew well, and the excellence of the Lipizzaner horses compared with the brilliance of their own Lipicia stud of which one of the men was a devoted follower.

Only over coffee did they touch on the original reason for Christine's arrival in Kranjska Gora. "So, what was thought of the Vitranc in London, then?" asked the woman earnestly.

"It was considered a first-class addition to their concession hotels," Christine answered honestly.

"And now?"

"As you can see," she gesticulated around the dining-room. "The high standards have been more than maintained. The food is greatly improved. It really is a very good hotel."

"Another brandy?" Mitja interjected smoothly, picking up a bottle with a good French label, and both men assented at once.

"I particularly like the view from this side of the hotel," Christine said to the woman. "Do you ski?" She excused herself soon afterward, sensing that the business, whatever it was, would now become specifics.

Mitja escorted her to the door. "Thank you," he said simply. "You were a great help."

"Thank you for my lunch," she replied, "but I didn't do much."

"Precisely. That was what I wanted." He touched her shoulder briefly and went back to his guests.

Mitja tended to spend an hour or so each evening either at the hotel or in the village. That night he invited Christine to accompany him.

"Two invitations in one day?" teased Alex.

She was rewarded by a frosty look from her brother who said nevertheless, "You can come, too, if you like."

She felt plainly that it had been issued grudgingly for she said a little huffily, "Oh, I'm a bit tired. Another time, perhaps?"

Mitja raised his eyebrows slightly but his only reply was, "It's freezing fast. Wrap up warmly, Christine. We shan't be late, Alex."

They walked over to the hotel, their breath steaming in little white clouds as they talked. It had not snowed for several days and the packed snow underfoot was becoming treacherously slippery. At the bar Mitja ordered *veniaks* and when they had been served he said, "About the lunch, Christine."

"I don't have to know, if you would prefer it," she said quickly.

"I wouldn't be telling you anything if I did," he replied testily. "I'm thinking of selling," he told her. "They were prospective buyers."

"The Vitranc? Oh, Mitja! Why?"

He did not answer immediately but shrugged. Then he said, "During lunch I realized they wouldn't do. So, thank you, Christine. Let's leave it at that, for now."

They did not stay very long. "Alex will be waiting for her hot chocolate," was Mitja's excuse.

The air, as they left the hotel, took Christine's breath away, catching in her throat with its chill and making her eyes water. She had decided not to be offended by his reticence and had him laughing with her over a shopping incident that afternoon.

"Let's hope it snows again soon," he said,

grasping her arm and holding it tightly against his side.

She was glad of the support. "Will it, snow, I mean?"

"In about twelve hours, I should think."

"That'll delay Mrs Martinovic, won't it? She'll love the excuse to stay on with her daughter."

"Will you mind?"

"Oh, no," she replied instantly. "I've enjoyed this week immensely."

"So've I. I wish . . ." He stopped suddenly in the middle of the road and she skidded on the ice beside him.

"Whoops!" she exclaimed, laughing as he righted her instantly. "What do you wish, Mitja?" she asked curiously, feeling that the answer might be important.

"Oh . . . nothing," he replied evasively. "Come on, it's too cold to hang around tonight." But on the doorstep he held her back momentarily. "Thank you, Christine."

"For what?" she asked, tilting her face up to see him properly.

"Everything . . ." His kiss was meant only as an impulsive gesture of friendship – for it *was* too cold to linger outside – as he touched his lips to hers. Their breath mingled as he drew her closer, then with a soft exclamation his mouth closed over hers hungrily, his face blotting out the night sky in which not a single star shone. He held her suffocatingly tightly – as if it had been far too long since his arms had embraced her – and for a second she was tempted to pull away, but as before her body knew better than her mind what she needed. Treacherously, as treacherously as the icy ground under her feet which made her cling to him as something solid, her body responded as it had always done before, her female senses reveling in the readiness with which, once more, she was compelled to answer his demands despite her mind which continued to insist that this was madness after all he had stated.

"Christine . . ." he murmured.

"Mitja . . ."

He raised his head. "God. It's cold out here. We must be crazy! Come inside."

Madness, that's all it was. He didn't love her, or—or anything. Womanless, he had turned to her momentarily. Could she – dared she think of this as a tentative beginning? Her blood was singing in her veins in a way that had nothing to do with the sting of the icy air as she followed him inside the house. But, "Hot chocolate," she said prosaically, "that's what we both need," and she had the satisfaction of reading puzzlement in his face as he took her coat – as she slipped out of it, evading him. It didn't matter, for once, that she was not sure if he had wanted to continue what he had started on the doorstep, or not. At least now he had ceased to consider her an open book.

Mitja and Christine were washing up together the next evening, for the most part silently, except for such asides as, "Excuse me," and, "There's a dry towel over there." Then, as Christine dried her hands, Mitja observed casually, "You do know I'm leaving in two days?"

"Leaving . . ." she faltered, dismayed, because

however difficult it might be sometimes, living in
the same house as Mitja, at least he was there.
On the other hand, they were used to Mitja
announcing he would be away for several days.
His tone of voice this time suggested it would be
for longer.

"The national ski championships at Sarajevo.
Surely Alex told you I like to go and watch
them?"

"Of course," she replied promptly, "but I'd
forgotten." Some years before, Mitja himself had
won a place in the national team. He still watched
the championships every year, for a few days,
renewing old friendships, meeting the up-and-
coming young people. It was because of that he
was able to attract the best instructors to Bohinj
– had been able to this season for the Vitranc
also. "You won't worry about Alex while you're
away, will you?" she asked. "Anyone can see
how much better she is. And Mrs Martinovic will
be back as soon as the roads are clear enough for
the buses."

"I know." His eyes were on her face, serious,
remote. "Because you are here." Then he caught
hold of both her hands, towel and all. "Thank
you, Christine," he said. "I keep having to say
that, don't I?" He smiled. "I rather like it."

She liked it, too. His hands were warm on hers,
strong and full of life and vigor. Her pulses raced
and she was sure he must feel the pounding of
her blood through those sensitive fingers that she
grasped firmly with her own slender ones, the
towel now on the floor at her feet. "How – how
long will you be away?" she stuttered.

"A week or so. Maybe longer. I have people to

see. One or two feelers have been put out – the interest is definitely there – this may be the time to find a buyer for the Vitranc. I still haven't told Alex about that first, abortive attempt. I think I'm slightly afraid she might have sentimental family feelings about it. After the championships we shall definitely have to have a talk."

"Will she need much convincing?" Christine asked him.

"Probably not," Mitja answered. "I keep forgetting Alex is very shrewd, for all she is young still. Besides," he paused. Then he said, "In spite of all I said about disliking the hotel trade myself, I do see there is a need for something to be attached to the sports center before I can expand it any further."

"Accommodation?" Christine suggested.

"More than just accommodation. Good quality self-catering units and a series of small restaurants . . . I've already commissioned a feasibility study. So . . . I shall be very busy in Bohinj for the next few years. What is more, if Alex . . . when Alex is better," he said firmly, "there will be a job for her somewhere in my organization."

He had it all planned. Already she knew he would succeed. Lucky Alex. "So, we may not see you for some time?" she commented bravely.

He shrugged. "Who knows?" His face softened. "I'll keep in touch, Christine."

Of course he would. For Alex. "Then I wish you good luck," she said, as they left the kitchen together. Soon afterward he put his head round the living-room door to say good night. Christine and Alex were reading. Christine suppressed a sigh. No invitation for her tonight.

"No invitation tonight," Alex observed, "for either of us," she corrected herself, reddening as she realized how hurtful her remark could have sounded to her friend.

"No," Christine answered shortly, confirming Alex's fears that she had been hoping for one.

Mitja was starting his journey before dawn. He had said goodbye to Alex the previous evening. Christine got up to make him coffee, throwing on a track suit and brushing her hair hurriedly the moment she heard him stirring and catching her alarm before it woke Alex in the room below.

"You needn't have bothered," Mitja observed, though he drank the hot liquid gratefully.

"I know," she replied serenely, "but before dawn is a miserable time of day. "So," she said, as he came back into the house for the last time, "goodbye, and safe journey," and she held out her hand.

He put down his brief-case again to take hers. He seemed to reflect for a moment, then he raised his eyes to hers and the old, teasing merriment was there again. "Don't you think the occasion merits a goodbye kiss?" he dared her.

Christine did not think twice: if she had done she would probably have fled. She stepped forward, closing the gap between them, lifted her face and placed her mouth on his in a gentle caress. That was all she intended, but when she would have stepped back she found herself prevented by arms like steel.

"I think you can do better than that," he said, his mouth inches from her own, and proceeded to demonstrate how right he was as she awoke to molten pliancy in his embrace, the promise of lissom flesh all melting submission driving them both instantly to a height of passion. Her fingers acted as if they had a life of their own as they played with the soft hairs that curled on the nape of his neck. She knew that his hands would drive her crazy, if he did not release her, soon. He did, slowly. "After all," he said, "a man needs to have something to remember on cold, lonely nights, away from home," stepping back from her with reluctance, but she swayed toward him and his arm went round her waist again. Again their expressions were dazed, as if neither could quite believe, after all that had gone before, just how swiftly their senses had ignited.

"Christine . . ." he began.

"I . . ." she said, and swallowed convulsively.

"You . . ." he shook his head.

But in that house there was no privacy. The bedroom door opened unceremoniously and Alex called out, "Are you still here, Mitja? I thought I heard the front door."

"I'm still here, dear," he answered. He laid a gentle hand against Christine's cheek as he let her go. Then he bounded up the stairs. "You'll catch your death of cold," he scolded his sister, "without a robe."

"I just wanted to say goodbye again," she said, and they hugged each other warmly.

"Take care, both of you," he said. He hesitated, bent and kissed Christine's cheek, where his hand had been. "See you soon," he said cheerfully, and then the door had closed behind him.

The following afternoon Mrs Martinovic returned home. "It is good to be back," she sighed, as she relaxed over a cup of coffee.

"Don't tell me you didn't enjoy every minute away," Alex said provocatively.

"Of course I did, especially the first few days when I had the babies to myself. But it's not the same as having your own, is it, and sweet as they are, I'm not so young as I was, nor so agile. I was quite glad when their mother was well enough to take over again, I can tell you."

"Agile enough for them, I'll be bound! And your daughter is fully recovered?"

"Ooh, it was a nasty operation!" Mrs Martinovic launched herself into gruesome detail that had Alex shuddering visibly. ". . . But it is nice to be home," she ended, "in peace and quiet."

"For us, too. We missed you," said Alex.

"So tell me what has been happening while I've been away." They told her, and her wise old eyes read a great deal more into what was not said than either girl imagined. "Let's hope Mitja returns soon," was all she replied.

They did not hear from Mitja for over a week, except for a brief card. It was Christine who took his phone call when eventually he made contact.

"Mitja! How disappointed Alex will be to have missed you." She was breathless, but more from realizing who was at the other end of the line than from running downstairs to answer the call.

"I should have got in touch before. How is Alex?" he asked.

"Fine. We got your postcard."

"Good. And you're all right?"

"Fine," she repeated. She thought, what a trite conversation. She had so much to say to him, and could think of none of it. "Mitja?"

"Yes?"

"We've been following the championships from the papers. They sound exciting."

"You don't want to believe everything you see in the papers," he replied guardedly.

"No?" She was puzzled, then she remembered a certain picture. "No," she agreed dryly.

Mitja chuckled.

"But you have enjoyed them?"

"Well enough. That's why I'm phoning. I've made some useful contacts which I have to follow up."

"That sounds good news."

"It could be."

"I see," she said.

"The only thing is, I have to go off straight away. I won't be coming home for a week or so."

"Oh." She paused. "Alex will be disappointed not to have spoken to you." Then she realized that her own disappointment at not seeing him was likely to be far greater than Alex's.

"Will you miss me?" he was asking softly.

"Of course," she answered stiffly.

"No, I mean, will *you* miss me, Christine?"

"Yes." She felt, down the wires, rather than heard, his satisfaction. Her answer had been too forthright, too revealing, "Especially the wet towels you leave on the bathroom floor," she ended pointedly.

His laugh had an element of satisfaction in it. She guessed that her afterthought had come too late for him to be put down by it. This conversation was becoming dangerous. How to end it neatly?

"See you in a while, Christine," he said softly, "and I'm sorry that sounds so vague. Don't go away while I'm gone, will you? I think, when I get back, it will be time we had a long talk. And in the meantime, please take care of yourself. And Alex," he added hurriedly, and before she had time to think how, or what, to reply, "Bye," he said.

"Goodbye, Mitja. Good hunting." Her mouth was dry with excitement as she replaced the receiver. Suddenly the wait, all that had gone before, seemed worth it.

The weather grew milder; the snow was now mushy, unpleasantly wet underfoot, the streams rushing torrents swollen by what was melting fast. Skiing was impossible except on the highest runs, walking in the valley was difficult. Except for a couple of postcards from Mitja they heard nothing more from him. He had moved from Sarajevo to Zagreb, from there to Bohinj. It was spring in the valley before he appeared, and when he came, shortly on the heels of a cable, he was not alone. He breezed in through the front door, sun-tanned, fit and healthy as though he had spent much time in the open air, very much alive and bringing with him a draft of cold, spring air as he carried in piles of expensive-looking luggage which he dropped on the floor to hug his sister.

"Alex!" he exclaimed. "How well you look. And Christine!" and the next moment the girl found herself enveloped in a warm, friendly embrace, somewhat different from the one she had dreamed about since she had known he was returning. "Come and meet Eva. She's come to stay," he announced, stepping back from the doorway he was blocking. Behind him they saw a girl, tall and elegant and slim, with long black hair curling over the collar of an expensive fur coat.

Alex and Christine had exchanged shocked glances before they realized the silence was being prolonged beyond politeness. "How nice," Mrs Martinovic said, bridging the gap valiantly, "and how long will *Gospodica* Eva be staying?"

There was a tinkling of soft laughter. "I haven't quite decided," Eva answered, "but Mitja didn't mean I am staying here. Half those bags are his. The rest are going to the Vitranc."

The indefinable tension relaxed. Mrs Martinovic appeared to approve of Eva, Alex to be won over by the charming exterior. Exterior? Christine castigated herself for her jealousy – for that was what it was – and petty-mindedness. If Mitja liked to bring a young woman back to Kranjska Gora, it was not her concern. Unfortunately. He wouldn't, if it were!

"Do you recognize her?" Alex hissed as, eventually, the last of the baggage belonging to Eva was hauled back outside and into the waiting hotel van.

"Should I?" she asked, surprised.

"It's the girl in the newspapers, the one looking as if she could eat him," Alex answered, with sisterly candor. "You must remember that picture."

It was indeed, and of course she did; it was

such a good one of Mitja. The girl was hanging on his arm and gazing up into his face, and next to her name in the caption were the words, "Ladies' Champion."

Christine promptly forget that Mitja himself had told her not to believe everything she saw in the papers. That was that, of course. Eva was such a good choice for a man who ran a sports center, a skiing champion who also appreciated the good things in life. Mitja couldn't fail with a woman like her behind him. And a quiet despair descended on her.

# 8

Mitja returned from the Vitranc later that evening, alone. Alex had already gone to bed and Christine was tidying the living-room when he walked in, tall and bronzed and very handsome. "How nice it is to be home," he declared, his voice full of contentment. "It's so quiet and peaceful." Then he looked at Christine. "I could have wished for a more heartfelt welcome from you," he said reproachfully.

"Whatever do you mean?" she replied cagily.

"Pulling away from me as you did," he answered. "At least I expected a welcome kiss."

Christine's heart began to thump. "Why?" she demanded frostily, edging further away from him.

"Because you kissed me when I went away all those weeks ago," he replied evenly. "For friendship's sake, if for nothing else," he said, and moved deliberately toward her.

Christine almost panicked as his arms closed round her, steel hard, pressing against the long, lithe length of his body. If he kissed her he would know just how much she had missed him, she thought desperately. "No!" she exclaimed, tilting her head sideways, outraged that he should have come to her from Eva. It was the wrong move, for instantly his mouth claimed hers in a kiss that devastated her so that she was participating in it joyfully before she knew what she was doing. It was almost as if he were starved of kisses, she thought dazedly as his mouth burnt its way to her earlobe, down her throat and back to her mouth, a notion that was perfectly absurd, under the circumstances.

Then she became aware that diabolically knowing fingers were giving her a new pleasure as they caressed the swell of her breasts, that somehow Mitja was stroking bare, heated flesh. "No!" she protested, her face flaming. "No!" she said faintly, then more firmly, her eyes saucer-round with shock.

"Christine . . . darling," he murmured, pressing little nibbling kisses on her forehead and cheeks.

She was horrified – at herself for wanting to succumb – by what he was doing. Hadn't he said she could never be anything to him? "Go away," she panted, "go back to your Italian woman! Leave me alone!" and at last she wrenched herself from his arms.

"Christine . . . Eva is . . ." he began, a smile lurking around his lips.

"I don't want to hear!" she cried, putting her hands over her ears as she fled, but the bark of laughter that was his answer, which she could not entirely shut out, was neither sardonic nor furious. Strangely, it sounded amused, satisfied, as if her reactions were just as he had predicted.

It appeared Eva was not disposed to leave Kranjska Gora, yet. "It's so restful, after all the exertions of the championships," she told the girls, though they knew quite well that Eva was up dancing until the small hours each night with a group of young men who had gravitated to her within hours of her arrival. Very often her partner was Mitja. "You ought to join us," she cooed to Alex on several occasions, usually in Mitja's presence.

"I don't much care for dancing," Alex always replied, stiffly. Christine loved it, but nothing would have persuaded her to join Eva, unless she were invited specifically, by Mitja.

They saw very little of him. Sometimes Christine wondered why he had bothered to come back at all. Each week he disappeared to Bohinj for two nights. Building work needed to be supervised, he told them. He was still looking for a buyer for the Vitranc. Occasionally he showed strangers around, but he never again requested Christine to act as his hostess. Once or twice she recalled the conversation they had had over the phone about needing a long talk. So far all he seemed to be doing was avoiding her.

And Eva remained.

One June morning Mitja announced, "There's a picnic up at the Erika on Sunday. Shall we all go?" The Erika was a small, old-fashioned family run hotel above Lake Jesna. The lake itself was an idyllic spot, sandy-rimmed and aspen-fringed and reflected in its depths the high peaks where the river which filled it had its source. Christine loved its beauty. "During the summer the Erika puts on the occasional grand barbecue with folk dancing and games and anything else you can think of," he added, "and it doesn't finish until the last person leaves. I think we should all go. Mrs Martinovic too."

"Well, why not," that lady agreed.

On Sunday morning Christine appeared at breakfast wearing jeans and a shirt. Once Mitja had gone, Mrs Martinovic, attired in her best black, admonished her. "You'll be warm enough in a dress if you take a thick cardigan," she said severly. "No girl looks anything but a ninny dancing in trousers."

They traveled there in horse-drawn carts, hay wagons lent for the day, long and narrow with a raised portion running the length of the wagon on which they sat, their clothes protected by an old piece of carpet. Along with several others from the Vitranc, Eva was there too, looking gorgeous in loose casual trousers, a silk shirt and a lot of gold jewelry. She climbed nimbly into the cart and Christine, hampered by her full-skirted pale blue dress covered with tiny daisies, felt impossibly rustic beside the elegant sophistication of the other woman.

By the time everyone had been handed down at the Erika, Eva had disappeared. Christine expected that Mitja would leave them to go and find her but he merely grinned and remarked, "I see Helmut is a very determined young man. She only met him yesterday," as he offered his arm to Mrs Martinovic.

They ate large portions of succulent pork, fragrant with herbs, and drank beer and finished the meal with chunks of cake. Then they sat in the sun replete, with music lulling them to somnolence in the background. Christine felt lazy and content and quite prepared to let the many children run and laugh and dance around them.

Then the folk dancers appeared. The men were

dressed like the bandsmen with red shawls under their vests, the long fringes draped over their shoulders. The girls were in calf-length, full plain-colored skirts, white blouses, embroidered aprons and pretty shawls. Some had chain-belts round their hips and all were wearing white caps with heavily embroidered bands, and as they flew past in the arms of their partners, their hands resting lightly on the men's shoulders, there were flashes of white petticoats and glimpses of white-stockinged thighs.

"The dances tell a story," said Mitja, bending toward Christine, his hand resting against her wrist. "Usually it is of a boy who is courting a girl; sometimes she loves him, sometimes she spurns him, sometimes he courts many girls and they all laugh at him."

"How cruel," said Christine, without thinking.

"Love can be cruel," answered Mitja, but in a low voice so that only she heard. "Don't you think so?" he asked her.

"I—I don't know," she prevaricated.

"The one who is spurned is always made to look a fool." Then his voice lightened, "But I daresay it was his own fault for not making his intentions clear from the first."

"Oh, to be young again," sighed Mrs Martinovic, oblivious to the conversation beside her. "Mitja, you should be with the dancers. Weren't you one of the best in the village when you were a boy?"

"They've already asked me," he replied, "and I think I might . . . on special occasions."

"Have you found a partner?" Mrs Martinovic asked alertly.

"I think I've found just the one," and something in his voice, in the way she knew he was looking at her, gave Christine the impression that it was not Eva to whom he was referring.

The dancers stopped and were applauded. The couples split up, each one choosing a new partner from among the audience. Mrs Martinovic was claimed by a young man. "My nephew," she explained, flustered. Alex was chosen by his friend.

Mitja took Christine's hand. "Come on," he exhorted her and pulled her to her feet, and all at once her full skirts and frilly petticoat seemed entirely appropriate, and she could not have cared whether Eva was there or not. Raddy had danced like this, with Mrs Raddy at Christmas at the Children's Home party and he had taught all the girls the old-fashioned waltz so now, her hands on Mitja's shoulders, his on her waist, Christine swung lightly around the concrete floor as though she were on a cloud.

Afterward he fetched more beer while the uninhibited played silly games and he lay on the grass, stretched out with his eyes shut against the sun, and she sat beside him and steeled herself not to put out a hand to stroke his face or smooth the dark hair away from his forehead, and longed fiercely for the afternoon not to end.

Mrs Martinovic and Alex came away from the games still laughing. "We are going home now," Alex said. "The hay wagon is returning for the last time."

"I'll get my things," and Christine started to rise.

"Don't go," and Mitja's hand imprisoned hers

unerringly though his eyes remained closed, his face turned away from her.

"Certainly not," declared Alex. "I've had two dances and that is quite enough for me, but you and Mitja must stay until the end."

"Perhaps for a little longer," she capitulated without difficulty.

"And don't wait up for us," said Mitja.

The folk dancers returned and Mitja released Christine for just one dance, into the arms of the troupe's leader who complimented her on how well she followed him. Just before dusk the smell of food began wafting across the dance floor and Mitja dragged Christine away to eat again. Fairy light twinkled in the trees around them and the atmosphere changed, for with the darkness there came a dreamy quality over the dancing that had nothing to do with the music or the couples on the concrete circle. Suddenly the pairings seemed less arbitrary, and not all the couples who faded from the light did so for mere food and drink while those who were left had a languid look about them.

It was a night for enchantment, for the fulfillment of impossible, romantic dreams and sensual longings. Christine knew that if, when, she was swept into the protective darkness it would be willingly, so deeply had she fallen under the spell of Mitja's arms and the music. Just as her secret longings were being formulated, Mitja stopped. She stumbled. "You're cold," he said. "We must find your sweater," and, his arm warm round her waist, he led her away.

So easy to go with him, so simple to do as he wished, but, "I'm not cold," she protested.

"Nor tired?" She shook her head. "Then you should be, for I am," he observed. "So I shall wrap you in your thick wool sweater and we shall sit and watch the others, under the stars." He spread his anorak under a tree and they sat on it, close, with their backs to its trunk, his arm around her, her head on his shoulder, listening to the music in the distance.

"You haven't danced with Eva," Christine said, in a small voice into a long silence. For the life of her she couldn't think why she had to introduce the woman's name, then. She had been thinking of the long walk back. The question had come to her lips unbidden, and couldn't be recalled.

"Eva came with Helmut," he replied quietly. "They left a long time ago. Didn't you see them?"

"No," she whispered.

"And I came with you, and I danced with you." She knew he was going to kiss her even before he finished his sentence. "And now I am going to kiss you, as all pretty girls should be kissed at picnics, so don't imagine you can prevent it."

Far from preventing it, she turned in his arms and kissed him back. She kissed him with all her heart, such was the magic of the night, and when he lifted her so that she sat in his lap she went willingly, with a sudden, fierce desire that his kisses would never stop.

"Beautiful, beautiful Christine," he murmured against the hollow of her throat, his fingers sure at the dainty shaped buttons of her bodice and the lace that covered her underneath, and when he bared the full curves of her breasts, pearly-white in the moonlight, to his ardent gaze, she could only gasp in delight as he kissed them to a rosy glow.

Elation flared in her; elation that she could so stir him. Without thinking, she undid the buttons of his shirt and pressed her lips to his warm flesh and ran her hands over his muscular frame before returning to caress his cheeks with a delicate touch. Her whole body glowed, warm and giving, but her mind, ever more cautious than her body, won the battle with her senses and the little moan that escaped her lips conveyed to Mitja that she was scared; scared, perhaps, not so much by him but of her own reactions to the way in which he was making her feel.

Reluctantly, his breath ragged, Mitja rearranged the frothy lace and maneuvered buttons clumsily into buttonholes before he set her on her feet. Then he stroked her neck and kissed the corner of her mouth and said with a not quite steady voice, "Pretty girls get kissed by the lake, too, on picnic nights."

"How do you know?" her own voice quivered.

"I've heard a thing or two."

Would he, one day, be telling about the English girl he had kissed on a picnic night? She took his hand, because that seemed an unfair assumption, and not even pretending that she could not see, and he squeezed it and kept it clasped firmly in his, and when they had left the lights of the Erika far behind and she really could not see he drew her close to his side as they wandered slowly down the road.

They came upon the lake and they left the road and went down to the water's edge, and they looked on the lovely scene, the moon high in the sky, the silvery reflections of moon and tree and peak and cloud, and she did not wait to be kissed but held her face up to his in silent invitation and put her arms around his neck and wished the moment would last for ever.

"Moments like this should last for ever," he whispered against her lips.

"Memories of them do," she assured him.

"That sounds sad, as though nothing ever comes of them."

"Perhaps that depends."

"On what?"

"Oh, on the phase of the moon," she replied guardedly.

"And will you grant my wish, beautiful moon maiden, or will you flee from my arms like a wraith?"

"Perhaps," she murmured, unable to decipher what his steady gaze was telling her.

Mitja sighed abruptly. "I wish . . ." he began.

"Only kisses," she answered at once, uncomfortably, for suddenly his seriousness alarmed her. "Kisses on picnic nights, not wishes. Do girls get kissed anywhere else between the lake and home?" she queried, totally unaware she was courting danger.

Mitja's breathing became ragged as he answered, "Some get spanked for flirting outrageously," he warned her, "the rest get kissed at the front door," he added quickly, the startled-fawn look in her eyes squeezing his heart-strings painfully. In the moonlight it was impossible to see into the depths of those eyes. His arm went

around her again, protectively. "Come home,
Christine."

For Christine the euphoria of the picnic lasted a
mere three days. Alex and she had just ordered
coffee in the square after a walk when Christine
remembered that Mrs Martinovic had asked her
to fetch something from the supermarket for that
evening. "I'll only be five minutes," she told
Alex. "So stupid, when we've passed the shop
already, but I might as well get them now as
later."

The supermarket was crowded and Christine
could not find what she wanted at first, then
while she was hesitating over sizes a familiar,
disembodied voice said, "This is what you want,
isn't it?"

She looked up startled. Mitja! But she was
alone, for the moment, and the voice was coming
clearly from the other side of the stack.

"Yes, that's right. I'd better take two of the
small ones." Eva!

"Why bother? You'll get it in Rome easily
enough."

"Too much of a nuisance. I'll be too busy to go
shopping."

"Ah. The life of an Italian socialite," he teased.
"I'll miss you," he told her, then, but not so
quietly that Christine did not hear every inflec-
tion of his voice. Her heart missed a beat. She
had to go – this was a private conversation – but
they would see her.

"Perhaps, for a time," Eva conceded. "Not for
long, though, my dear. You have too many distractions."

"Tourists come, tourists go," he agreed. "Not that many are all that distracting."

"I wasn't thinking of the tourists," and she made the term sound an insult, "more of your little friend."

"My . . . ? You mean Christine?"

"Your little friend. Not that she's all that little. One might almost call her Amazonian."

"Some men prefer their women not to look as though they would break at a touch," Mitja said, almost defensively.

Eva laughed mockingly. "And you just like to have the handling of them, I know. Well, when I'm gone you may devote all your time and energy to her. Shall I hazard a guess just how long it will take you to bring her to boiling-point? Why, Mitja *darling*, I do believe you're embarrassed," and her laugh trilled out above the babel of the supermarket shoppers.·

Christine leant her forehead against one of the uprights in front of her. She felt a little dizzy and quite unable to move. "Are you all right, *Gospodica*?" an anxious male voice asked above her right shoulder.

Christine nodded numbly, then felt impelled to explain. "The heat . . . you know. I'm going in a moment," assuring him that she was not going to faint on his shop floor.

She quite missed the angry altercation that had broken out in low tones on the other side of the stack and only caught Eva's final, dulcet reply, " . . . men like you. So, good luck, Mitja dear," before she swept down the aisle and out of the shop.

Christine, sick at heart, humiliated, *furious* with

herself at having fallen into the age-old trap of staying to listen when she should have known she would hear no good of herself, did not stop to consider the ambiguity of Eva's last words. Righteous anger sparkled in her eyes as she recalled how near to succumbing to Mitja she had been at the picnic. How he must be rejoicing at his conquest! Eva and he deserved each other, predators that they were. What a pity she was leaving, and Christine prayed that one of Eva's countrymen would hoist her with her own petard, and soon!

As for Mitja . . . at least now she knew exactly where she was with Mitja Minic! A long talk, indeed! All he had ever wanted was a talk that would end in bed!

Alex regarded the two spots of color on Christine's cheeks when she rejoined her and remarked, "You look flustered. You were ages. I thought at least you must have been abducted."

"The place was full," Christine replied. "I loathe supermarkets!" she said.

"So I see. This coffee's cold. Want another?"

"Why not?"

"Did you know Eva is leaving tomorrow?" Alex, who had also seen Eva and Mitja come out of the shop, asked casually.

"I had heard," dryly.

"She made a sudden decision the morning of the picnic. I talked to her then, did you know? Apparently her family wants her to marry the son of a banking family they've known for years. She has decided the time has come to agree – retire at the top of her form, so to speak."

"Poor banker. I hope he knows what he's getting." As she said it Christine's conscience smote her. Had she misjudged the situation? No, of course not.

"She's quite nice, really. Has—has anything happened to upset you?" she asked hesitantly at Christine's snort of disbelief.

"No. No, nothing. So you had a little talk with Mistress Eva?" Her speculation that the title was apt was like a barb.

"She said Mitja had a lot to do with her decision – that she had been very depressed after the championships and that he had helped her through a difficult period. He would. He's like that."

Again Christine wondered . . . but the conversation she had overheard had been real enough, the meaning of the words clear, to her.

"I expect Mitja will miss her," Alex observed, dead-pan.

"Then we must make sure he has other . . . distractions." Once more Alex gave her an odd look, but Christine finished her coffee and gathered up her purchases. "Mrs Martinovic will want these. We'd better get back now."

# 9

Christine found she could not be angry with Mitja for long – especially when he seemed not to know how furious she was with him and acted as though he were not missing Eva a bit. On the other hand she knew she must be wary of him from now on. Then, not long after Eva's departure he asked Christine to partner him in the folk dancing at the next picnic at Erika.

"Me!" she expostulated. "I can't."

He raised an eyebrow. "Why ever not?"

"One, I don't have a costume; two, I don't know the steps . . ."

He roared with laughter. "I'm glad you put first things first. Naturally it will be far more difficult to find you a costume at short notice than for you to learn the steps."

"No problem about either," Mrs Martinovic, who was present, said complacently. "Certainly not about learning the steps from what I saw of Christine's dancing at the first picnic, and as for the costume, she may have mine." Then she burst into merry laughter at the look of incredulity on the faces of the girls. "If you could see those expressions . . ."

"I'm sorry, Mrs Martinovic," Christine apologised contritely. "We didn't mean to seem either rude or ungracious but . . ."

"Though we're about the same height I'm three

times your weight," Mrs Martinovic leant across
the table and patted Christine's hand. "Don't
fret, dear. I was slender, like you, on my wedding
day, and tucked away in the attic is the costume
I wore then. When I grew too fat for it I put it
away. I always hoped my daughter would wear
it one day, but she isn't in the least bit interested.
So . . . so, I should be very happy for you to
borrow it and wear it as it should be worn."

Christine was very moved. Alex became practical. "Mitja, you must find out which dances
they're doing."

"We'll try the costume on at once," insisted
Mrs Martinovic, "just in case there are a few
alterations to be done."

She was right about the fit. The skirt was green
and heavy and swung like a bell about Christine's
slender legs; the shawl was green, too, and
embroidered with pink and gold roses and
fringed with black silk. The petticoats were still
stiff and smelled sweetly of lavender and, along
with the cap and its headband, heavily encrusted
with gold thread, only required pressing. Mrs
Martinovic shook her head sadly over the blouse
which had turned yellow but Christine said she
would use one of her own.

Christine was convinced the rehearsal was
going to be a disaster, but her body picked up
the rhythms and her brain the steps so easily,
despite her nerves, that, with the occasional
nudge in the right direction from a partner who
knew exactly what he was doing, she made fewer
mistakes than couples who had been dancing
together for years.

Josip, the troupe leader, took her to one side

after the rehearsal. "Mitja was right," he told her. "You are good and will do very well on Sunday." He regarded her steadily, though a little apprehensively. "There is just one thing . . . you are not Slovenian. One forgets. You do not . . . forgive me . . . you do not dance with your whole body, only your feet. You must always remember that the dances tell a story. In the story your partner is wooing you, you are willing to be courted. You must not be so stiff in Mitja's arms. I would swear you were not stiff in mine. Could it be that you are out of sympathy with Mitja?" he asked delicately.

Her face flamed. "N-no," she replied hastily. "Perhaps I was thinking too much about my feet . . . the steps," she said, not altogether untruthfully.

"Then that is all right. On Sunday you will look as though you enjoy being in his arms, that you would rather be in his arms than those of any other young man. Then you will dance beautifully."

Relax and look at him, she told herself on Sunday as they stood under the trees waiting for the band to strike the opening bars of the first dance, that was all Josip meant, and it was not hard to look at Mitja, and she did so under her lashes, covertly, as he stood beside her, handsome in loden green knee breeches, the pink in his shawl, partly hidden by his black vest, matching hers, his red feather standing cockily at the side of his hat. She would not have changed places with any other woman there.

The other couples, she noticed, were equally absorbed in each other, standing close together,

one or two of the women smoothing imaginary
wrinkles out of her partner's costume, the men
touching a wrist, a cheek, proclaiming proprietor-
ial right. Mitja's arm stole around Christine's
waist and without conscious thought her body
curved toward it. It was almost as though she
belonged there, in the circle of his arm, the two
of them together in a patch of dappled sunlight,
waiting to dance for the entertainment of others
in an idyllic mountain retreat.

There was a rustle as the musicians settled
themselves. Mitja turned her face toward him,
putting a finger under her chin, bringing it close
enough so that her eyes were forced to meet his.
"Just relax and look at me," he said, "meltingly,
like that, and forget your feet."

"You won't like it if I forget them altogether,"
and she tried a chuckle that didn't quite work for
the idyll was only an idyll and it was necessary
for her to remember to keep her feet firmly on
the ground, metaphorically, for she could not
bare her heart again and risk it getting trampled.

He gave her a little shake as if he knew what
she was really thinking and said, "Your feet will
be all right, so relax and enjoy the dancing. You
were as stiff as a board at the rehearsal."

"Oh, so sorry," she began in mock outrage,
but the finger under her chin moved swiftly to
cover her lips and then, in full view of the troupe,
it was replaced by his mouth in a long, hard kiss.

Christine could not prevent the instant soften-
ing of her lips as they responded to him, nor
could she help the melting of her limbs that
seemed to flow into his, but through her heightened awareness of Mitja and what he was doing

to her she heard, distinctly, a titter and a female voice say, "Well, there's a first time for everything. I've never seen Mitja kiss a girl in public before," and her partner answer, "You must admit he has very good taste," in a tone full of admiration.

She grew hot with embarrassment and tried to pull away, only it appeared that Mitja had other ideas and it was a long minute before his hold on her slackened sufficiently for her to release herself.

"That's better," said Josip beside her, before she could regain her equilibrium, laughing openly. "Now you look like a girl who's just been kissed very satisfactorily and expects to be kissed again, very soon. That's much better. Now you can't help but dance as though you're enjoying yourself."

She looked from Mitja to Josip and back again. They were both laughing at her. Men, she thought disgustedly, and her lip curled! They all seemed to think a crook of the finger, a touch of the lips and you were theirs for the taking without strings, and for a moment she was sorely tempted to pick up her full skirts and flee.

"Not laughing at you," Mitja said softly, "with you, I promise," and at the put-on, purposefully hang-dog expression on his face, her insides turned over. A crook of the finger, a touch of the lips, and she would do anything he wanted, and that was what was so dangerous, for her peace of mind. But the music had begun and Mitja's arm around her waist was compelling and she hadn't the strength to do anything but follow where he led . . . and she was enjoying herself:

the rhythms, the steps, the music, and the man who partnered her so well.

Was it all play-acting? Were they both pretending with their speaking glances, the delicate turn of the head? If so, it was very heady stuff for, true to the story the dances told, he seemed to be wooing her. His gaze said eloquently that he found her beautiful and the downward tilt of her eyelids said that she knew he did and was glad. His hand lingered on her slender waist and told her without words that he found her desirable, and the curve of her hip, the brush of her breast against his arm said that she knew it to be so. The smile on his lips, tender and for her alone, said that he was waiting for the moment when no one else was there, and the teasing glance she gave him as they were parted in the dance told him he would have to catch her first – but that the capture would not be hard and the conquering very sweet. And at the end he took her hand and kissed her wrist and his eyes seemed to say that he wished he was kissing her mouth; and in the applause that followed she came back to earth with a little bump.

"Those two were very good," Christine heard herself and Mitja identified by a middle-aged couple as they passed. "It takes practise to dance together so well, or . . ."

But what else was said she missed for Josip was clapping Mitja on the back and nodding his approval at her. "That was good. You may be sure I'll be in touch for another session, very soon."

It must have been only play-acting, for once again Mitja was coolly formal. "Twenty minutes of general dancing now," he reminded her as he led her toward the audience. "I'm going to find Mrs Martinovic," he said as they separated, "and you may find yourself a gorgeous young man," but then to her amazement he added, "though if you look at him in the way you looked at me I'll thump him and wring your neck!"

He was only joking, naturally, but the good-looking young man in front of her, grinning hugely and obviously waiting for her to choose him, appeared to have taken the warning literally, for his manner was most respectful, much to her amusement.

Both Mrs Martinovic and Alex were very complimentary. "You might have been dancing together for years," commented Alex, "you looked so sure of yourselves. Or at least have done a sight more practicing than I know you have."

"Or have a close rapport," said Mrs Martinovic. "Dancing partners are born, not made, a little like marriage partners," she ended, and gave a tiny sniff.

"What do you think, Christine?" Mitja asked over her shoulder, making her jump for she had not seen him join them. "Do you think marriage and dancing partners are made in heaven?"

She could not look at him but she did believe in marriage, and in marriage for love, and he deserved a truthful answer. "I don't know," she said, "but I don't think anything comes easily."

"Quite right," said Mrs Martinovic approvingly, but then her attention was caught and both she and Alex drifted away.

"So you have strong ideas about marriage,"

Mitja observed casually. "I like that," he added, not at all casually.

"Certainly I do. Don't most women?" asked Christine firmly.

"Perhaps, eventually, but they can lead a man who loves them a pretty dance, to coin a phrase, before they capitulate, even in a dance," he said, his voice low but full of meaning.

She felt his eyes boring into her, his will setting out to destroy the barriers she had erected as soon as they had come off the concrete circle. She gritted her teeth. As often as he wanted her to she would seem to play-act the village maiden in love – just so long as no words of confession were to be expected afterward. It might be masochism on her part but it had to be like that for her self-preservation. After all, how could he expect her to trust him? First he was attracted to her, then he decided she would not do, then it was second thoughts and *then* Eva came on the scene. He must not be allowed to trample all over her again. Yet she did love him.

So, if they were to dance regularly now, she would just have to make the most of each precious moment.

Then, one evening when the weather seemed set fair for a few days, Mitja suggested an expedition to Christine. "You've been working too hard recently," he observed. "You need a day off, and so do I."

He had it all planned. They took an early morning bus to Ratece and struck off up the Planica valley. At their first halt he spread the map out in front of her. "At the top of this valley we turn off the road and go up into the mountains," he told her.

"Are you expecting me to do any rock climbing?" Christine asked cautiously.

"Goodness no!" he reassured her. "Only the sort of walking anyone could do."

"One day I think I'd like to try. If I'm still here," she added quickly.

He glanced at her strangely before answering. "One day I'll take you," he promised, "but today we'll walk up to Vratica then come down the drovers" road to finish at Jesna with the evening sun in the right place for the best reflections in the water. I thought you'd like that."

"Yes," she agreed faintly. Then a small imp of mischief prompted her to add, "Was it just Jesna in the evening sun you were aiming for?"

There was a twinkle of appreciation in his eyes that dried her throat in trepidation. *Why* had she said that! "I could have thought of a shorter route," Mitja answered. Then he said, "But, yes, pretty girls do get kissed at Jesna in the setting sun."

"I'll remember that when I flag," she managed, thinking how weak were her resolutions.

"It's an easy walk, you'll not do that," he said as he hauled her to her feet, "only it might be starlight at Jesna if our stops are too long and too frequent." Casually, he stooped and plucked a small cerise cyclamen that was growing by the side of the path. "Wear this for me, Christine," he urged her, and his fingers were not quite steady as he fastened the little flower into her buttonhole, and for once he avoided her eyes,

and she held her breath, but he did not kiss her,
then.

The drovers' road was deserted. "This is the
way the animals were herded to and from the
high pastures," Mitja told her when they stopped
for lunch. "There's another one on the other side
of the mountain."

"Is it used nowadays?" asked Christine inter-
estedly, handing him a chicken joint. The road
was wide enough for two small carts to pass and
descended in a series of hairpin bends at a gentle
gradient. It was grassy and its edges were delin-
eated by boulders and, after some of the terrain
they had been walking on, it was soft to the feet.

"I doubt it," replied Mitja, accepting a hunk of
bread. "It's so much easier to transport animals
by road now, though I daresay local farmers use
sections of it."

Christine would have liked to have lingered in
the companionable silence that fell then, warmed
by the sun, where the high peaks seemed close
enough to touch. She wished he would always
be like this, safe, undemanding. When he had
finished the last of his fruit juice they packed
away their things to go.

"For a girl used to a sedentary life, you don't
do badly in the mountains," he commented.
"Here, let me," and he knelt down to adjust a
bootlace which had loosened.

"I'm sure it's the thought of my reward that
keeps me going," she answered demurely,
entirely without thought.

"Reward?" He paused in what he was doing,
and glanced up at her.

"At Jesna," she said into the smiling dark

brown eyes at her feet, her heart beginning its familiar thump.

He chuckled as he stood up. "I could so easily be tempted into dalliance here and now, my dearest Christine, but if we dally here, I shall not have you off the mountain before dark . . . and then what would Mrs Martinovic say!"

She understood neither herself, nor him, truly she did not, she thought as she paced him down the drovers" road. He spoke airily of dalliance, *dalliance indeed*, in the same breath as he called her his "dearest Christine." He knew how she loved the lake at Jesna and he had chosen deliberately to finish their walk there, had even promised to kiss her at Jesna, and the thrill of physical longing that swept over her then caused her to stumble where the road was smooth.

Mitja shot out a hand to grasp her elbow. "Careful!" he warned.

"My ankle does that sometimes." It was, after all, the one she had broken. "I was miles away," she added truthfully.

He nodded. "So was I. At Jesna," and there was that in his expression that turned her heart over. "I'll not get you there if you break an ankle."

After what Eva had said, she was sure the night of the picnic had meant no more to him than any casual encounter, she thought as she had thought before, or any of those other times he had kissed her. Everyone knew that men kissed girls unthinkingly. So it had been the first time any man had caressed her as Mitja had done. He could not have known that; could not possibly have guessed how the feel of his lips and hands

on her breast had ignited what had hitherto lain
dormant. Often, after they had danced with the
troupe, since that night she had waited with
anticipation/trepidation for him to make the
opportunity for them to be alone together; had
wondered why he had not. His behavior had
been circumspect, entirely proper, too proper,
almost indifferent.

"You're flagging, Christine," he remarked,
stopping.

"Just admiring the scenery," she prevaricated.

"I'd rather you admired me," he said, "or at
least took notice of me," and he took her hand
in his, his thumb warm on her quickened pulse.

She wished the summer was over, that both he
and Alex were gone, that she had never met
either of the Minics! No, that was untrue, and
ungrateful. She wished . . . that they were at
Jesna and she could cause the world to stop.
Dalliance? She had never wanted dalliance with
Mitja, nor a light-hearted kiss, kisses. Somehow
she did not think she could ever dance with him
again, pretending to be the village maiden in
love. The game was over. And the summer was
almost gone. She accepted her reward at the end
of a tiring day, her lips cool to his touch. She
decided her heart was breaking.

"I had hoped . . ." he murmured afterward,
"I've tired you out, haven't I? You've quite gone
away from me. And you dropped my flower,
too." He sounded so sad she could have wept,
except that she would not have known why.

"I had it in my buttonhole. I'm sorry," and she
was not just apologizing for the lost flower.

He kissed her on the forehead. "Now is not

the time, is it . . . you are too tired . . . maybe tomorrow?"

For a moment hope flared in her eyes, but he could not have meant what she needed to hear, she knew that. "Or tomorrow . . . or tomorrow," she agreed lightly, as if there were all the tomorrows anybody could every want.


Later she thought, if only she had known what was to happen she would have answered him differently. But she was tired, almost exhausted.

They arrived home to find Alex waiting with two telephone messages for Mitja. "There was a call from a man in Ljubljana this afternoon," she told her brother. "He wants you to call him back immediately. And Igor Fattuta phoned from Bohinj."

Mitja consulted his watch. "I'd better call them both straight away," he said.

"I'll have a bath while you're making the calls," said Christine, suddenly determinedly cheerful. "Then we'll both have a beer and tell Alex all about our splendid walk." She was also being tactful as she sensed the brother and sister wanted to speak privately.

When she emerged again twenty minutes later feeling considerably less jaded, the atmosphere was charged with barely suppressed excitement. "Do I get the impression it would be considered more polite to ask what it's all about than to keep quite?" she inquired cautiously.

"Mitja has had a wonderful offer for the Vitranc," Alex burst out.

"Not only is the money right," said Mitja, "I

like the people very much. I think they will do really well for the place."

"It means we can both go back to Bohinj almost immediately. Such a relief."

"Oh Mitja!" Selfish dismay warred with pleasure for him. "That's what you wanted all along, isn't it? You must be so pleased. I am glad for you, both," Christine said, her pleasure for him winning hands down after all.

"I shall probably be ready to move in a few weeks," Mitja said. "Let's drink to success and the end of summer. Wine, I think," and he handed the girls a glass each and raised his own in a toast.

Christine smiled at the two. "That's marvelous," she said softly, her eyes not quite meeting anyone's.

"What will you do at the end of the summer, Christine?" Mitja asked abruptly.

"Yes, Christine," Alex said uncomfortably. "What about you? What will you do?"

Christine shrugged. "I've been thinking about that," which was true enough. Winter, she thought, began for her that moment, cold and dreary.

"I'd forgotten about you," Alex said miserably.

"You needn't worry," Christine said firmly. "I shan't give up the translating . . . it's going far too well. I might get a flat in Zagreb . . ."

". . . and come and visit us? That would be fun," commented Alex.

"Or I might go back to London," Christine continued, as if Alex had not interrupted. "The publishers don't really mind where I work from. On the other hand, I might even do some tour-

ing. I'd rather like to see something of Montene-
gro and the south. I'll let you know when I've
made up my mind finally, but I wouldn't count
on me being around after, say, the middle of
September," she finished, as though she were
discussing catching a local bus.

"Well, that sounds reasonably final. At least
we know where we all stand, don't we?" Mitja's
face and voice were carefully controlled and only
an observant onlooker could have noticed the
disappointment at the back of his dark eyes.

Christine was looking at the crestfallen Alex.
"I expect I shall turn up, like the proverbial bad
penny," she said, "so you won't be getting rid
of me completely. But that's enough about me. I
want to hear more of your plans for Bohinj."
Mitja must be angry with her, she decided,
because she had not consulted him about her
future plans. She was quite amazed. How
unreasonable of him!

Adroitly Christine managed to avoid any direct
confrontation with him that evening. He would
have cooled down by morning, she thought, and
come to the conclusion that she was doing the
sensible thing. Then their showdown would be
less acrimonious. Common sense told her that
face him she would have to, sometime soon.

# 10

Christine was preparing for bed when there was a knock at her door. Mitja was glowering at her when she opened it a crack and he was inside the room with the door securely fastened before she had time to protest. "I want to talk to you," he began, in a low, fierce voice.

"So I see," she observed, as coolly as she could in the face of such unmannerly behavior. She had the presence of mind to realize that if she were inadequately dressed at least her summery cotton gown held up by thin straps was opaque.

"You knew I wanted to talk to you!" he accused her. "Why did you avoid me deliberately this evening?"

"At the lake you said it would do tomorrow!" she hissed, outraged. "I'm not going to talk to you about anything, here and now, and if you think I'm going to let you browbeat me at all because you are angry that I never consulted you about my plans, you are very much mistaken, so get out of my room before you wake the whole house!"

"Mrs Martinovic sleeps like a log," he smiled wolfishly, and unaccountably her heart missed a beat, "and Alex . . ." he shrugged. "What I have to say won't take long."

"Tomorrow . . ." she pleaded faintly, feeling

sure she knew what he wanted to say, and not wanting to have to find an answer, yet.

"Things have changed. At the lake I thought there would be plenty of tomorrows . . . I didn't expect Igor's call . . . I have to leave very early tomorrow . . . after all this time, how dared you announce casually that you have plans to go south in the middle of September!" He was pale under his tan. There were lines of strain etched deeply around his mouth.

She saw this as she began to protest mildly, "I didn't . . ." This was not what she had intended.

"Christine . . ." he interrupted, "how could you think of making plans like that without consulting me first!"

"I haven't!" The denial was hot, emphatic.

"You must know I have plans."

"Oh, I was hearing about them the entire evening," she replied, a little bitterly. "Mitja, will you leave this room, at once, please?"

"Plans concerning you," he finished doggedly.

"And I can guess what they are," she said frantically, "and I don't want to know." Dalliance, she thought wildly, turning toward the door.

"That's not what you've made me believe these last few weeks," he said sharply.

"I don't know what you mean," she was almost there.

Quick as a flash he moved, and she found herself imprisoned with her back to it, his body hard against hers, preventing any movement, his hands either side of her head so that she was forced to look him in the face. "Oh, yes you do," he answered softly. "You've flirted openly with

me all summer, Christine. Are you telling me
now that you're nothing but a little tease?"

She did not pretend to misunderstand him
again. "That was play-acting," she replied
instantly, loftily.

"And what is this?" His hands held her face
imprisoned, uptilted, as he bent and claimed her
lips. It was a cruel kiss, savage in its intent to
master. Christine beat a fist against Mitja's
shoulder, once, twice . . . and then there was no
more fight left in her and she hung against the
door, held upright only by the man's strength.
Then, knowing her mastered, his hands moved
swiftly from her face to her body with sweeping,
intimate caresses of neck and breast, waist and
hip and thigh that caused her heart to beat suffocatingly, her skin under the thin cotton night-
gown to glow burningly hot and her senses to
reel.

There came a moment when he took his lips
from hers and she moaned his name. "*Mitja!*" It
was not a plea to be set free but a more female
cry, to be claimed, and in that moment she did
not care whether it was only dalliance in mind so
long as he made her his.

Then he spun her around violently. "Look at
yourself!" his harsh voice grated in her ear, his
hard fingers grasping naked shoulders. "Is this
play-acting?"

There was a figure in front of her, disheveled
hair, swollen mouth, purple-dark eyes. Herself.
Reflected in the mirror. One strap of the night-
gown had broken and one white breast was
exposed, the nipple brown and throbbingly taut
against the paleness of her skin. The image of

herself cleared her head and a gasp came from her lips. "Mitja, please!" and she had no idea whether it was in pleasure from his handling of her or pain from the humiliation of it.

"Play-acting?" he demanded, again.

"No," she moaned.

The next moment she was lying across the bed. "There won't be a tomorrow, will there Christine," he stated bitterly. "Perhaps tease is the wrong word. I think you're a coward, a woman who won't ever acknowledge her feelings for a man because she's afraid of getting hurt. You know, I almost think I prefer the Evas of this world. At least they are totally honest about what they want."

Regardless of her state of near-nudity, Christine had hauled herself upright. "You've done it again!" she raged. "Every time you've ever been-been nice to me, you've always succeeded in bringing Eva between us. I think it's a great pity you didn't marry Eva!" she snapped. "Then at least I'd have been spared your attentions," she added melodramatically.

"Nice to you! *Nice*," he growled, and she flinched at the sound of his voice.

"I didn't ask Eva to marry me," he said coldly, his hand on the door knob, "because it wasn't Eva I fell in love with. It was you. That was the real pity because now I realize that has absolutely no future in it. I wouldn't marry a woman who couldn't bear to have me touch her, a woman who is incapable of loving me as I love – loved her."

She sat there, her mouth inelegantly agape, and the door opened and closed with an awful finality. After a moment she lay down again, sobbing her heartbreak into the feather pillow.

Why speak to her like that then cast her aside? Why show her herself at her most vulnerable and not take advantage of the situation? How unkind he was. How cruel of him not to have taken advantage of her . . . No. No! She shot off the bed and sat down weakly at the dressing table. That was not what she had meant . . . it was a slip of the tongue . . .

A Freudian slip, she grimaced. The only play-acting she had ever done with Mitja had been this evening when she had pretended she could walk away without a backward glance in mid-September. She must have been convincing, she supposed. He had believed her anyway. It was all to do with pride, of course, his and hers. How easy it would be to give in to pride, give in to the wave of tiredness that was urging her to sleep and in sleep to forget her humiliation. But the summer was almost over, and quite suddenly her pride seemed a most unattractive thing. What if she went to him now, without pride, and told him she really didn't want to go; that she wanted nothing more than to stay, with him, for as long as he wanted her, and in whatever way he wanted her?

A tremor shook her. How terrible it would be if he really did prefer Eva. And if it were dalliance? At least her initiation would leave her with memories. Resolutely Christine refused to consider a third alternative, that Mitja had been deceiving them both, that he loved her still. So she knotted the broken strap of her gown, opened the door softly and tiptoed down the stairs to Mitja's room, thinking as she did so: what of Mrs Martinovic? But she was a heavy sleeper, and Alex was down the corridor. Then she thought: what if Mitja were already in bed and asleep? Then she berated herself for the coward he had called her, and the next minute she was inside his room.

He was standing by the window, his back to the door, a dejected droop to his strong shoulders.

It was going to be all right, she knew exultantly. He was as miserable as she. "Mitja . . ." she whispered, and it turned out a croak.

He spun around. Instantly a blaze of hope – joy – swept over his features. He was, unmistakably, glad she had come.

She thought: I'm not going to get away with just explanations.

He said, not very evenly, "Have you come to call me more names, or have you come for another reason, Christine?"

She thought: he's making it my choice, not forcing me in any way, this time. She was glad it didn't make it any easier. She said, "Not to call you names, at least, not rude ones." His mouth quirked. Suddenly his tiredness was gone. She went on bravely, "You were right. You've always been right, Mitja. I've come because I . . ."

He didn't allow her to finish. "Then, stop talking, love, and come here."

She went into his arms, and there were no explanations needed. His need for her was in his kisses and caresses, the intent expression on his face as he slipped off the torn gown and laid her on his bed. Then he was all gentleness, all tenderness as he touched and caressed, bringing her to a frenzy of longing that opened her to him; and he took her with a ferocious tenderness that had her gasping and clinging to him frantically until the world that was their two bodies subsided into a small sigh, and two tears that were entirely joyful escaped out of the corner of her eye.

She lay in his arms, with her eyes closed, held to his heart. He stroked her face and discovered the moisture and he shifted so that he could gaze down at her and kiss away the dampness. "Poor love," he murmured. "You took me by surprise. I was a lot rougher than I intended to be."

"Intended to be?" she parried, archly. Held against him, she was self-confidently provocative.

He caught his breath. "Intended . . . intend. Christine . . . if you look at me like that I . . ."

She smiled up at him.

At first she was sweetly responsive but it wasn't enough – not for Mitja who demanded her total surrender, nor for Christine who now gave, joyfully.

Afterward he said, wonderingly, "I never knew a woman could be like you, so generous, so ardent."

She said, "I never imagined there could be such ecstasy."

For a time they were gentle with each other, their hands stroking, their lips brushing softly across the other's skin. Then Mitja said consideringly, "Though I always knew you had it in you to be passionate."

*How* did he? Well, loving Mitja that would have

to follow. She would have liked to have said so but she was still a little shy of him. Instead, "You intended to find out?" she gurgled.

His kiss was swift, urgent. But, "It shouldn't have been the result of a quarrel," he said remorsefully.

She had quite forgotten. It would do, tomorrow. "Something had to resolve it," she said practically. "I'm sure it was as good a way as any."

"Quite the best," he agreed. "Remind me to quarrel with you frequently," but the way he held her and kissed her told her almost better than his words of endearment that their energies were in future to be used to please each other rather than rowing, and as he bent his head to her breast she felt suffused with love.

She woke cramped, just before dawn. Mitja was sleeping on his stomach, one arm flung across her thighs, the other trailing over the edge of the narrow bed. She smiled with pure happiness, settled him with infinite care, and crept back to her attic room. When she woke the second time it was with the same feeling of intense happiness. Tomorrow was here. Today Mitja would tell her he loved her . . . it came to her that he had said many things in the night, but not actually that. She would give him the opportunity very soon. Then she saw the time, and realized with a sinking heart that Mitja had said he was leaving early. Could he have gone already? He could.

"You look rough," commented Alex with devastating frankness when Christine finally appeared.

"I feel it."

"Was yesterday too much for you?"

"A great deal too much!"

"My brother should have known better."

"Yes!" She was stiff and sore and the *double entendre* made her eyes fill with tears but the worst hurt lay elsewhere.

"Have I missed something?" Alex asked, mystified.

Christine sniffed. "No." She blew her nose. "What is there to miss?"

"That's what I ask myself." Then her eyes widened. "Mitja went up to your room last night. I thought it was Mrs Martinovic – except she doesn't usually stir after ten. I hope everything is all right?"

"So do I," Christine answered softly, not trying to deceive Alex. "Relationships can be very complex," she commented obscurely, and sighed. So he had gone without saying goodbye. He had said he had loved her. In the night she was almost sure he loved her still. Now it seemed it could only have been dalliance.

Like the tomorrow he had promised her once before, it was long in coming. Mitja remained in Bohinj, his reasons unexplained. Even Alex, to whom he had spoken on the phone, was uncommunicative. "Some business or other, I expect. He'll be here eventually."

Eventually. But that wasn't enough. Not after what had passed between them. So, the one time in her life she had gambled she had lost. So be it. She began to make arrangements. The sooner she could leave the better it would be, for everyone. She decided to make Sarajevo her base for the next few months since it was essential to have an address to which her professors could send their articles for her to translate. She went to the university to discuss it, and it was made so easy. Within forty-eight hours it was all fixed: somewhere to stay, addresses of people to meet, a whole new life opening up for her. It was what she wanted, wasn't it?

"You can't go without saying goodbye to Mitja!" Alex protested fiercely, when Christine explained she would be leaving Kranjska Gora earlier than she had expected. "He'll be devastated! He'll be furious, with me, for letting you go! Christine, please change your mind!"

Almost she wavered. But, "It's all arranged," she said, obdurately, "for the day after tomorrow."

Alex continued to try to dissuade her for a while, but realizing then it was no use she subsided to a somewhat sulky silence. After telling Christine roundly that she was a fool, it was Mrs Martinovic who helped with the packing.

Dinner that final night was a subdued meal. After it, Christine decided she could take no more. "I'm going for a walk," she declared.

"Anywhere special?" inquired Mrs Martinovic.

"Probably Lake Jesna," Christine shrugged. "It's a lovely night."

It was: peaceful, quiet and serene, with the moon reflected in the still waters of the lake. It was so beautiful she could hardly bear it. Into the quiet, moonlit night, under the stars, there came a crunch of gravel. Christine hoped whoever it was would leave her alone. She did not feel like company that night.

"There you are," he said.

Mitja!

She gasped, swung around and the next minute she was in his arms, not knowing how she had got there or who had made the first move, but in his arms where she had always wanted to be.

"Oh! I love you! I love you! I love you!" she cried urgently, over and over again.

She felt, rather than heard, a muffled chuckle. She stopped, appalled, horrified, humiliated. Would she never learn!

"That's better," he declared. "Now, perhaps, I can get a word in?"

"Mitja . . ." she murmured uncertainly, and began to pull away from him.

He tightened his grip. "Christine! Dearest Christine . . ."

Then his lips were on hers, hungrily, bruisingly, his fingers hard on her cheeks and throat as if only by the roughest contact could he prove to himself that he was with her again; and she was kissing him back wildly, matching his ferocity, the tears of joy streaming down her cheeks and wetting his hands.

The salt of her tears alerted him to her distress. "My love. How I must have hurt you," he muttered brokenly, and tenderly he touched the point under her jaw where his thumbs had dug into her softness.

"Hurt me!" she exclaimed dazedly. "But I love you!" as if the other were therefore an impossibility, and he caught her to him again and rained kisses on her cheeks and eyes and throat and lips until the stars reeled above her head and she had to beg him to stop.

He released her instantly and she was cold and bereft and moved closer to him, catching his hands and replacing them from where he had let them fall, one around her body, the other on her right breast, under the sweater she had thrown on after dinner – at least, that was where she thought his hand had been. It certainly seemed the natural place. "That's better," she sighed, when she had sufficient breath, and in her sigh was all the satisfaction in the world.

"Much better," he agreed, and she could sense that he was smiling as his hand, cool against her heated flesh, stroked her. Gradually, and in unison, for both could feel the other's heart-beat, the first passion of their reunion subsided.

"Say it again!" he demanded, at last.

"Say what?" she asked almost drowsily, entirely demurely, knowing very well what it was he wanted to hear but, perversely, denying what she yearned to give.

"What you said when you fell into my arms and I had to wait patiently until you'd finished."

Incoherent, but she understood him very well! "I like that," she cried indignantly. "You grabbed me!"

"Let's not argue," he answered amicably. "I like that," he said.

"So do I," she agreed, and her voice trembled as she moved under his seeking hand. "Oh, Mitja . . . I love you."

Presently he moved his cheek from her fragrant hair. "We should go back. You must be freezing."

"I'm warm enough, with you here," she murmured dreamily, her cheek against his shoulder. Then she asked, raising her face, flushed and rosy to his, "Does Alex know you're back?"

"She told me where to find you."

"Mitja, you may recall certain declarations I've made?" Christine reminded him softly, boldly, certain that now was the moment she had been waiting for and intent on not letting slip another, precious opportunity of hearing what she wanted to hear.

"One or two," he replied cautiously.

"I've yet to hear one from you . . . if that doesn't sound too importunate."

"You be as importunate as you like," he grinned, "but you actually want a declaration along with all that kissing?" aggrievedly.

"Yes," she answered stubbornly. "Please, Mitja."

"What sort of declaration?"

"That you . . . Mitja!"

But her lips were claimed once more and then the words, low, vibrant, charged with his passion and need for her, rang in her ears. "I love you, Christine. I love you more than I can ever say!"

Later she sighed, "It has been a long time. I'd given up hope after you were so furious when I returned, and with a job."

"There was a reason for that. You see, by then I was in love with you. It happened when you first came to look after Alex. No, I think it probably happened soon after we met – which was why I thought of you immediately when we needed someone to look after Alex – but I only realized what was happening to me gradually.

Yet while I was, I still knew how stupid it was –
or thought so. You had your own life in your
own country. How could I expect you ever to feel
the same way about me and mine! And you were
about to leave us. I tried to distance myself from
you, tried to discipline my emotions before it
really was too late."

"You succeeded only too well," she broke in,
feelingly.

"To the extent of making us both miserable,"
he admitted. "And then you came back. I thought
it was perverse of you. That was why I was
angry. I thought that if you believed I felt nothing
but anger you would go away, and then I could
get over you. I didn't stop to think you had
nowhere to go. And then I was so glad you'd
stayed. I just tried to hide my feelings from you
in exactly the same way you were hiding yours
from me, it seems," he smiled ruefully, "so much
we were at cross purposes. I thought, maybe,
you just wanted an affair . . . an affair with the
man who taught you to ski . . . like so many of
the female tourists who come each year for so-
called sport."

"Dalliance!" she exclaimed, laughingly. "You
did think that of me. I knew it all along!"

"No!" he protested. "I never, ever, thought of
you in terms of just an affair. Oh, I don't deny
that I wanted to take you to bed then, and I do
now, only more so," and he held her to him fast,
caressing her fiercely as if only with difficulty
could he keep his passion for her in check. "What
do I have to do to prove dalliance was the last
thing on my mind?" She shook her head against

his chest. "Dear heart, I know," he murmured. "Marry me?" he asked tenderly.

"Oh, yes, Mitja!" she replied fervently. "Mitja," she said, after a pause, "I never flirted with you, ever. I mean, I meant every look, every gesture, always." She kissed the corner of his mouth and the base of his throat and he caught his breath as he watched her face in delight, as she undid the buttons of his open-necked shirt and pressed her lips to his bare skin. "How stupid to think reticence a virtue," she said.

"And now I have a wedding present for you," he said as they reached Mrs Martinovic's door. "We have a visitor. Can you guess who it is?"

She couldn't. It was Raddy. It explained Mitja's absence. Some weeks previously inquiries he had initiated had produced a man called Petar Radivojevic. Petar had evidence to prove Josip had been born in Kranjsk Gora as he had maintained, but that he had been taken away by the Nazis along with his family. No one had ever discovered what had happened. There was no immediate family left, but Petar was a nephew and there were cousins. Mitja had gone to London to bring Raddy back for a reunion.

If there was anything needed to convince Christine how much Mitja loved her it was this, holding Raddy in her arms while she smiled through her tears. Later, when the tears had been dried, the champagne drunk and they were alone together, she said, "How may I ever thank you!"

"A kiss or two will do for a start," he smiled at her complacently.

"A thousand or more," and she punctuated her words with a few of them. "A lifetime of love." then she said shyly, "Did you hear Mrs Martinovic offering me her Slovenian costume for our wedding? Would you like that, Mitja?"

"She asked me first. I told her I didn't mind what you wore at the wedding," and his gaze was both mischievous and adoring, "so long as I had the pleasure of removing it." Once again she read in his face the desire that was mingled with the love he had for her, and all the while his hands were adoring her, too, and under them her body turned immediately to the molten fire of passionate longing.

"Just dalliance!" she whispered teasingly, though for once suppressing the delicious tremblings that shook her.

"Never just that!" he declared. "Christine! . . ."

"Mitja . . . I love you so." Such power he had to make her respond, so easily she could arouse him, so sure of each other they now were. So careful of each other they must be. She stroked his cheek. "Such a short time, now, and we shall never be parted."

"My wife . . . with every sort of love that there is," he promised, "passion and tenderness and children and happiness, if we work for it, and love always . . . not tomorrow, but now," and as she melted totally into his embrace, he cried, "I love you, Christine."